Praise for the
Vampire Memories Series

Hunting Memories

"A gripping tale. The action moves the story along while the characters, with their skills and secrets, keep the reader's full attention. *Hunting Memories* is a must read in the series, and it provides many answers in the overall story line. I'll be looking forward to the next book in the Vampire Memories."

—Darque Reviews

"One of the year's better vampire novels . . . with realistic characters, including ghosts and vampires, who have plausible problems; an intriguing, if standard, plot; historical literacy; and a style of writing that encourages turning pages. Both fantasy and romance fans should enjoy Hendee's commendable effort."

—*Booklist*

"Filled with action, a bit of politics, and plenty of character-building interactions, this is a strong addition to the series. . . . Those looking for an alternative to Patricia Briggs or Ilona Andrews won't be disappointed with Hendee's newest series."

—Monsters and Critics

"An enjoyable and creative (not just of new vampires) cocktail cleverly blending urban fantasy mixed with strong horror elements . . . a thriller of a vampire tale."

—*Midwest Book Review*

Blood Memories

"A satisfying story line coupled with engaging characters, fast action, and a hint of things to come make this a winner."

—Monsters and Critics

"A good vampire story for the Halloween holiday; the story is fast-paced and intriguing."

—*News and Sentinel* (Parkersburg, WV)

continued . . .

"Well written . . . a fascinating tale with wonderful characters and delicious villains who solicit the readers into loathing them. The story line is character driven, although there is plenty of action throughout. . . . [Fans of] the vampire subgenre will enjoy this work as an exhilarating tale of death visiting the undead."
—SFRevu

"A terrific vampire stand-alone thriller that fans will enjoy . . . the story is filled with action, but also contains a strong cast who ensure vampirism in the Northwest seems real. . . . The heroine especially is an intriguing person. . . . This [is] a fine tale that the vampire crowd will appreciate."
—Midwest Book Review

"Intriguing. . . . Ms. Hendee's fans will be gratified to know she writes just as well on her own as she does in tandem."
—Huntress Book Reviews

"A blend of fantasy and horror mixed with the story of one young woman's path to independence and true knowledge of self, Blood Memories is a unique story guaranteed to intrigue. . . . Readers won't be able to resist Eleisha's charm. . . . If you enjoyed Buffy the Vampire Slayer but were far more interested in where the older vamps came from than in the human heroine herself, this story should certainly catch your fancy. Cunning, stealth, guile, sheer evil, and a surprising amount of goodness make all of these characters alive and unique. A story line that travels from modern-day Portland, Oregon, to England in the 1800s adds interest as well. If you like vampires, then you're certain to enjoy Eleisha's story. Don't miss Blood Memories, the first in what promises to be a fantastic new series."
—Romance Reviews Today

"I personally liked Blood Memories quite a bit. I am pleased to say that it is in no way a Buffy clone, nor is it anything like the goofy paranormal romances that turn vampires into some kind of harmless nonmonster with strange eating habits. I like how Hendee explores the personalities of her characters."
—Fantasy & Sci-Fi Lovin' Book Reviews

"An engrossing tale of vampire death and evolution."
—Patricia's Vampire Notes

MEMORIES OF ENVY

A VAMPIRE MEMORIES NOVEL

BARB HENDEE

A ROC BOOK

ROC
Published by New American Library, a division of
Penguin Group (USA) Inc., 375 Hudson Street,
New York, New York 10014, USA
Penguin Group (Canada), 90 Eglinton Avenue East, Suite 700, Toronto,
Ontario M4P 2Y3, Canada (a division of Pearson Penguin Canada Inc.)
Penguin Books Ltd., 80 Strand, London WC2R 0RL, England
Penguin Ireland, 25 St. Stephen's Green, Dublin 2,
Ireland (a division of Penguin Books Ltd.)
Penguin Group (Australia), 250 Camberwell Road, Camberwell, Victoria 3124,
Australia (a division of Pearson Australia Group Pty. Ltd.)
Penguin Books India Pvt. Ltd., 11 Community Centre, Panchsheel Park,
New Delhi - 110 017, India
Penguin Group (NZ), 67 Apollo Drive, Rosedale, North Shore 0632,
New Zealand (a division of Pearson New Zealand Ltd.)
Penguin Books (South Africa) (Pty.) Ltd., 24 Sturdee Avenue,
Rosebank, Johannesburg 2196, South Africa

Penguin Books Ltd., Registered Offices:
80 Strand, London WC2R 0RL, England

First published by Roc, an imprint of New American Library,
a division of Penguin Group (USA) Inc.

First Printing, October 2010
10   9   8   7   6   5   4   3   2   1

 REGISTERED TRADEMARK—MARCA REGISTRADA

LIBRARY OF CONGRESS CATALOGING-IN-PUBLICATION DATA:
Hendee, Barb.
    Memories of envy: a vampire memories novel / Barb Hendee.
    p.   cm.
    ISBN 978-0-451-46353-1
    1. Vampires—Fiction. I. Title.
    PS3608.E525M46   2010
    813'.6—dc22   2010022363

Set in Dante MT
Designed by Alissa Amell

Printed in the United States of America

Again . . . for Jaclyn and Susan.
I could not write these books without you.

MEMORIES
OF ENVY

prologue

Eleisha Clevon sat in the garden outside the church. She was cross-legged on the ground, right beside Robert's grave. The moon was nearly full.

"I wrote down all four of the laws," she told him, holding a sheet of ivory paper toward the granite headstone. "But I still think only the first one applies."

Of course, she hadn't been able to bring his body home, only some of his ashes that she'd carried in his sword case. But at least he had a proper grave, and she'd wanted his headstone to be clean and straightforward—like him.

It read:

ROBERT BRIGHTON
PROTECTOR
1491 TO 2008

Strangers never came into the churchyard, but even if they did, she didn't care who saw the dates. His existence required recognition.

"We haven't found anyone else yet," she said. "But we will soon, and when we do, I promise to teach them the laws." She pointed back toward the redbrick church. "And Rose is settling in nicely."

She knew that her companions, who lived with her at the church, found it odd when she sat outside sometimes, talking to Robert, but she couldn't just leave him all alone. He had opened her eyes to the history of her own kind, to what they once had been and could be again, and she would not allow him to be forgotten.

"I hope I worded these correctly," she said, drawing the sheet back and looking down at it. "I tried to remember exactly what you showed me."

First Law: No vampire shall kill to feed. This ensures our safety and secrecy.

Second Law: No vampire shall make another until reaching the age of one hundred years as an undead, and no vampire shall ever make more than one companion within the span of one hundred years. The physical and mental energy required is so great that any breach of this law will produce flawed results.

Third Law: No vampire shall make another without the consent of the mortal.

Fourth Law: The maker must teach the new vampire all methods of proper survival and all four of the laws in order to protect the secrecy of our kind.

She finished her scan and then read them to him aloud.

Lowering the paper, she looked at the headstone. "I promise to teach them, Robert. I promise you didn't die for nothing."

She reached out and put her hand on his grave, thinking she should plant a white rosebush beside it. He'd never talked about anything so trivial as flowers, but something told her that he would like white roses.

chapter 1

"Remember to look for cars parked in the shadows of columns or trees," Eleisha said, glancing around the Lloyd Center parking lot.

"I know," Rose answered—rather shortly. "But I fed only a week ago. I don't see why we keep going back out so soon."

Eleisha looked away and didn't answer, as they should not be having a chat about feeding practices in the open.

They stood on the sidewalk near a theater complex with a warm night breeze blowing past, both of them appearing to be typical Portland citizens. Eleisha looked about seventeen, dressed in jeans and a tank top, her dark blond hair in a loose braid.

Rose de Spenser looked about thirty, an elegant lady, tall and slender in a linen dress. Though her face was smooth, she had several streaks of white running through her long brown hair.

Yes, the two of them appeared quite normal.

But Eleisha was beginning to wonder whether these training sessions would ever get any easier.

"I can't see Philip," Rose said, looking across the street toward the nearest light-rail stop. "Is he still watching us?"

"Yes, he's watching."

And that was another thing. Due to recent encroaching dangers, Eleisha couldn't go hunting alone—not without a guardian—as if she were a child instead of a two-hundred-year-old telepathic member of the undead. She gritted her teeth.

Things *would* improve.

They had to.

However, right now she faced the daunting task of teaching Rose to feed without killing. Eleisha had learned that vampires were latent telepaths—they could replace the memories of their victims, and in centuries past had always fed without killing.

She was determined to reinstate this practice.

"Okay, the movie's getting out," she said, watching people pour from the main theater doors. "Just let the crowd thin and then look for someone alone."

Watching the flow of human traffic, she was tempted to point out a few good prospects, but she wanted Rose to learn on her own. This drastic change of hunting methods hadn't been easy on any of them, as they'd all fallen into deeply set patterns decades ago, relying on the power of their gifts to draw victims away . . . and then drain them and hide the bodies.

Eleisha knew that Rose was still struggling with this new way of hunting.

"There," Rose said softly, her brown eyes following a young man moving toward the far edge of the parking lot.

She had a tendency to choose men.

But Eleisha didn't care as long as the potential victim was alone and moving toward a car in the shadows.

Without a word, she and Rose fell into step about ten feet behind him. A row of willow trees lined the edge of the lot, and Eleisha was beginning to think Rose had chosen well, until the young man took out his keys and pressed a button to unlock a green Toyota pickup.

Trucks weren't the best option.

But Rose didn't stop.

"Excuse me," she said, letting the power of her gift flow outward. "Could you assist us?"

Within a few nights of becoming undead, a specific element of their previous personality developed into an overwhelming aura that could be turned on and off at will. Rose's gift was an aura of wisdom. When she used her gift and spoke, her victims fell under a spell of the absolute sense and truth of her words.

The young man stopped and turned around. He was clean shaven and wearing a Mariners baseball cap.

"My friend and I have been out walking, and we must have taken a wrong turn," Rose went on. "We hoped you could direct us to the Doubletree Hotel on Multnomah Street."

He stared at her, listening. Eleisha found this to be a poor opening on Rose's part, as she was *asking* for something instead of making a suggestion.

"Yeah," he said, still moving his eyes up and down Rose's face. "It's not far—just a few blocks."

"It's so dark out now," Rose said. "We would not be safe. It would be best if you drove us."

Oh, well, that's better, Eleisha thought. She'd been half tempted to turn on her own gift but changed her mind. The young man's expression shifted to concern, and Eleisha could see his mind working under the influence of Rose's suggestion. Of course it was too dark now. Of course the only wise choice was for him to drive them back to their hotel.

As if letting two strangers into his truck was the most natural thing in the world, he hurried over to the passenger door and opened it. "Here, I'll take you."

"I am Rose," she said, smiling.

"Jason," he said, holding the door open.

Eleisha shook her head slightly to clear it. The problem with hunting in teams was that they were not immune to each other's gifts, so when Rose spoke and let her aura of wisdom flow, Eleisha could be seduced by an absolute belief in Rose's words as well. She needed to keep sharp and focused.

Rose climbed in first, so that she would be in the middle, and Eleisha climbed in afterward, pressed up against the passenger-side door.

As Jason ran around the back of the truck, Rose whispered, "This is difficult! I'm not hungry yet."

"We can't wait until you're starving again," Eleisha whispered back, and then fell silent as Jason opened the driver's-side door.

This was an issue Rose had not been able to overcome. Since being turned in the early nineteenth century, she'd regretted killing so much that she always pushed herself to the very edge of starvation before leaving her house to go out and feed. So, while a part of her seemed to welcome Eleisha's training, another part found using her powers to hunt nearly impossible unless she was hungry to the point of weakness. But . . . when she was that starved, she also had a tendency to lose control and drain blood too quickly.

Put him to sleep, Eleisha flashed telepathically. *You know what to do.*

Though Rose was skilled with her gift of wisdom, her telepathic abilities were coming along more slowly. She was just beginning to master putting a victim into a deep sleep and holding him there.

The truck was covered by shadows and the parking lot was nearly empty. Jason reached over to put his key in the ignition, but Rose touched his hand.

"Wait," she said softly. "You're tired. You need to rest first."

He blinked slowly, looking at her face, and then he closed his eyes, his head lolling back against the seat.

The action was faster and smoother than Rose had managed in the past, so at least she was gaining better control.

She had the rest of the routine down fairly well. She simply lacked drive and motivation unless she was starving.

Lifting Jason's wrist to her mouth, she punctured his skin carefully with her teeth and began sucking in mouthfuls of his blood. Eleisha slipped inside Rose's mind, tasting the blood, seeing images of Jason's recent memories as Rose consumed some of his life force. . . . His father had cancer, and his mother was a doctor; they lived in a sky blue house on the outskirts of the city; he'd come to the movies alone because of a stupid fight with his girlfriend, Patricia. . . .

Rose stopped feeding.

She bit at the skin between the wounds her fangs had made, making it a ragged cut instead of two punctures. Then she slipped further inside Jason's unconscious mind, taking him back to the moment he'd left the theater and altering his memories. He'd walked to his truck alone, but just before reaching it, he'd slipped and fallen hard, cutting his wrist on a broken beer bottle. He'd climbed into the truck before realizing how badly he'd cut himself, and then he'd passed out.

Eleisha monitored all of this in Rose's mind.

"Good," she said quietly, opening the door to slip out. "Be sure to lock his door."

They would leave him asleep, locked inside his truck, but he would wake up soon, almost as soon as they left him. He had given up some of his life energy, and yet he would still live.

This was how Eleisha's predecessors had hunted for centuries, and this was how anyone she found, anyone she helped, was going to hunt.

Rose followed her back toward the light-rail stop.

"That was good," Eleisha said again. "I didn't have to help you at all."

"It's getting easier."

Philip? Eleisha flashed.

Here.

Philip Branté stepped from the dark trees behind the light-rail stop. He was so tall, Eleisha had to tilt back her head.

"Is baseball-cap boy still breathing?" he joked, his French accent blending the words together.

His skin was ivory, and his eyes were a shade of light amber. He wore his red-brown hair in long layers down to the top of his collar—and he spent a small fortune on products. But even in the warm night, he wore a long Armani coat to cover the machete fastened to his belt.

"Still breathing," Eleisha answered. "We should move to a different part of the city so you can feed, too."

He'd taken her downtown a few nights before, so she didn't need to hunt again yet.

"No," he answered. "I'll see you and Rose back to the church and then go out by myself."

She frowned. They'd all made a pact not to go out at night alone.

Philip was the only one who ignored this agreement. He believed he could take care of himself.

She didn't argue with him, as she was well aware that he'd become very adept at putting victims to sleep and altering their memories on his own. He didn't need her training anymore.

Besides, her relationship to him was growing . . . complicated, so she picked her battles carefully.

"Okay, but don't come back here," she said.

They varied their locations every week.

"I'll go to the riverfront."

She nodded and followed him down the street, with Rose walking beside her.

Wade Sheffield sat in the office he'd set up on the main floor of the church, scanning his computer screen for any news stories of people being checked into hospitals with unexplained blood loss.

Summer was passing quickly—nearly over.

Both windows were open, allowing the night breeze to carry in a scent of roses, lilacs, and hydrangeas from the garden. He lifted his eyes from the screen, gazing outside at the wrought-iron fence.

He'd been living here for several months with three vampires and a ghost. He was probably the only mortal in the world more comfortable with the undead than he was with normal people, but he'd been able to read minds all his life, and "normal people" did not enjoy his company.

So now the five of them were trying to make this abandoned old brick church into a home and, to his surprise, they were succeeding.

They dubbed the church "the underground."

The main floor comprised a large sanctuary, complete with stained-glass windows and two offices. Wade now occupied one office, and Rose had turned the other into her bedroom.

The upstairs was not currently in use, but it sported six rooms that had once been engaged for Sunday school classes, and later, these would be used to house any lost vampires they found.

The basement comprised a three-bedroom apartment where Wade, Eleisha, and Philip lived, as well as an industrial-sized kitchen the old congregation had once used for potluck dinners.

Rose and Wade had overseen much of the recent remodel.

They'd replaced shabby carpets and refinished several hardwood floors. Fresh paint covered the walls, and thick shades covered the downstairs windows. Philip had wanted to board those windows up, as they were close to the ground and too accessible, but Eleisha talked him out of it, so he'd opted for bulletproof glass and stronger locks.

While working on the church, they'd all at least felt busy, felt that they were making progress. But for the past week, Wade had sensed a restlessness vibrating from his companions, and he couldn't help viewing himself as a failure in their true goal: to find other vampires in hiding and bring them here . . . before Julian Ashton could intercept them on the journey back.

From what Wade understood, nearly two hundred years ago, Julian had realized that, even as a vampire, he would never develop telepathy—would never be like his peers—and out of fear, he'd gone on a killing spree, beheading telepathic vampires but leaving the younger ones, who had not yet been trained, alone.

Almost two centuries passed.

But when Wade had first met Eleisha, connected with her, and awakened her latent telepathy, they'd set a chain of events into motion, and they were now in a position to try to repair small, dangling, leftover remnants of the damage Julian had done, to find others still in hiding and create something akin to the way Eleisha's predecessors had once existed.

Their strategy was for Wade to search out any online news stories of homicide victims drained of blood or of living people checked into hospitals with cuts or gashes that did not warrant an unexplained amount of blood loss. He'd once worked as a police psychologist, and he knew a good deal about *where* to search for such stories.

Then they would attempt to make contact, travel to meet the vampire, and try to bring him or her safely home to the church before Julian came out of the shadows swinging a sword—as he had done before.

However, two months had passed and, as yet, Wade had not uncovered a single story that panned out. He knew Eleisha was becoming afraid that maybe they'd been wrong—maybe there was no one else left.

But Wade was doing his level best to find a lead and start a new journey. He'd also been attempting to drag his companions, kicking and screaming, into the twenty-first century. In addition to having a computer and Internet access installed in the church, he'd purchased and set up cell phones for Rose, Eleisha, and Philip. Only Eleisha had shown interest. Rose was daunted by the prospect of learning to check her voice mail—and she'd simply put the phone in her top dresser drawer. Philip seemed to view his as some kind of "leash" and didn't care for the prospect at all.

Wade was determined to keep trying.

"Anything?" a masculine voice with a Scottish accent asked.

Wade half turned. "Not yet, but I've only just started tonight."

Seamus de Spenser, the final member of the group, was standing behind him, looking over his shoulder. Seamus' body was transparent, as always. Though long dead, he looked like a young man, his brown hair hanging to his shoulders. He wore a blue and yellow Scottish plaid draped across his shoulder and held by a belt over the black breeches he had died in. The knife sheath at his hip was empty.

He was Rose's nephew, and he'd died the same night she was turned—but had come back as a spirit, forever tied to her.

Wade and Seamus got along well.

Although all four of Wade's companions possessed some exotic element to their appearance, he viewed himself as rather common—in his early thirties, with a tall, possibly too-slender build. His only outstanding feature was a shock of white-blond hair. He hadn't bothered to get it cut for almost five months, and it was now long enough to tuck behind his ears.

"I've just finished the New York papers, and I'm moving to Europe again," he said.

"I hope you find something soon, even if it comes to nothing again. I'd like to go out looking."

Seamus was a key component of their strategy. Once Wade located a possible location, he would send Seamus to investigate. As a ghost, Seamus could zero in on a vampire—or anything undead—once he was in the being's general vicinity. Unfortunately, he couldn't stay too long, as his spirit was tied to Rose, and the longer he stayed away from her, the weaker he became.

She was the anchor that grounded him.

Wade had sent him out twice in the past few weeks, once to Alaska and once to Barcelona, but any hints in the news stories had been thin at best, and Seamus had found nothing unnatural on the other end.

"What's this one coming up?" Seamus asked, leaning closer.

"The *Evening Standard*," Wade answered. "From London."

"Maybe looking in such big cities won't help us—too many other stories to cover. Can you seek out smaller papers, for smaller towns?" Seamus floated backward, drifting toward the door.

Wade tightened his mouth for a moment and then said, "I have. This is more complicated than just . . . oh, wait, listen to this." He squinted, leaning closer to the screen, reading a headline. "POLICE CHASING MADMAN ATTACKED BY OWN DOGS NEAR KING'S CROSS STATION."

"I don't see how that—"

"Hang on. Just let me skim this."

Saturday night, a disruption occurred near Euston Road outside of King's Cross Station when the sound of a woman screaming sent two policemen racing through pedestrians. Both policemen had dogs in tow, and according to several witnesses, a grizzly scene awaited them in the alley between Crestfield and Belgrove.

They came upon what one witness described as a "wild man biting a woman." The attacker had blood smeared upon his face and hands, and as the police arrived, he is said to have "snarled like an animal and then run out the other end of the alley."

Police gave chase, only to have their own dogs suddenly break away and turn upon them, stopping any possible pursuit. Within moments, the dogs ceased their attack and are being held for observation, pending destruction. The names of the policemen have not been released, but one is in Whittington Hospital with multiple bite wounds.

The female victim, identified as Gloria Melika, is expected to recover. Her attacker has not been apprehended.

Wade stopped scanning. Then he read the article aloud to Seamus. They both fell quiet for a few moments.

"What do you think?" Wade finally asked, but he really wasn't speaking to Seamus . . . more to himself. A wild man biting a woman? Two police dogs turning on their own handlers? And near a busy station in London?

"I think you should open up our maps," Seamus answered.

In addition to the desk and the computer, the small office was dominated by several large bookshelves that Wade had been filling with travel literature and maps. Seamus had found that by studying a detailed map and then "wishing" himself someplace, he could travel quickly from one point to the next if he could keep the line of travel clear in his mind.

"Here," Wade said, hurrying to the nearest shelf. "Start with the atlas."

Since Seamus couldn't physically touch anything, Wade began pulling materials off the shelves. Moving among several maps, they began with a large image of America and England, then worked their way down to London, and finally to a street schematic around King's Cross Station.

"You got it?" Wade asked.

Seamus nodded his transparent head.

Voices drifted in from outside: the light tones of Rose and Eleisha talking as they came through the wrought-iron gate.

"They're back early," Wade said. "Do you want to wait and tell them where you're going?"

"No, you tell them . . . but try not to get their hopes up."

Although he'd been dead many years, Seamus retained a good deal of his humanity, and he still worried over the feeling of others.

"I'll be careful," Wade promised.

The air around Seamus wavered, and he vanished. Wade watched the empty spot a little longer, and then he left the office, heading to meet Eleisha and Rose.

As he passed through the door into the sanctuary, he wondered, *Where's Philip?*

Philip walked along Naito Parkway above the Willamette River. He'd never been one to become fond of places, but he liked hunting down here—all the dark shadows and the rushing water made it easy to dump a body.

On the parkway's west side, a row of towering hotels cast more darkness over the river.

Most of the time, he hunted exactly as Eleisha wanted him to. He'd even become good at it.

But sometimes, like tonight, he grew overwhelmed by the need to drain an entire life, fill himself with blood, and feel a heart stop while he was still drinking.

Eleisha could not find out about these nights. If she did, she would not forgive him, and he could no longer exist without her. She fed him something he'd never even known he was starving for, and he had no intention of ever being without her again.

Everyone had secrets. As long as he kept his, all would be well.

He walked along, looking down at the river, reveling in being alone. Although he'd come to need company, being alone once in a while was good, too. It meant he could do anything he wanted.

As long as he wasn't alone too long.

Eleisha and Wade had shown him that there were other things to do with his nights besides just hunting, such as playing poker with plastic chips or watching movies together using the DVD player. Since settling in the church, Eleisha had also started a bizarre practice of reading books to them aloud. At first, Philip expected this to be boring beyond belief . . . but it wasn't. She chose detective novels by Robert Crais or humorous books about an inept woman bounty hunter by a writer named Janet Evanovich. She even read older books by P. G. Wodehouse, which made Wade laugh out loud. Philip didn't always understand what was so funny, but he liked watching Eleisha make Wade laugh.

This last thought stirred up images of the church, of home, of Eleisha waiting there for him, and he walked faster.

He passed a few maple trees when a familiar sound tickled his ears.

Someone nearby was weeping softly.

He stepped off the sidewalk, into the small park beside the river, and looked around, stopping for a moment to listen with his eyes closed. Then he walked behind the line of trees.

A woman sat on the ground, her arms wrapped around her legs, her face pressed into her knees as she tried to cover her sobs.

"You are sad," Philip said, letting his gift begin to flow.

She jerked her head up in surprise.

She was not young, perhaps mid-thirties, with dark red hair and blond highlights. But even tear streaked, her face was pleasing. She seemed overdressed to be sitting on the ground, but then he noticed that her black velvet gown looked like something from a Nordstrom Rack, and yet she wore a slender Rolex and Prada pumps.

She was interesting.

"What's wrong?" he asked, using both his gift and his heavy French accent to make her study him in turn.

Philip had never given much thought or appreciation to his gift. He couldn't remember anything about his life as a mortal—as if his existence began the night he was turned—so his gift had always seemed a part of him.

He exuded an overwhelming aura of attraction. The moment he spoke, his victims were fascinated by him, longing to touch him, to please him.

She stared at his face as he moved closer and crouched down. He reached out and wiped away her tears with his fingers. She let him.

"Tell me," he whispered.

"I was going to get married," she whispered back. "Finally. To a stockbroker here in the city. We were happy."

He waited, cocking his head to one side.

"He ran a credit check and found out . . . I don't come from money," she went on as if she knew Philip, as if he were a friend. "I owe fifty thousand dollars on all my cards to . . . to look like this. He broke it off over dinner." She let out another sob. "I couldn't go home alone to my apartment."

She was in pain and, to his great surprise, she moved him.

He didn't like the feeling. He'd come out alone so he could hunt to please himself.

Leaning closer, he let the full power of his gift engulf her, and she gasped, reaching out to touch his hair, her eyes shifting back and forth across his face.

"It's all right," he said.

He kissed her, like a mortal would. He did this often while hunting alone.

But always before, when he killed to feed, he liked to take the experience to a certain point and then turn off his gift so he could feel attraction shift suddenly to terror. He liked to feel his victim struggle and fight and scream. He fed on fear as much as blood.

Tonight was different.

He didn't turn off his gift. He didn't want to terrify her. Instead, he moved his mouth down to her throat and gripped the back of her neck. In a flash, he bit down hard, but he didn't rip her throat, just drove his teeth in to feed. He let himself drink as quickly as he pleased, swallowing without care or concern. She bucked once, but he held on to her easily, letting his gift calm her while he consumed her life, her memories, everything that she had been.

He saw a childhood of poverty in a filthy mobile home. A mother smoking cigarettes and watching television. He felt a longing to escape. He saw a series of cubicles and computers as she typed in data at various jobs. He saw a chain of boyfriends that stopped at a square-jawed man in a gray wool coat. The stock-broker. Matthew. She loved him. He represented everything she'd ever wanted. Then Philip saw a posh restaurant, and Matthew was speaking coldly, telling her to leave, as if she mattered little more than the empty wineglass in front of him.

The woman's heart stopped beating, and Philip raised his head, looking into her dead face.

He'd never fed like this before—killing a victim without revel-ing in pain or fear.

Even though the choice had been his, he suddenly felt . . . unsatisfied. He didn't allow himself the luxury of killing very often, for fear of Eleisha finding out, and now he'd just wasted a chance. What was wrong with him?

A flash of hot anger surprised him as much as his earlier mo-ment of pity had.

Eleisha was *doing* something to him, and he knew it. But he needed her more than he needed his freedom.

The anger passed.

Still looking down at the dead woman, he picked her up and carried her toward the river. Several of her memories stayed with him for the entire walk to the water.

Strange.

He leaned over and dropped her, watching her slip beneath the dark current, still thinking of Matthew's cold face when he'd sent her away.

Then he straightened and forgot about Matthew and forgot about the woman.

Eleisha was waiting for him to come home.

chapter 2

Eleisha was alone in her room, sitting on her bed, mulling over the news Wade had just shared.

Had he really found something this time?

In London?

That seemed too close to Yorkshire—where Julian kept a town house—to be promising. Wouldn't he have already found someone existing in England? But perhaps not. Wade relayed the phrase "wild man" from the news story, and she had no idea what this might suggest about their potential find.

But what if . . . what if they really had found someone else? Someone who needed help, who needed a home and other undead companions?

Someone who needed the old laws.

Eleisha would keep all her promises to Robert.

She stood up, trying to push her hopes away until they learned more.

This room pleased her in a way no other bedroom had before. She liked that it was halfway underground. She liked the antique sloped ceiling and the cream-colored walls and the white trim. Walking over to the closet, she opened one side and looked up.

A small cardboard box peeked over the top shelf's edge. She

took it down and went over to her dressing table, sitting in the walnut chair and looking into the mirror.

Slowly, she opened the box.

Inside was a set of antique silver brushes, a mirror, and a comb. Eleisha had brought them with her from Seattle. They had once belonged to a vampire named Margaritte Latour—Maggie. Philip had made Maggie in the early nineteenth century—only a year or two after he was turned himself. She had been his lover in their mortal days and his closest companion afterward, but they'd abandoned each other when Julian's killing spree began.

Maggie moved to America soon after and then later, much later, had become a close friend of Eleisha's.

But Maggie was dead now, turned to dust, like so many others.

Eleisha fingered the largest silver brush. Maggie would have liked this church, this home. She would have liked the company of her own kind.

Pulling the brush closer to her chest, Eleisha tried to shake off the unwanted feelings of sorrow and loss. Everyone living here in the underground had lost people they cared about. Wallowing in regret would not change that.

But her sadness wouldn't pass away so easily.

The bedroom door opened, and Philip walked in. He never knocked. He didn't need to.

She smiled at him and then noticed his black T-shirt, remembering that he'd been wearing an Armani button-down earlier in the evening.

"You changed your shirt. You didn't get blood all the way through your coat, did you?"

He shrugged. "A little." Upon seeing her expression, he held up one hand. "Don't worry. I was careful."

She nodded. Such things could happen even when one was most careful.

After closing the door, he walked toward her. He was quite probably the most handsome man she'd ever seen.

But that didn't matter. She didn't care about aesthetics. In the past, the person she'd loved most in the world had been tragic to look upon.

She also knew it was quite unexpected that she should now prefer Philip's company to anyone else's. Before developing his telepathy and learning how to alter memories, he'd been a savage killer who hunted for pleasure.

He was also vain, self-centered, and easily bored.

But . . . he had a great capacity for living and enjoying himself—something Eleisha lacked. He had come into her life when she'd needed him; he'd protected her from Julian and then stayed to help with the underground when he could have gone anywhere in the world. He'd stopped killing mortals and adapted to feeding in the manner of their predecessors, even though this change of practice was difficult for him. Most important, when Eleisha was with him, she was distracted from dwelling on sad thoughts, and she didn't feel alone.

"What are those?" he asked, looking down at the brushes and hand mirror.

She hesitated. Philip didn't like talking about the past.

"They were Maggie's," she finally answered. "I brought them in my suitcase from Seattle."

He frowned. "*Pourquoi?*"

Why had she kept them? She didn't know what to say, and he crouched down beside her. His ivory face had a little color tonight, and his skin glowed. She couldn't talk to him about this. He wouldn't understand, and he already thought she'd been half mad for bringing some of Robert's ashes home and burying them in the garden.

"I just . . . I wanted us to keep something that was hers, so we wouldn't forget," she said.

He shrugged and stood up.

"The sun will be up soon," he said.

Summers in Oregon weren't exactly conducive to being a vampire. Winters were perfect: The sun was down by four thirty in the afternoon and stayed down until seven thirty the following morning. But the nights in summer were short—the sun stayed up until nearly ten at night and seemed to rise again a scant few hours later.

Philip walked over to the bed and sat down, taking his boots off and pulling his T-shirt over his head, tossing it to a chair. He glanced over to make sure the shade was tightly closed and then leaned back against the pillows. Eleisha was barefoot. She was still wearing her tank top from earlier but had changed into a pair of faded gray sweatpants.

Leaving Maggie's silver brushes on the dressing table, she moved to join Philip, crawling up the bed until she was close enough that he could reach out and pull her down against his shoulder. She suddenly remembered that she hadn't told him Wade's news—and that Seamus had gone off to London. But her eyelids were heavy, and his skin felt . . . almost warm. She hoped he hadn't taken too much blood from his victim.

"Did your hunt go well?" she asked carefully, not wanting to sound accusatory.

"*Bien*," he murmured, rolling onto his side and using one arm to pull her against his chest. "Sleep."

Pressing the top of her head beneath his chin, she closed her eyes.

*   *   *

The nights here were so short in the summer that Wade spent more hours awake and alone than he had in the spring.

He was back at the computer again, but hearing footsteps out in the hall, he looked up and saw the sky slowly turning gray. Was it near dawn already? For a moment, he assumed the footsteps must be those of Philip returning, but then he noted the light, quick sound and realized they belonged to Rose. He got up and went to the door.

She was coming toward him down the hall, heading for her own room, and she smiled.

He smiled back, still surprised by how quickly his affection for her had developed. Rose was odd, even for a vampire—a strange mix of calm wisdom and manic anxiety. She was a lovely woman, from her long flowing dresses to the white streaks in her hair, and she shared his and Eleisha's vision of finding other vampires and returning their kind to the old ways of practicing telepathy and feeding without killing.

But Rose's smiles were always a little lost, a little hesitant, and Wade still felt sorry for her. She was a creature of deeply ingrained habits, and she feared change more than anything else. She'd settled in San Francisco in 1870, and although she'd wanted to join Eleisha and Wade desperately, this new home in Portland must still feel so foreign. Her apartment in San Francisco had been small and cozy. The church was large and drafty, with winding staircases and three distinct floors.

"I didn't realize how late it had grown," she said. "Will you keep watch for Seamus?"

"Of course." He reached over and opened her bedroom door. "Did you see Philip come in? The sky's getting light."

"No, but I'm sure he's here. Have you checked Eleisha's room?"

At those words, they both fell into an awkward silence. But her eyes were fluttering. Once the sun began coming up, she could not fight collapsing into dormancy.

"I'll see you tonight," she said.

He nodded as she slipped inside, and then he closed the door behind her. Turning around, he tucked his white-blond hair behind his ears, wondering what to do with himself now. Although he'd become accustomed to sleeping during the day, he needed only six or seven hours, and he wasn't tired yet. He looked toward the stairs down to their apartment. Maybe he should make some food and watch the morning news.

But even as he walked down the stairwell, he knew what he was going to do first.

It was a twisted habit that he couldn't seem to break. He promised himself every morning that he'd stop. But he never kept the promise.

The stairwell exited directly into the living room of their apartment. To his right was a small family kitchen. To his left was another hall leading to their bedrooms. He walked to Philip's bedroom and opened the door.

The room was empty.

He knew it would be.

All of Philip's clothes and furniture and personal belongings were here—just not Philip.

Something in their little world had altered, and Wade still wasn't entirely sure what it meant. He thought back to a brief period of time when it had been just him and Eleisha—before Philip.

After a somewhat rough beginning, Philip's entrance had not been unwelcome. He was unbelievably strong and a skilled fighter.

They needed him. Wade had awakened his telepathy and taught him how to read memories . . . to share memories. They had both seen down the lines of each other's pasts and knew far too much about each other.

Back in Seattle, the three of them had shared Maggie's old home, all settling into different bedrooms and existing simply as a group of somewhat lost individuals who relied upon one another for different needs.

Then Rose contacted Eleisha.

Eleisha bought the church here in Portland.

She and Wade began making plans for the future, to find others like Rose.

They went to San Francisco and stayed a few nights in Rose's apartment, but she had only one guest room, so Wade offered to sleep on the couch and let Philip and Eleisha share the guest room, as they both preferred to be shut away during daylight hours. This had seemed only sensible, but Wade could not forget the jolt he'd experienced the first time he'd opened the guest-room door and seen Eleisha curled up asleep on Philip's shoulder.

He didn't know why the sight bothered him so much. He wasn't jealous. He just suddenly felt like he was standing . . . outside. Since returning home, Eleisha and Philip had kept their own rooms, but Philip seemed to sleep in his less and less often.

Wade closed the door to Philip's empty room and walked a few steps farther down, opening Eleisha's. She never locked it.

He went inside, finding his two companions asleep on top of Eleisha's white lace comforter. They didn't move. They didn't breathe.

They were deep in their dormancy; nothing would wake them, which made Wade's secret intrusions seem even worse. He had a PhD in psychology and was well aware that his behavior bordered on dysfunctional at best. But he couldn't seem to stop doing this.

He just stood there, looking down at them.

Eleisha was sleeping up against Philip's chest with the top of her head pressed into the hollow of his throat, her long hair tangled around one of his arms.

As always, Wade felt like an outsider looking in. He didn't belong with other mortals anymore—as he made them too uncomfortable. In his heart, he knew he belonged exactly where he was and that he was following the correct path. But even here, he was still somehow in between.

Eleisha and Philip valued him, made him feel accepted.

But he was different from them and he knew it. Worse, they knew it.

He was a mortal living among the undead.

Someday, one of them might openly acknowledge this. But not today. Turning, he walked out of the room and closed the door.

Vale of Glamorgan, Wales

Julian Ashton galloped his new horse down the path leading up to Cliffbracken Manor, his home. The night sky was showing the barest hint of gray. He would need to get inside the house before long.

Almost two centuries ago, his family had lived here, hunted here, danced and held banquets here. He'd always preferred his town house in Yorkshire, and so this place had long been empty but for a few servants cleaning the cobwebs.

Recent events had brought him back here, and he was beginning to find some peace in having the entire estate to himself. He'd purchased a horse, a decent hunter from a stable outside of Cardiff. Riding each night had brought back memories, making him more aware that with his father truly gone, he was now lord of the manor . . . whatever that meant.

The old stable loomed before him, and he pulled up his horse, jumping down with a thud. Julian was a large man with a bone structure that almost made him look heavy. His dark hair hung at uneven angles around a solid chin, and he pushed it back, away from his face.

The horse stomped, kicked, and snorted in agitation, pulling on the bridle, trying to rush toward the stalls.

"Stop," he ordered, taking a firmer grip. Julian always expected obedience.

The horse stopped kicking, and Julian led it inside the stable. Just as he'd tied off the animal to remove its saddle, the air shimmered beside him and a transparent teenage girl appeared.

His spy: Mary Jordane.

In addition to being transparent, the most striking things about her were her spiky magenta hair and shiny silver nose stud. She was thin, with a hint of budding breasts, wearing a purple T-shirt, a black mesh overshirt, torn jeans, and Dr. Martens boots.

"They've sent their own ghost to London," she blurted out immediately, "to look for some wild guy who bit a lady in an alley."

He tried not to wince.

Mary's penchant for babbling the instant she appeared had never ceased to grate on him.

"Stop!" he ordered.

Julian used this word with great frequency.

She pursed her mouth and crossed her arms—as she often didn't seem to realize she was a ghost. By performing a ritual séance several months ago, he'd called her from the other side, manipulating her into cooperation with a mix of promises for the future and threats of sending her back to the gray, in-between plane where he found her.

In spite of the fact that she was American, she'd proven quite useful.

"Slow down," he said. "What's happened?"

The meaning of her initial outburst was sinking in, and he wanted every detail of her report.

She glared at him petulantly a little longer and then began speaking. He was beginning to suspect that she enjoyed bringing him relevant news.

"Wade found a news story in London," she said. "He sent Seamus off a little while ago. What do you want me to do?"

"What was in the story?"

One of Mary's strengths was her amazing memory. She could recall conversations almost word for word. "I couldn't listen in when Wade was talking to Seamus . . . 'cause Seamus can sense me if I get too close, but I listened through the stained-glassed windows when he was talking to Eleisha and Rose."

She went on to recount the events of two policemen with dogs coming upon a man biting a woman in an alley near King's Cross Station, the man fleeing, and the dogs turning upon their handlers.

Julian put his fist against his chin, thinking. "Any description of the man?"

"Nope. Not that I heard."

If the attacker was described as "wild," that would suggest someone who appeared both mad and unkempt. Julian was interested in locating only vampire elders—those who'd existed before 1825.

But perhaps one of the elders had escaped him and gone feral. It was possible.

In the past, for centuries, his kind had existed by four laws, and the most sacred of these was "No vampire shall kill to feed." They retained their secrecy through telepathy, feeding on mortals, altering their memories, and then leaving the victims alive. New vampires required training from their makers to awaken and hone psychic abilities, but Julian's telepathy had never surfaced. He lived by his own laws, and so the elders began quietly turning against him. His own maker, Angelo, had tried to hide this news from him, but he *knew*. He heard the rumblings, and he acted first, beheading every vampire who lived by the laws, including Angelo, who would have turned against him sooner or later.

Julian had left a small crop of younger vampires, untrained vampires like Eleisha and Philip and Maggie, alone. They were not telepathic and did not know the laws and were no threat to him.

Then, with no warning, Eleisha suddenly developed fierce psychic abilities, and she began actively *looking* for any vampires who might have escaped Julian's net and remained in hiding.

She found one who didn't count: Rose de Spenser, another uneducated creature who knew nothing of her own kind.

But then Eleisha found Robert Brighton, a five-hundred-year-old elder who had practiced the laws like a religion. Robert had come out of hiding for Eleisha, who was so very easy to trust. Julian could not allow him to contaminate the others, to start the whole nightmare over again, and so he'd tracked Eleisha down and taken Robert's head.

The fact that Robert had survived and hidden for so long told Julian he couldn't possibly be the only one. Now Julian was simply waiting for Eleisha to find more elders, to lure more of them out . . . and to lead him right to them.

"Have they arranged for plane tickets?" he asked.

Mary shook her transparent head. "No, they're waiting on

Seamus. It could be nothing, like the last two times they thought they'd found something. You want me to go to London and check it out myself?"

"Not yet. Go back to the church and keep watch. If Seamus finds anything, come tell me immediately."

His eyelids felt heavy.

"Okay." She turned around and looked out the stable door. "Oh . . . sorry. I don't think you can get back up to the house."

He gazed past her and saw that the night sky was growing lighter, and the manor was still a good walk away.

But it didn't matter. He could sleep in the old groomsman's room out here. Once, he would have found such an act unthinkable, but now, he didn't mind sleeping in the stable.

"Come tell me immediately," he repeated. "Do you understand?"

"Yeah, yeah, I got it."

Useful as she might be, she still grated on his nerves.

She vanished.

He quickly put his horse away, with buckets of grain and water, and then headed deeper inside the stable, stumbling once, hoping he'd make it to the bed before falling dormant.

chapter 3

The following night, Wade sat at the dining room table in their apartment's kitchen, drinking tea and working with Rose to develop her telepathy.

In part, they were also trying to keep busy. Seamus had returned several times since sunset, looking exhausted. While Seamus possessed the ability to feel an undead presence among the fabric of life—if he got close enough—his spirit was tied to Rose, and he was having more and more difficulty being away from her. So he'd teleported back to try to regain some strength, and then blinked out again. As yet, he'd found nothing in London.

The news was not encouraging.

Wade took a swallow of his orange spice tea and set the cup back down. Except for the office, he found this kitchen the most pleasant room in the church. The round table was dark stained oak, but Eleisha had painted all the cupboards white, and then Rose had created an indoor herb garden from a variety of brightly colored pottery containers.

He'd been allowing Rose to read his thoughts intermittently and then pushing her out so she could learn to feel when his block was intentional. The most fundamental element of telepathy involved the ability to block another psychic when necessary. She would not be able to hone her abilities properly until she mastered this skill. It had come naturally to Eleisha, and almost as quickly to Philip.

But Rose was having trouble, and until she could block another telepath, she lacked too much control, and she would not be able to feed without Eleisha's close supervision.

Wade was doing everything he could to help.

Rose was dressed casually tonight in a gray sleeveless sweater and long skirt, sitting with her legs crossed and her palms on the table.

"Okay, now, this time, I'll read your thoughts, and I want you to try to force me out," he instructed. "Don't worry. You won't hurt me. Just push me out as hard and as fast as you can."

He, Eleisha, and Philip had all become so mutually adept at reading one another's thoughts that they'd made a pact not to even try without express permission—basically out of good manners. So he always gave Rose plenty of warning.

He reached out carefully, pressing into her mind, seeing flashes of her concern over mastering this skill, and then he felt her trying to push him out.

Good, he flashed. *Try harder.*

The skin over her cheekbones tightened as her expression grew more intense. He felt her resistance to him increase, and he decided to make her work for this. He pushed back. A flicker of uncomfortable surprise crossed her features, but she continued trying to force him out.

Then without meaning to, he suddenly broke through her barrier and caught a barrage of deeper images and thoughts he had not intended to see, nearly all of them focusing upon worry about Eleisha.

He pulled out. "Oh, Rose, I'm so sorry. I didn't mean to—"

"It's all right," she cut in, gripping the edge of the table tightly with one hand. It wasn't all right. He began to apologize again.

"No," she interrupted. "I don't mind you seeing my thoughts, but I should be gaining faster. Eleisha could keep you out almost right away."

He wanted to take her hand and offer comfort, but he didn't. "Eleisha might be an unusual case. I . . . I haven't done this enough yet. But you're doing fine. You'll get it."

He looked around, still feeling the effects of having suddenly invaded Rose's mind—and what he saw there.

"Where is Eleisha?" he asked, then paused. "Oh, God, she's not out in the garden talking to Robert again, is she?"

That particular penchant of hers was beginning to worry him.

"No, I heard her tell Philip she was going to take a bath, but I haven't heard any water running," Rose answered. "She's just been so distant these past few nights. Something's wrong." As if these words brought her to a decision, she stood up. "I'm going to go check on her."

Explosions and gunshots sounded from the television in the living room. Philip was watching *The Replacement Killers* with Chow Yun-Fat.

Wade stood up, too. "She's just getting worried because we haven't found anyone yet." He moved around the back of his chair, stepping closer. "But I've read a lot of minds, maybe too many, and Eleisha's one of the most solid people I've ever known. That's probably why Julian turned her in the first place. She faces things as they come."

"I hope you're right."

She walked out of the kitchen, through the living room, toward the hall. As she passed Philip, he didn't even look up. Although they had reached a level of mutual tolerance, like two strange cats forced into the same home, Rose and Philip didn't exactly like each other. Then again, the only two people Philip *did* seem to like were Eleisha and Wade.

Rose vanished down the hall.

Wade sighed, went into the living room, and dropped down on the couch next to Philip, who seemed pleased to see him.

Philip didn't like watching movies alone.

"Eleisha's in the bath," he said. "She'll be out soon."

"How far in are we?" Wade asked, looking at the screen. He'd seen this film before, but it was pretty good.

"Not far. John Lee has just gone to get his fake ID and passport."

As the next round of gunshots exploded from the screen, Wade was still feeling the psychic aftereffects of Rose's concern over Eleisha.

Eleisha sat at her dressing table, in her robe, staring at Maggie's silver brushes, knowing she should take her bath and go check on Philip.

But the mere effort of getting up almost seemed too much.

A soft knock sounded on the door, and she knew who it was without asking. Wade's knock was brisk and loud, and Philip wouldn't have bothered.

"Come in," she said.

Rose just cracked the door first, then opened it a little wider, looking at Eleisha with something akin to concern on her face.

Was Rose concerned? Why?

They were both quiet for a few moments, and then Rose said, "I didn't hear the water running."

Communication was not a strong point for any of them. They had all lived on the outskirts of humanity far too long. But Rose's words spoke volumes to Eleisha . . . that Rose had been listening, had been worrying, had been waiting, had been watching. Could she feel Eleisha's sadness? Did she know?

"Come in and close the door," Eleisha said.

Rose did. She walked over and looked down at the silver brushes and the hand mirror. "Those are elegant. Are they antiques?"

"They were Maggie's."

"You brought them from Seattle?"

The sorrow inside Eleisha began to build, threatening to spill over. "Yes. They're all I have left of her."

All she had left of Robert were his ashes and his sword.

Rose suddenly reached out and grasped her wrist. "Come over here."

She pulled Eleisha up and led her to the bed, where they could sit facing each other.

"Are you in mourning?" Rose asked. "Because you did not have time before? Now that we have too much time, with little to do, is the past coming back upon you?"

The open—blunt—nature of these questions threw Eleisha off balance. Although she had become accustomed to exchanging telepathic thoughts with Wade and Philip, this type of verbal confrontation was uncomfortable.

But Rose's eyes expressed only concern. She wanted an answer, and Eleisha had no idea what to say.

Was she in mourning? She didn't know what that felt like or how to define it.

She let her mind turn inward. "No, I . . . just can't stop thinking about them, about how we're looking for others like ourselves, so we can exist together, become what we once were, and Maggie and Robert won't share any of it with us because they're gone." She choked on her words. "If I had just seen things more clearly, acted faster, done even a few things differently, they'd still be with us."

She looked at the floor. "Maggie would have loved it here. When I found her, she was so lonely, and she didn't even know it."

Eleisha knew that Rose was not given to sympathy. Rose had been a midwife back in Scotland during her mortal life. She relied on knowledge and wisdom, not on emotions.

"That is why you suffer?" Rose asked in clear surprise. "Self-blame?"

"I don't know! I just know they're not here, and I can't stop going over what happened to them in my head. And I can't stop thinking that they should be a part of this."

"Eleisha, look at me." Rose's voice was hard now. "Listen to me. I spent far too many years wishing I could change the past, alter one or two things that happened, and then imagining how different the future would have been. But the past is like stone! It's set and done. I'm not telling you how to feel, only that regret for what can't be changed won't serve you."

Her tone softened again, and she touched Eleisha's hand. "But that doesn't mean we forget." She stood up. "Come to the dressing table and tell me about Maggie."

Talk about Maggie? There was so much to tell.

Eleisha moved across the room, looking down at the silver brushes. "She was beautiful. I know people use that word all the time, but Maggie was so beautiful that when she was in a room, nobody even noticed Philip."

Rose raised an eyebrow.

The sight washed away some of Eleisha's sadness. She almost smiled. "No, really. You should have seen her." She hesitated, wondering about mentioning the next part. "And she'd lived a more normal life than you or me before she was turned. She'd had lovers and . . ."

She stopped, not sure how to finish the sentence. Due to circumstances, neither Eleisha nor Rose had ever married or known romantic love.

"I understand what you mean," Rose said calmly.

"She liked clothes and jewelry and going out to nightclubs. She liked company. She used to do my hair and dress me up like a doll . . . and I just let her do it. But she also liked staying home by the fireplace and playing chess."

At this, a flicker of something, maybe pity, did cross Rose's face. "Oh, Eleisha, I didn't realize. . . . You're distraught tonight; perhaps later, you can show me some memories—let me know her better."

Eleisha looked up. Show Rose memories of Maggie? The prospect brought comfort. Philip would never have allowed that.

"Here," Rose said. "Sit down. I've always wanted to dress you up like a doll, too, or at least do something with your hair."

She might have been joking, but Eleisha sat down in the chair anyway.

Rose picked up one of the brushes, and she was moving it toward Eleisha's head when her face suddenly contorted and she made a gasping sound. She dropped to her knees, staring at nothing.

Eleisha slid instantly from the chair to the floor. "Rose!"

Rose seemed beyond speech, and then she mouthed one silent word. "Maggie."

She gripped the brush tighter.

The brush.

"Drop it!" Eleisha cried.

But Rose didn't, and Eleisha almost knocked it out of her hand before recognizing the expression on Rose's face . . . the same expression Wade and Philip wore while reading each other's memories.

Rose was locked away inside a memory.

Without waiting a second longer, Eleisha reached out and grabbed Rose's free hand, sinking into her mind, into the memories. At first, she was lost in a haze, not at all like her previous experiences of seeing someone else's life in Technicolor from their own point of view. The haze cleared, and she felt more like an . . . invisible ghost or intruder standing on the edge of a room and looking in.

She could not believe what she saw there, but nor could she break away.

Maggie walked down the hallway of her house in Seattle, tightly gripping the silver brush.

She looked the same, exactly the same as Eleisha remembered, wearing a snug black dress, her mass of dark brown hair falling to the small of her back.

But her face was tense and frightened at the same time, and the house looked different. Maggie stopped at one of the guest rooms and reached out to separate strings of beads hanging in place of a door.

Beads?

Maggie looked inside. There was no one in the room, but the décor was startling. The room had been painted red, and strange curtains with a colorful diamond pattern hung over the windows. The bedspread matched the curtains, and the dressing table was white, but gaudy with gold inlay. Everything seemed to be decorated in some garish color. A guitar leaned against one wall, but it was gathering dust. A boxy television set on top of a dresser was showing a Doris Day and Rock Hudson movie with the sound turned off.

None of this reflected Maggie's taste. None of it reflected the house in which Eleisha had once lived.

"Simone," Maggie called out, her voice tight. "Are you here?"

No one answered, and Maggie walked down to her own bedroom. The door was open, and someone sat at the dressing table, holding Maggie's silver hand mirror. The slender figure in a gauzy purple dress half turned. Two large suitcases rested beside her.

Even lost inside the memory, Eleisha almost gasped as the girl turned.

She was lovely, like something from a bygone photograph. Her starkest feature was her shining black hair, cut into a razor-straight bob about chin length. It swung whenever she moved, creating an illusion of near constant fluidity. Her skin was white, her eyes were china blue, and her tiny nose was spaced perfectly above a small, red heart of a mouth. She wore flat shoes and a string of black beads around her neck. She reminded Eleisha of a flapper from the late twenties or early thirties . . . and yet this memory of Maggie's was clearly from later than the thirties.

"You didn't come to the club," Maggie said, her voice still tight. "Neither did Cecil. I waited two hours."

The girl shrugged, as if bored by the conversation. "I'm sick of going to the Showbox with you," she said. "Everyone there knows me already. I want new people."

"Your face is glowing, Simone."

"Is it?"

"Yes." Maggie walked farther into the bedroom. "Did you decide to finally feed on one of your conquests?"

Even lost in the memory, Eleisha could feel her own body grow stiff with shock. Maggie was speaking to another vampire.

Simone shrugged again. "He seemed ready."

The tightness in Maggie's voice broke, and she glanced at the suitcases. "Then come out with me. I'll take you someplace new. I promise."

She sounded desperate, almost pleading, as if she hungered for Simone's company.

"There are no new places here," Simone answered coldly. "I'm sick of Seattle. I'm going home to Denver."

"You hated Denver." Maggie's voice betrayed nothing now, but she gripped the brush in both hands as if terrified to let it go.

"Not anymore. Parts of it are quite posh now. Have you seen photos of the Brown Palace Hotel? I think I'd like to go home." She turned and looked back in the mirror, pleased. "Let them get a load of me for a while." She paused for effect. "But I'm never coming back here. Do you hear me? Never."

She swiveled her head to watch Maggie's expression crumple in pain.

"You promised," Maggie whispered.

"I don't care."

"I made you!" Maggie shouted suddenly. "You'd be an old woman without me!"

"And I'm sick of you reminding me!" Simone shouted back. Then she calmed and shrugged again. "I want new people. All new people."

Maggie didn't answer, but the sorrow on her face pulled at Eleisha's heart.

Simone stood up. "Oh, and Cecil stopped by. I left you a present in the closet. Just so you know, he *was* my last conquest, as you like to say. He stopped caring for you months ago."

She picked up the suitcases and walked out of the bedroom. Maggie didn't try to stop her. Instead, Maggie walked slowly to the closet and opened the double doors.

A tall man in a dark suit lay on a pile of shoes. His throat was torn and his eyes were still open. Maggie just stood there, staring at his dead body.

Eleisha's horror at this psychic voyeurism increased, and she wanted to pull away, to stop looking . . . but she didn't.

She couldn't bring herself to leave Maggie all alone.

As *The Replacement Killers* ended, Wade glanced at his watch, wondering what Rose could be saying to Eleisha all this time.

Philip stood up. "Is she still in the bath?"

He took a step toward the hall, and Wade was about to stop him when the air shimmered and Seamus appeared, looking exhausted and even more transparent than usual. Recently, Wade had begun trying to press Seamus for more specific answers regarding the physics of his connection to Rose and the possible dangers of him staying away from her for too long, but as yet, Seamus either couldn't or didn't want to answer.

Forgetting Philip, Wade turned to Seamus in concern. "You're not going back out. Not yet. You should see yourself."

"I think I found something, but I'm not sure," Seamus said weakly, his Scottish accent blending the words.

Wade froze. "What? What have you found?"

Seamus shook his translucent head. "Something. I've searched London. I can feel death on the edge of my range—not a ghost—but I can't find it."

He had a strange way of wording his abilities. He was seeking the signature of an undead presence, something outside the fabric of life.

"And you've never had trouble finding a vampire before?" Philip asked.

Wade had almost forgotten that he was standing in the hall archway, but his question was perfectly sound.

"No, I found you almost right away," Seamus answered, "once I reached Seattle."

Wade took a long breath. They certainly couldn't abandon this lead, but he wasn't sure what they should do. Should they go to London themselves and search?

"Let me rest, stay by Rose a few nights, and I'll try again," Seamus said.

For now, that seemed sensible, but again, Wade wished he understood more about Seamus' strengths and limitations.

Wade nodded. "She's in with Eleisha. Let's go and tell them."

Philip's eyes narrowed. "In with Eleisha? Why?"

Seamus ignored him and blinked out.

"Come on," Wade said, walking down the hallway. "Rose just wanted to check on her."

Philip followed, still looking less than pleased. "Rose doesn't need to—"

"Wade!" Seamus' voice echoed around them. "Hurry!"

Wade bolted into motion, running down the hall and jerking open Eleisha's door. It took a moment for the scene before him to sink in. Both women were kneeling on the floor. Seamus stood beside them. Rose's skirt was crumpled beneath her, and strands of hair stuck to her contorted face. She was gripping a silver hairbrush.

Eleisha was wearing a bathrobe, and the bottom was open, exposing her slender legs. She was gripping Rose's wrist, and her expression was equally disturbed.

What was happening? What should he do? He feared disengaging them by force and causing them further shock.

But in this split second of indecision, Philip pushed past him, moving almost faster than he could see. Before Wade could take another breath, Philip had one arm under Eleisha's back and another under her legs.

"No!" Wade cried, too late. "Wait!"

Philip had already swept her up into the air, and then he stumbled backward, falling to sit with his back against the side of the bed, crushing her up against himself in a panicked embrace.

"Don't hurt her," Wade yelled at him, running to Rose.

"Help Rose!" Seamus was calling in the same moment.

"Take the brush away," Eleisha choked out.

Too many things were happening at the same time. The brush?

Wade dropped down beside Rose, entering her mind while he was still moving.

I'm here! he projected.

He could feel her pain, but he didn't read her thoughts, as he could not allow himself to get lost in whatever she was experiencing. Instead, he tried to break her focus, to create a bridge.

Wade?

She could feel him.

Open your hand.

She dropped the brush.

She blinked and then choked at the sight of him.

"Rose, are you all right?" Seamus asked.

She leaned forward, closing her eyes.

Wade could not help reaching out to touch her shoulder. "It's okay."

He looked over to see Philip's arms still tightly gripping Eleisha, but her eyes were open, and she was staring back at Wade.

"The brush," she whispered. "It was Maggie's."

*   *   *

Twenty minutes later Eleisha was sitting at the kitchen table as Wade handed her a cup of very hot tea. She set it down.

Rose sat beside her, still looking somewhat shell-shocked. Seamus hovered directly behind Rose.

Philip was standing by the sink with his arms crossed, his expression dark. Eleisha knew he hated any type of discussion that involved his own past—especially anything that included Maggie.

"Psychometry?" Wade asked Rose. "You picked up memories from touching Maggie's old hairbrush?"

Even though everyone was calmer now, more composed, underlying tensions still filled the room, and Eleisha's back teeth kept clicking together. She was having difficulty accepting that Maggie had made another vampire and kept it a secret.

"Yes," Eleisha answered Wade. "I've held that brush many times, and I didn't flash to a memory." She looked at Rose. "You have a power that none of us do."

Rose blinked, as if this had just occurred to her. "It's not one I would ask for."

No, certainly not. Being forced inside Maggie's past must have been terrible. At least Eleisha had chosen to look. Rose had simply been sucked into the vision, an unwilling voyeur to Maggie's pain.

"You're sure it was Maggie?" Wade asked.

"Of course I'm sure," Eleisha answered, somewhat shortly. "But the house was so different, gaudy and garish, like that Austin Powers movie you showed me."

He moved closer, "Maybe the sixties or seventies?"

"Maybe . . . but the girl, Simone, she didn't fit. She looked more like someone from the twenties or thirties."

"Well, if that's the case, they were together a long time."

No one spoke for a few moments, but Philip's expression

turned darker, like he was fighting to keep from walking out of the room.

Eleisha hated to drag him into this, but she had little choice. "Maggie never told you?"

He wouldn't look at her. "You saw it wrong. Maggie made no others."

"I *didn't* see it wrong," she answered quietly. "Simone said she was leaving to go to Denver, but she seemed . . . to like new things. I doubt she's still there."

Again, they fell silent for a short while, and finally, Wade said, "Seamus is in no shape to go out again, but I say we forget the lead in London for now." He turned to Seamus. "Can you stay with Rose a few nights, until you feel like yourself again, and then go look in Denver?"

Seamus had faced a great many changes in recent months, and he seemed to be having difficulty at the moment worrying about Rose's newfound ability. Eleisha shared his concern. Would it get worse? Could Wade teach her to control it?

"I can look in Denver," Seamus answered.

"She was so cold," Rose whispered. "Simone. Even if we find her, will she want to join us? Will she follow Robert's laws?"

Eleisha did not understand her questions. Of course Simone would want to join them once she knew they existed.

"We're bringing back the old ways, where we can live safely with each other and still keep our secrets," Eleisha said. "She'll want to come."

Rose glanced away.

chapter 4

Three nights later Seamus materialized in an alley near Market Street in Denver, making sure he was alone in the darkness. He wasn't up to full strength, but he was strong enough to do a search, and he instantly began sensing for an undead signature . . . for a black hole in the fabric of life.

A presence, or perhaps an absence, hit him almost right away, close by, and he blinked out, rematerializing in another alley on Larimer, peering across the street into a little tea shop.

There.

He sensed a vampire in that shop. Rose's vision had paid off—and quickly. Seamus wasn't certain how he felt about her new ability, but he wasn't sure how he felt about many things these days. He'd spent nearly two hundred years alone with Rose, never letting her see how a part of him longed for true death, how he'd suffered through the empty nights, one after the next, where nothing ever changed. Yet another part of him could not bear to leave her all alone. She was his blood and kin, and he endured the endless sameness for her sake.

Wade and Eleisha had changed all that, and now Seamus was a part of something bigger. . . . The underground wouldn't even exist without him. He was the seeker, the searcher, the one who brought everyone together. They could never have found one another without him.

But this *joining* had brought great upheaval for Rose—and for him as well.

The tradeoff was more than fair. Seamus had not realized how hungry he'd been for friendship, and Wade was a true friend, the best of men, in Seamus' eyes. Eleisha had won his affections, too, for she was always kind to Rose.

But Philip . . . did not belong among them. Seamus hated him as he hated the vampire who'd turned Rose so many years ago. Philip was the same breed. He'd been a thoughtless killer in the not-too-distant past, and sometimes, Seamus suspected he had not changed at all. Sometimes, Seamus even considered following when Philip went out alone. He hadn't yet, but the thought had occurred to him more than once.

It was galling that Rose had to live in the same house with such a creature—and even more that Wade and Eleisha could not see the truth of Philip's character.

For now, Seamus did not wish to rock the boat. He liked his new existence too much, but as he became more and more integral to the group, he planned to make himself heard.

The tea shop across the dark street appeared nearly empty. He could see a garish, abstract painting on the back wall, and he sensed an open space behind it. Blinking out, he materialized in a narrow, one-stall bathroom. He was alone for now, and should someone try to enter, he could whisk himself into nothingness in seconds, hopefully quick enough to avoid being seen.

He had no wish to frighten anyone, and the sight of a six-foot-tall Scottish Highlander from the early nineteenth century could rattle the stoutest heart.

He drifted closer to the wall, already feeling himself beginning to weaken.

This was something else he'd hidden from Wade . . . that within moments of being separated from Rose, he began losing his hold on this world.

All ghosts on this plane were tied to a place or a person. Their spirits remained here due to strong—overwhelming—emotion at the time of death. Seamus was no exception. Rose was his only reason for remaining here, and whenever he left her, he could feel himself slipping away, being pulled to the other side.

He fought back, using all his strength to remain . . . so he could be useful to Wade and Rose and Eleisha.

He told them that being away from Rose simply weakened him. He did not tell them the truth. Once he returned to her, he was most comfortable dematerializing and slipping into what he called "nothingness," where he could drift unseen near her and draw strength from their connection.

And this was exactly what he planned to do as soon as he had some solid information for Wade. In the past week, Seamus had pushed himself further than before, twice almost succumbing and being pulled from this plane to the other side . . . which he had never seen. The effort to remain was agony, like pulling an entire house filled with stones. But he'd fought to remain.

He had a new purpose now, and tonight he had succeeded. He'd located a new vampire.

Drifting even closer to the wall, he tried to position himself behind the painting he'd seen from outside. Then slowly, ever so slowly, he let just the surface of his face pass through the colors of the painting, so he could see out into the room—without being noticed himself.

Two women sat together over large pottery cups, leaning close as if huddled in conversation.

One of them—the vampire, Simone—was lovely, just as Eleisha had described her, with milk white skin, china blue eyes, and black hair cut in a straight line at her chin.

But the other woman, although older, possessed beauty of her own, with long blond hair and a slender form. She seemed anxious, gripping the cup tightly, and her eyes were tinged red.

"I'm sure it's nothing, Hailey," Simone said. "He's probably just working too many hours."

Seamus almost floated backward. Simone was having tea with a mortal and consoling her? That hardly sounded like the woman from Rose's vision.

"No, it's more than that," Hailey answered, her voice shaking. "We've been married fifteen years, and Alex has worked long hours before. This is different. When he's with me now, it's like he's not even there, like he doesn't see me."

To Seamus' further surprise, Simone reached out, grasping Hailey's hand.

"I'm here for you," Simone said, her face awash with concern.

Tears gathered in the corners of Hailey's eyes. "I know. Your friendship these past months has meant so much to me." She looked at her watch. "I need to go. I'm hoping he'll come home for dinner tonight. Maybe . . . maybe we can talk."

"That sounds good," Simone agreed, standing up to hug her friend good-bye.

But the second Hailey's back was turned, and she began walking away, Simone's expression shifted. All traces of sympathy vanished, replaced with a hard look of triumph, like someone who had just won a deeply satisfying victory.

Seamus watched her in confusion. She didn't appear to be hunting. What was she doing?

After Hailey was gone, Simone waited about five minutes and then headed out of the tea shop, taking a left and heading toward Sixteenth Street.

Seamus blinked out and rematerialized high in the night air over the tea shop. He drifted along the tops of the buildings, following Simone as she walked quickly down the street until she reached a collection of professional buildings.

She stopped.

Seamus spotted a one-story bank annex and a six-story architectural firm. He moved toward the edge of the bank annex's roof, lowering his body to a position as if he were lying facedown. Then he peeked over, so he could see below and listen without being seen himself.

"Simone," a man called, stepping out the glass doors of the firm. He was tall, wearing a polo shirt and sport coat.

She ran to him, letting him grab her . . . letting him kiss her on the mouth. She kissed him back.

"Alex," she said, pulling away, her voice full of longing.

Seamus couldn't believe the name she'd spoken. She was dallying with Hailey's husband? How could she do such a thing? More important, why would a vampire even want to?

"You're late," he said.

"I'm sorry. I was . . . I was with Hailey." She reached out to him again. "We have to tell her."

"No. You don't know what it would . . ." He shook his head. "I can't."

"Then we have to stop this," she said, her voice full of pain.

She took a step to walk away, but he grasped her arm, gently, and lifted his right hand to her face.

"Simone," he mouthed.

She looked up into his eyes.

And then the strangest feeling began to slowly envelop Seamus. Suddenly, he began to envy Alex for touching Simone, for even standing so close to her. Seamus envied Simone's beauty so much, he wanted to posses her, to make her his own.

The drive was almost overwhelming, and he struggled to hold himself back.

But through the haze, he also fought to focus on Alex's face . . . and he saw the same emotions reflected there: the envy, the need.

"I love you," Alex said raggedly. "Do you hear me?"

Then Seamus understood what was happening. . . . Simone had turned on her gift.

She melted into Alex again. "You mean it? You do?"

"Yes."

"Say it again."

He held her against himself, so that her face looked over his shoulder, and Seamus could see her clearly.

"I love you," Alex repeated softly.

Alex could not see her face, but again her expression altered to a look of cold, wild triumph. Had she been waiting for those words?

Then, just as quickly, her expression shifted to open adoration, and she pulled back slightly to look up at him. "It's no one's fault, Alex. It just happened."

His eyes moved up and down her delicate face. "I have to go home tonight, but I'll call you later."

"And we'll be together soon?"

"Soon. I promise."

She smiled at him, like a joyous young girl. "You make me so happy. I'm going home, too. I'll wait to hear from you."

Alex kissed her again, more deeply this time, and then he walked toward a parking garage. Simone watched his back, her blue eyes glowing with triumph again, her face a hard, perfect mask—hiding whatever seethed beneath.

The feelings of envy vanished from Seamus.

He had no idea what she was playing at, but now, the mere sight of her made him feel like small insects were crawling up and down his transparent arms. He wanted to shudder.

She began walking in the other direction, and he followed.

If she was going home, he needed to see her address.

Philip went looking around the church for Eleisha, knowing that if she wasn't in the kitchen or reading in the downstairs living room, she was probably out in the garden. He found her near the front gates, down on her knees, clipping faded buds from a climbing yellow rosebush.

She didn't hear him coming, and he stopped to watch as she worked intently. She was wearing a long broomstick skirt and a thin flannel shirt. Her hair was loose, hanging almost to the ground where she knelt. She never wore makeup, but her ivory face glowed in the darkness.

She looked small and fragile.

He'd never known anyone like her. She represented the present for him, the *now*, and he didn't want to look back on the past. He didn't like the chain of events that was unfolding, and when he'd agreed to help Wade and Eleisha in this bizarre "search," he'd never expected to find anything remotely connected to himself.

"Seamus is back from Denver," he said. "I think he found something. The others are waiting in the sanctuary."

She started slightly and turned her head. Her eyes seemed far away. Lately, she had been thinking too much. Much too much. He wasn't stupid, and he knew she was nearly bursting to talk to him but had so far managed to hold herself back.

Suddenly, kneeling there on the ground, she appeared anxious, almost afraid of him.

"Since you made Maggie," she asked without any warning, "and Maggie made this girl . . . this Simone, does that mean she is related to you?"

The question stunned him. "What?"

This was what he didn't want! Discussions like this.

But the half-frightened look on her face kept him from turning around and walking off. He didn't want her to be afraid to ask him questions.

"No," he said with effort. "I don't think it works that way."

"Did you turn Maggie because you loved her?" she rushed on. "Only because you loved her?"

He went rigid, grinding his back teeth, but her expression had changed to hope now. For some reason, she needed to speak aloud of these things. He walked over and crouched down, with little idea what to say.

"I don't know," he answered. "You know I can't remember anything of my life before Angelo turned me. Julian said that Maggie and I were going to be married, even though my family was against it, even though she was common and had no money."

"Then you must have loved her."

"I must have."

"But you turned her afterward. Why?"

"I don't know."

He did know. Perhaps he couldn't remember anything from before being turned, but he was keenly aware that he'd been very different before and that Maggie didn't like the new version. She was repulsed. He thought that by turning her, he could change the way she looked at him.

Eleisha reached out to touch his fingers. "Can you show me?"

He jerked his hand away. "No!"

Her eyes widened, and he cursed himself.

"No," he repeated more calmly. "I cannot show you anything from before, and after . . . after, you don't want to see. I don't *want* you to see." How could he possibly explain this? "I like the way you look at me now."

To his great relief, she pulled her hand back. "Oh, Philip, I'm sorry."

He studied her face. She did understand. He placed great importance on what he saw in the eyes of others, but the reflection in Eleisha's was most important.

She saw him as strong, resourceful, and good company. She trusted him.

That could not change.

In his memories, she'd already seen some of what he had once been, in the early days. But Philip had discovered that he possessed the best control over what he did and didn't show Eleisha and Wade in their memory exchanges. He couldn't filter or change a memory, but he'd been careful with what he'd shown her, and there were entire decades he wanted to lock away and pretend never happened.

She stood up. "We should go in. The others are waiting."

Even more relieved, he followed her back to the sanctuary.

Mary Jordane hovered on the opposite side of the church.

Whenever she decided to fully materialize, anyone nearby could see her, but she'd learned to be cautious, and she knew the

layout of the churchyard by now, so she could initially appear behind rosebushes, shrubs, or one of the few small trees in the darkness, just to be sure she was alone.

Yes, she knew every inch of the garden and most of the church
quite well. After all, she'd been stuck here—on and off—for
months, waiting for Eleisha or Wade to stumble across another
vampire and set up a meeting.

So far, they hadn't found zip.

How long could this take?

But she wouldn't abandon her "post," as she liked to call it.
Julian had a temper, and making him mad was never a good idea.
He'd managed to call her spirit back from the gray, in-between
plane, but unfortunately, this gave him almost complete power
over her. He could call her to him at any moment—whether she
wanted to go or not—and he could send her right back to the other
side.

She wasn't going back there . . . so she obeyed him.

Still, even here in the real world, she longed to go someplace
else, anyplace else, and she hoped Eleisha would find something to
investigate soon.

In the meantime, in addition to spying on Eleisha's group, Mary
had been practicing her abilities.

One of the first things she'd learned was that she could "blink
herself" right inside the walls of a building. This didn't hurt her,
and no one could see her. The problem was that she couldn't see
or hear either.

So she was still working on new ways to spy and eavesdrop
without being spotted, and she was gaining a much stronger grasp
on wishing herself into "nothingness," or a state of limbo in which
she was invisible to people until either she wished to materialize
again . . . or Julian called her.

But she'd also learned that she had an advantage over the other spirits who'd remained here in what she called "the real world." From what she understood—from talking to other ghosts—spirits of the dead could exist on three different planes: (1) the real world of the living, (2) the gray in-between plane, and (3) the Afterlife. She had no idea what the Afterlife looked like, as she had never seen it, but during her time on the gray plane, she'd come to believe that the vast majority of ghosts ended up in the Afterlife, as she once could have . . . had she been willing to leave the in-between plane of the spirits who refused to accept death, who still longed to find a way back here, back to the living.

But all of the few ghosts she'd met here in the world of the living had been trapped the moment they died by strong ties to either a person or a place. Being tied down to a person or place, they could not move with the ease that she could. As yet, she hadn't met a single spirit who'd crossed back from the other side, like she had.

Mary was unique.

She could go anywhere she wanted and stay as long as she liked, or as long as Julian allowed.

She floated a little higher up the walls of the church and peeked in through a stained-glass window. Then she froze, on the verge of wishing herself away into nothingness.

Wade, Rose, and Seamus were all gathered in the sanctuary. She knew their behavior patterns by now, and a gathering in the sanctuary normally meant some kind of meeting.

But Mary didn't like being this close to Seamus. Sometimes he could feel her presence and would try to find her. As yet . . . she had no idea whether another ghost could hurt her, but she'd never waited around long enough to find out. She could easily whisk herself away before he spotted her—as he was tied to Rose and had more trouble moving around—but he sometimes picked the worst moments to feel her on the edge of his senses.

Julian wanted Eleisha's group completely unaware that they were being spied on, so Mary had to bolt if she felt Seamus coming. He couldn't be allowed to see her now.

She forced herself to remain in place, peering through the window. He looked preoccupied and tired and well . . . kind of faded. She knew he hadn't been around much the past few days. Where had he been?

But he didn't seem to know she was even there.

Good.

Just then, Eleisha and Philip walked through the main doors.

Mary moved her left ear through a bit of red stained glass so she could listen.

Eleisha knew that Seamus had found something the second she saw Wade's face: excited and tense at the same time. Poor Seamus looked exhausted, and she could barely make out the yellow and blue tones of the plaid draped across his shoulder. He also looked slightly . . . unsettled. She wondered why.

The sanctuary always felt so large to her, even when they were all gathered here. At first it had just been a big empty room, with a big empty altar. But she and Rose had slowly been turning it into a mix of a library and sitting room, with couches, small tables, lamps, and bookshelves. The six arch-topped stained-glass windows created a warm effect, even at night. She, Rose, and Wade all liked to read. So did Seamus if Wade turned the pages.

But the sanctuary also functioned as a meeting place—like right now.

She hated to launch into questions, but if they had finally found someone, she wanted to get started right away, especially in this case, because Simone would not know she possessed telepathic abilities and was still killing to feed.

"You found her?" she asked, but it came out more as a statement.

Seamus nodded weakly. "She owns a house on High Street, near some fancy public gardens. Her last name is Stratford, and I have her address."

Eleisha glanced around at the others. After all this time, Simone was still in Denver. This meant that in spite of her comments inside the memory, she was capable of planting roots. That was a good sign.

Philip stood stiffly beside a light brown couch, and he wouldn't look at anyone. But Wade and Rose both turned to Eleisha, clearly eager to get started.

"I should write to her," Rose said. "Let her get used to the idea that we are here, let her invite us to come meet her."

This had been Rose's strategy before—as she had contacted Eleisha first. Some element of her gift of wisdom seeped through into her letters, often causing the reader to be slightly seduced by her words. This hadn't worked on Philip, but Eleisha and Wade had both been affected.

However . . . with Simone, Eleisha was convinced that such an attempt would not be the best approach.

She steeled herself for the bomb she was about to drop. In the past few nights, she had been going over and over Maggie's memory, trying to get a better grasp of Simone. Although everyone changed and grew, from what she'd seen, Simone was selfish and violent . . . rather like Philip had once been. He never would have responded to a letter.

Eleisha had already decided on the best way to move forward if Seamus actually found Simone.

She shook her head. "I don't think so, Rose. She won't respond, and a letter might spook her. She could run, and then we'd lose her. I think an initial meeting in person might be best . . . so she can see we're not a threat."

"What?" Wade asked. "We just track her down and introduce ourselves?"

"Sort of." Eleisha hesitated. "But just me and Philip."

Wade blinked in surprise. "You and Philip?"

She rushed in before he could go on. "Think about it. Rose can't travel, so she'll have to stay here, and we shouldn't leave anyone alone." She paused again. "We don't want Simone spooked by a small crowd . . . and at first, I think she might be dangerous, not at all like Rose or Robert. You should stay here."

"No," Wade argued angrily. "You'll need me to help spark her telepathy."

Rose's expression crumpled, but surely she must have considered some of this before. She could barely handle the train ride from San Francisco, and she was terrified of airplanes.

The problem was that they all wanted to be useful. Seamus had already done his part. Rose had planned to help with initial contact, and Wade's main job was to help instigate the new vampire's psychic abilities. Both Wade and Rose must feel like the rug had just been jerked from beneath them.

"Of course we'll need you," Eleisha told Wade, "once we get her back here. But first, we have to *get* her back here, and I've only just realized that every situation is going to be different . . . depending on what kind of vampire we find."

Wade opened his mouth again, but Philip cut him off. "Eleisha's right. Rose can't come, and no one should be here alone. After we leave, you should load your gun and bolt all the doors. Don't go out until we get back. Do you have enough food?"

Wade stared at him.

Philip's job was to protect anyone they found from Julian long enough for a journey back here to the underground.

But Eleisha could see how much he liked her suggestion—that only he and she take this trip to Denver. He'd been uncomfortable with Simone's connection to Maggie from the start. Having only one other member of the group partaking in the search to find Simone seemed to put him slightly more at ease.

Frustrated, Wade glanced at Seamus.

"I'm in agreement with Eleisha," Seamus said. "From what I saw of this woman, Wade, I don't want you in the same city with her."

"Is she that bad?" Eleisha asked. "A thoughtless killer?"

"No, not like that. I didn't see her kill anyone, but she seems to like . . . playing games with people's lives, to hurt them slowly."

"What do you—?"

"I don't know!" Seamus nearly snapped. "I wasn't there long enough." He studied her face. "Her gift is envy. It's strong."

"Envy?" Eleisha had never encountered that before. "Did you learn anything else?"

"No." He paused, still seeming unsettled. "Just be careful. Don't trust her."

"We're not going to trust her," she promised.

Trust was not an issue, at least not at first. If Simone had spent forty years hunting with Maggie and then another thirty or forty hunting on her own, Eleisha's task would not be easy. But Philip had been the most savage killer in their entire history, and he understood the need for laws, for safety, for secrecy. He had learned to alter memories and to feed without killing. He had learned to value the opportunity to exist inside a community of his own kind.

If he could do it, so could Simone.

"So, we're agreed?" she asked. "Wade and Rose hold down the fort, and Philip and I go to Denver? Seamus, you might need to act as a go-between if we can't find her at her home. Can you do that?"

"I think so."

Wade didn't say anything, but at least he'd stopped arguing.

Rose still looked crestfallen. "I wish I could be more help. I thought I could at least write the letters, help arrange a meeting."

Eleisha reached out and grasped her hand. "Simone will need you as much as Wade when we get back."

Philip walked away abruptly, heading toward the door behind the altar. "I'll book our plane tickets. We should leave tonight."

"You bring that cell phone I bought you!" Wade ordered after him.

Eleisha found herself just standing there, holding Rose's hand and looking at Wade. He was stunned and angry.

But there was nothing left to say.

Julian paced the floor of his study.

He hadn't fed in more than a week, and he was hungry.

Normally, he didn't hunt near Cliffbracken, not even in the villages. Although he was adept at hiding evidence, completely disposing of bodies could prove difficult unless he was near either a large or a moving body of water.

A disappearance in a village caused a good deal more notice and concern than a disappearance in a larger city, and he didn't want an investigation focused within eighty kilometers of his home.

Mary had still not checked in, and although he did not wish to miss a report from her, he found himself growing hungrier each night.

So he pulled his Jetta out of its refurbished garage—from what had once been part of the stables—and drove toward Riverside. He could have afforded any car he wanted, but he'd liked this black Jetta. It was dependable.

Driving along the dark roads, he couldn't help dwelling on Mary's recent news that Wade had sent Seamus to London, seeking the truth about a madman biting a woman in an alley . . . and the two police dogs turning on their own handlers. Could this be another elder like Robert who had somehow slipped through Julian's net? If so, it would have to be someone who'd been hiding for so long that he had lost his grip on sanity. Julian had never heard of an elder who could use telepathic control of animals, but the idea seemed possible.

He was anxious for a report from Mary, and yet he feared calling her back in case she was in the middle of learning something important. If Eleisha's group had found an elder, he would need to act soon. Anyone from the distant past who'd practiced the laws, who might yet teach the laws, was a danger—mad or not—and he was anxious to know the outcome of Seamus' search.

So lost in his thoughts, he was surprised to realize he was nearing Riverside. He didn't plan to be here long, just long enough to feed.

He was aware that vampires like Philip sometimes liked to spend time with their victims, to talk and interact before feeding. But Julian had no interest in speaking with mortals. He fed on blood and fear and life.

That was all he required.

Pulling into the small city, he parked on Castle Street and left his car, walking toward the river.

It was after midnight, and the streets were nearly deserted. He walked along, passing a filthy old man with a bottle in his hand. Julian kept going. Farther down, he passed a group of teenagers engaged in a loud argument. Again, he kept going. He was interested only in someone alone.

Then he saw a figure walking toward him, up the sidewalk by the river. He could see her slender shape from a distance, and he heard her alternately humming and singing a tune in French. He moved off the sidewalk and stepped between two buildings.

The woman came closer, and he stared through the darkness. She was about twenty years old, with long light brown hair, wearing faded blue jeans, a T-shirt, and a backpack. He always preferred foreign travelers when possible, especially those traveling alone. It could be weeks before they were missed, and then friends or relatives often had no clue where to begin looking.

His routine was nearly always the same. He varied it only slightly based on the situation. Waiting there in the darkness between the buildings, he almost allowed her to walk past, and then he turned on his gift.

Fear.

Waves of fear flowed outward, surrounding her, engulfing her. She stopped, her eyes widening.

"In here," he said.

Her head swiveled toward him, and he could see the strong bones of her face. She looked healthy, with lightly tanned skin.

"Now," he said, allowing more fear to seep out until she was too terrified not to do as he ordered.

She took a step toward him and then wavered. He felt mild

surprise. It had been a long time since he'd encountered anyone with such a strong survival sense. But he let the power of his gift increase until her face twisted in fear and she came toward him.

The second she was close enough, he grabbed her arm and jerked her into the darkness between the buildings, moving farther back. Then he slammed her up against a brick wall. Her backpack cushioned the impact. Locked in fear, she couldn't talk, but her expression pleased him.

He didn't hesitate and bit down hard just below her jaw, holding her tightly while she bucked and struggled. She smelled of clean perspiration and vanilla.

Just as he began to swallow mouthfuls of her, he turned off his gift. He always did at this point, relishing most the feel of his victims' natural terror as reality set in and they knew they were about to die.

Suddenly, the feel of her body changed. She became more fluid in her struggles, trying wildly to push him away. He was drinking hard and fast.

But she managed to cry out, "No!" once before growing too weak to form verbal sounds, and then she stopped pushing at him. He was forced to hold her up.

It had indeed been a long time since he'd fed on someone this strong willed. He knew that other vampires saw the memories of their victims, pieces of the mortal's entire life while feeding. He did not. He had no telepathic ability at all.

Her heart stopped beating, and he almost regretted that the experience was over.

But he felt sated and strong again.

Still holding her up with one hand, he pulled back to look at her. Her throat was torn, and her head lolled forward. Blood still ran freely down onto her gray T-shirt.

He saw a small pile of aging bricks near the building behind him, and he dragged her over to them. Opening her backpack, he pulled out her wallet and her passport, slipping them into his pocket. He stuffed a few bricks into the backpack. After making sure the path was empty, he dragged her to the river and dropped her in, watching her body slip beneath the current. Then he washed his face quickly and made certain his shirt was clean.

Before he'd even reached his car, he'd forgotten all about the girl.

He got behind the wheel and started for home. Within a few kilometers, he was back to dwelling on Eleisha's progress, wondering whether she had found another elder.

The air beside him shimmered, and Mary suddenly appeared in the passenger seat, her silver nose stud glinting in the darkness.

"There you are!" she exclaimed. "I looked all over the manor. I even looked in the stables. I finally had to start searching for an undead signature."

Clenching his jaw, he wished they could devise some method of warning before she just popped into view like that. But he was more interested in hearing what she had to say.

"Eleisha and Philip are going to Denver," she blurted out. "Tonight."

This startled him so much that he briefly crossed over to the wrong side of the road.

"Denver?"

"Yeah, they—"

"Stop!"

Looking ahead for a clear area, he pulled the car off and put it into neutral, leaving it running. Then he turned his full attention to Mary.

"You said they were looking in London," he stated coldly.

"Yeah, but something happened. I'm not sure what. They pulled out of London and sent Seamus to Denver. He found another vampire, named Simone Stratford."

Julian's mind raced. Back in 1825, he had stolen a book called *The Makers and Their Children*, filled with detailed notes of all vampires currently in existence: their homes, their preferences, their companions. He had used this to hunt down all the elders—and he had studied it for countless hours. There was no vampire in the book named Simone.

"I don't think she's the kind that you're looking for," Mary rushed on, "'cause they were talking about waking up her telepathy."

Julian tensed.

He mentally separated vampires into two categories: (1) those who existed before his purge, who practiced the laws and who wanted him destroyed because he could not follow the first law, and (2) those who came after, who had no training in telepathy from a maker and no knowledge of the laws.

Vampires like Philip, Eleisha, and Maggie had fallen into a gray area of being created before the purge but left to develop on their own. They had posed no threat to him—until recently.

But he was interested, desperately interested, only in Eleisha tracking down the first type, and he did not want her distracted by running off after some vampire like Rose who fell into the second category.

"You're certain?" he said. "This Simone is young? She knows nothing?"

"I don't know. But Eleisha seemed to think so. And she's so worried Simone might be dangerous that she's leaving Wade and Rose behind. She's just taking Philip."

He sat straighter. "Dangerous?"

This was getting worse. First Eleisha finds some useless young vampire in Denver, abandoning the more promising search in London, and now she was approaching an unknown, undead, unpredictable creature?

He shook his head in frustration.

"You want me to contact Jasper and tell him to meet me in Denver?" Mary asked.

Julian put his fist to his mouth. He often forgot all about Jasper Nesland—a vampire he'd recently created to serve him.

"No. Go to Denver and keep watch."

Eleisha could be wrong about this woman they'd found . . . and she could still be an elder who'd simply changed her name.

"Find out what's going on and report back to me," he said. "But come straight back if you think Eleisha is in danger."

"'Cause you need her to keep hunting for the older ones, like that Robert guy?"

"Just keep watch and report to me."

She rolled her eyes. "Whatever. But we need to go to the manor first. I don't know how to get to Denver. You'll have to pull down some maps."

He took his fist from his mouth, knowing she was right, and wondering how recent his maps of America might be. He would have to order some new ones if Eleisha continued searching in the States.

"You go on ahead," he said, unable to stand Mary's company a moment longer. "I'll meet you there."

Thankfully, without another word, she vanished.

Julian sat there, still absorbing this unexpected change of events. Then he put the Jetta in first gear and pulled back out on the road, heading for Cliffbracken.

*   *   *

SAN FRANCISCO, CALIFORNIA

Despite Julian's orders, Mary to decided to go see Jasper before teleporting herself to Denver.

Of all the people in the world, Jasper was the only one that Mary considered . . . a friend. She spent as much time with him as she could, but even this relationship seemed to be changing.

For one, Julian had put Jasper into a gorgeous town house at the Infinity complex near the waterfront, leased him a BMW, and given him a credit line with Wells Fargo. Before Jasper was turned, he'd been a damaged, tasteless, directionless young man living in a rat-hole apartment with one chair and an old TV.

Mary had handpicked him for Julian, and so she kind of felt like he was "hers."

After being turned, Jasper adjusted to life as a vampire with amazing speed, and although he'd messed things up a few times on their last attempt to use Eleisha, he'd certainly proven he wasn't afraid to follow Julian's orders or to throw himself into a fight.

He liked the rewards too much: the town house, the money, the car, the clothes.

But after a few months of having money, he was beginning to look and act like a different person, and Mary found herself wishing he would go back to being more like he was in the beginning, when he was more like her.

She'd been an outcast in high school.

So she'd decided to live up to everyone's bad opinion of her by chopping off most of her hair in the bathroom one night, dyeing it magenta, and then going out and getting a nose stud. She'd acted out at school, driven her parents to the edge of sanity, and basically done everything possible to make herself *visible*.

She had a feeling that Jasper had done everything possible to make himself *invisible* back in high school, but that their social suffering had been pretty much the same.

She'd never asked him about this. They were both past all that now. A vampire and a ghost, working together.

At first, she felt like her condition gave her advantages over him. She could move anywhere she liked almost instantly. Disappear and reappear. Spy for Julian almost effortlessly.

Jasper couldn't do any of that. But then she found out he could do one thing she could never do.

He could change himself.

Teleporting from Wales to Jasper's town house in San Francisco, she found the place empty. This didn't surprise her. He normally went out at night. She floated just inside the door, looking around. The place was amazing, with marble-tiled floors and a state-of-the-art kitchen of stainless-steel appliances. One wall of the living room comprised a giant window overlooking the bay. The whole room was decorated in black and white.

Where had he gone? By now, she knew the specific feel of his undead energy signature—or perhaps his lack of an energy signature in the world of the living—and she tried to sense for him.

He was close. Very close.

She realized he was stepping off the elevator. She didn't sense any living person in the hall, so she blinked out and then blinked into the hallway. He was walking toward her.

"Mary," he said, glad to see her.

He was the only one who was ever glad to see her.

But he looked so different now.

When she'd found him, he'd been a shabby, skinny mess, wearing dirty pants and scuffed athletic shoes. His hair had been a tragedy.

She'd begun to believe the lyrics from that old song "Money Changes Everything."

A local stylist had taken in the shape of Jasper's face and then cut his hair very short, almost into a military cut—like George Clooney had worn for a while. Somehow, this suited Jasper, making the bones of his face appear more defined. He was wearing a simple pair of Levi's over some black boots, a Hugo Boss T-shirt, and a smaller version of the light Armani coat that Philip wore.

He looked stylish and confident.

He made Mary wish she could grow her hair out, dye it back to its normal brown, and go shopping for some new clothes. Although she'd never admit it aloud, he made her want to look like her old self again.

But she couldn't. She would always look exactly the same as she had the moment she'd died.

"What's up?" he said, unlocking the door to the suite.

He didn't bother asking her in because he seemed to think the place belonged to them both. That was something else she liked about him. He always acted as if they were a team who shared everything—well, everything he could share with a noncorporeal spirit.

"I just wanted to tell you to stay close and be ready to move," she said. Julian had not ordered her to give Jasper any messages, but this just seemed sensible.

"Where to?"

"Denver. I think Eleisha found someone. She took Philip, and they're flying out tonight."

"Just Philip?"

"Uh-huh. Wade and Rose are staying behind."

A new sword glistened in a rack over the fireplace. Jasper glanced at it. "Who'd they find?"

"I don't know. Some woman named Simone."

"Does he want me to take her head?"

"Not yet. I'm supposed to get more info first. Just stay close to the suite, so I can find you."

"Okay."

She wished she had more to share. She wished she had a reason to stay longer.

"I'll be back soon," she said finally.

He nodded a bit sadly, like he wished she could stay, too. But they both had to follow Julian's orders.

She blinked out.

chapter 5

S imone Stratford took a final look in the ladies' room mirror, pleased as always by what she saw.

The styles of the late 1920s had suited her to perfection, and she'd had the good sense to never become a fashion slave. She wore straight-cut, low-waisted, sleeveless dresses in vivid but solid colors—that accentuated her slender body—along with flat shoes and long beads tied in a knot below her collarbone. She liked black eyeliner and lipstick.

Rather than looking out of style in any given era, she always looked as if she were setting a style.

She'd never met a man who could resist the hint of an early-century flapper. Men were too drawn to the combination of color and energy and life.

Tonight, she was meeting Alex Barber at the Samba Room on Larimer Street. The place was slightly beneath them both, but she couldn't risk meeting him anyplace where they might be seen by anyone he knew. Besides, tonight she felt like dancing.

She'd arrived a little early to check her appearance and scout a table. As she stepped out from the ladies' room, she saw Alex coming through the front doors. He spotted her immediately, and she smiled, flashing white teeth and moving her head slightly so her shining black bob would swing.

He froze.

She knew he would.

She let him come to her.

"You're early," he said.

He was tall, with sharp features, still wearing his polo shirt and sport coat from work—as a partner in an architectural firm. He liked to be in charge, and she enjoyed the illusion of letting him think he was.

His wife of fifteen years was an ex–fashion model named Hailey. At present, Hailey was Simone's best friend.

"I thought I'd get us a table," Simone said.

"Have you?"

"Not yet."

She allowed a tiny bit, just a whisper, of her gift to leak out, making him envious of her beauty, of her entire life.

"I'll find us one," he said.

"No, I want to dance."

He cocked his head to one side. He wasn't a fool, and he wasn't given to falling for feminine wiles. That's why he made this exciting.

"Sure."

A Latino song was playing, soft and slow. He led her to the dance floor and pulled her close. She melted against him.

The place was packed. Normally, Alex didn't like such crowded venues, but she was in the mood to punish him a little.

He'd told her he loved her a few nights ago, which was good, but as yet he'd said nothing about leaving Hailey. Simone had been working on this game for four months! By now, he should be ready to leave his wife and beg Simone to live with him.

And then she would let Hailey find out about everything . . . everything. But Alex had to be disgusted with Hailey, tired of her, and mad for Simone first. Then she could feed on the shock and pain on Hailey's face as the truth finally hit her.

When Simone had first met these two, first seen the way Alex looked at Hailey—with a mix of love and desire in his eyes after fifteen years—she knew she'd found something special. Lately, the thrill of the contest had been losing its shine, but this was the most satisfying game she'd played in a long time.

As she danced, pressing her body up against his, she let more of her gift seep out, affecting the people around them. Heads turned her way as the people dancing near them were infected by envy. Women wanted to be her. Men wanted to be part of her life. She pulled her head back to watch Alex notice all the people looking at her.

She was the center of the world.

His eyes filled with need and longing. Maybe tonight he'd finally tell her he was leaving Hailey.

The dance ended, and she started to lead him off the floor, but a man standing near a table, staring at her, caught her attention.

He was taller than most men in the room, with amber eyes and red-brown hair hanging to the top of his collar. His ivory face was so handsome, it bordered on beautiful, and he wore a long Armani coat even through it was seventy-eight degrees outside.

Something about him frightened her—and she was rarely frightened.

Then a crowd of dancers exiting the floor crossed in front of him, and when she looked back he was gone.

"What is it?" Alex asked.

She shook off the eerie feeling. "Nothing."

Alex watched the cocktail waitresses nearly jumping among

numerous tables and then running back to the bar with drink orders to fill. "We'll never get served like this. You find us a place to sit, and I'll get us something from a bartender."

"Red wine," she reminded him, looking around for a table.

She spotted one that appeared empty, except for a few remaining beer bottles, and she headed toward it.

Then a young woman stepped into view about fifteen feet away, and Simone stopped again.

The woman—girl—seemed too young to be in a lounge. Like Simone, she looked out of place, like someone from another country or another time. She was small, with pale arms, wearing a tan tank top and matching broomstick skirt. Her dark blond hair was long and wispy, hanging loose. She wore no makeup, and the effect of her clothes and coloring created the image of a stalk of wheat swaying in a wind.

Simone backed up without knowing why.

Something about this girl frightened her.

Simone half turned, looking across the room for an exit, and she saw the ivory-skinned man in the Armani coat standing about twenty feet to her left. She whipped her gaze back to the front, and the girl was gone. The path to the front door was open.

Simone hurried across to the bar, grasping Alex's sleeve. "Forget the drinks. I don't like this place."

He frowned but let her pull him out the door and outside. She hailed a cab the instant her feet hit the sidewalk.

Philip followed Simone across the floor, and he stood in the dark doorway of the Samba Room, watching her taxi disappear down Larimer Street. He could still feel her gift washing over and through him, how he envied her, how he wanted to be like her.

In all his existence, he'd rarely been affected by the gifts of his peers. Julian's gift of fear could cripple him, but otherwise, he'd never been seduced, not even by Eleisha's.

Simone's life seemed so perfect. He wanted it.

The feeling began to fade, and he forced himself to step back inside the club.

Eleisha was still inside, waiting for him.

Mary had managed to materialize behind an oversized palm tree near a wall in the Samba Room, ready to blink out if anyone spotted her, but no one even noticed she was there. She'd watched Simone dancing with some corporate-looking guy in a polo shirt. Mary ignored the guy. Julian would want a detailed report on Simone and nobody else.

At the moment, Mary had no idea what she would tell him, but she struggled with an uncomfortable trepidation over the idea of Jasper getting anywhere near this woman.

Jasper had explained several things to her that Julian had not—such as how a vampire's gift worked—and Mary felt Simone's right away. It was strong. Even as a spirit, Mary couldn't help longing to be Simone, to look like her, move like her, live like her.

With effort, Mary managed to clear her thoughts and focus, but then she spotted Philip and Eleisha out among the crowd. She saw the way Philip was staring at Simone, like a hungry man looking at a rib-eye steak, and the situation seemed to be getting more complicated.

She knew exactly what Julian wanted to know: Was Simone a telepathic elder or one of the new breed like Rose?

As yet, Mary couldn't tell, but she wasn't sure it mattered. Something told her that either way, Simone was dangerous, and

Eleisha never should have come here. But how could she explain *that* to Julian?

As Simone fled from the Samba Room, Mary blinked out and rematerialized in an alley, watching the taxi drive past. She knew she had to concentrate on learning only the details Julian wanted to know.

Blinking out again, she materialized high in the sky, so her form blended in with the night air. She followed the cab.

When Rose awoke that night in her room at the church, she got dressed and stepped out into the hall, expecting to sense Wade's presence in his office.

She did not.

Cracking the door, she peeked in to make sure it was empty, and then she heard a clinking sound coming from downstairs.

"Wade?" she called out cautiously.

No one answered.

She moved quietly down the stairs, but the apartment was empty as well, and she began growing anxious. As far as she knew, Seamus was off assisting Eleisha and Philip. She and Wade had promised to hole up inside the church together. She heard the clinking sound again.

Walking down a back passage, she emerged into the industrial-sized kitchen that had once been used for potlucks and parties by the congregation.

She'd never been in here—as none of them needed to visit this room.

The first things she saw were a long stainless-steel counter and a sink. Stacks of folding tables were piled up against one wall. Then, on the other side of the counter, she spotted Wade, down on his knees in an open space, holding a screwdriver and attempting to construct some kind of contraption with pulleys and weights and a leather bench.

A large flattened cardboard box lay on the floor behind him.

He wore a pair of faded jeans with a rip in one knee and a tight navy blue T-shirt. His near-white hair had grown down to his chin, but the look suited him. Rose often thought he underestimated his own physical appearance—maybe from spending too much time standing next to Philip.

"What are you doing?" she asked.

He jumped slightly and looked up. "Oh, Rose." He waved the screwdriver in front of himself. "What does it look like I'm doing? I'm building a home gym."

She moved closer, examining the pulley system. "Why?"

"Why?" He sounded incredulous. "Because Philip seems to think I'm about as useful as a twelve-year-old girl, that's why."

She'd never heard nor seen him so frustrated before.

"You know that's not true," she said. "Philip needs you very much, and he's well aware of it. I shudder to think what he'd be like without you and Eleisha."

Wade turned back to tightening the closest screw with a vengeance. "Is that why he left me here to 'hold down the fort'? I don't want his gratitude or affection right now, Rose. I want his respect."

She hesitated, watching the sinews in his forearms as he worked, not knowing how to answer him. Was this really about Philip? Or was it about Eleisha? Wade seemed to be conveniently forgetting that Eleisha had been the one who insisted he stay behind. Philip had simply agreed—so had Seamus.

After a few moments of silence, Wade sighed and sat upright. "I'm sorry, Rose. Did you need me for something?"

Still concerned, but relieved at the change of subject, she said,

"There's no hurry. I just thought that since we're alone and we have nothing but time for the next few nights, you might work with me on this new telepathic . . . development."

He put down the screwdriver. "The psychometry? Has it happened again?"

She nodded. "Just in bits and pieces. I sometimes see flashes of memories when I touch things like teacups, Eleisha's bath towel, that kind of thing. I won't touch anything Philip's even been near, including the living room couch. If I can't learn to control this better, I might need to start wearing gloves."

His expression shifted to a mix of sympathy and guilt—not at all what she wanted from him. "Of course," he said. "I should have come to you. I should have realized you were going through this all by yourself."

"As I said," she told him, "there's no hurry. Finish your project, and we'll talk later."

He was clearly going through some kind of issue all by himself, too.

Eleisha and Philip had taken a parlor suite at the Oxford on Wazee Street.

Neither one had spoken on their walk back to the hotel. Simone had fled at the sight of them, and running after her would have drawn too much attention. So . . . they'd failed in their first attempt to connect with her.

Once upstairs, Philip unlocked the door to their rooms and led the way inside.

"Seamus was right," Eleisha said finally, clicking on a small lamp and dropping her canvas handbag on the floor. "Her gift is envy. Could you feel it?"

"Yes."

This was the first word he'd spoken since they'd entered the nightclub. She reached out and touched his arm.

"Are you okay?"

He nodded briefly but didn't answer.

"We startled her, didn't we?" Eleisha asked.

He nodded again.

"Do you think she'll run away? Leave the city?"

"No. She doesn't know what we are yet."

"We'll have to find some way to try again."

The suite was comfortable and old-fashioned, with round cherrywood tables and midnight blue couches. He walked over to the window and looked down at the dark street. Poor Philip. He hated this, hated having to deal with a vampire Maggie had created. It must bring back too many unpleasant memories from the distant past.

But Eleisha couldn't stop thinking about Simone, who was so graceful, so lovely. Maggie had always liked beautiful things. She must have loved Simone.

And Simone had left her.

Eleisha knew that sometimes even the closest of vampires felt compelled to go their own ways. She had loved Edward Claymore as a teacher and a companion, but in the end, she'd left him. His role as teacher had become smothering after seventy years. She had come to believe that unless the relationship felt equal, it could not last.

Had Maggie treated Simone like a student for too long? Was that why Simone had turned so cruel, feeding on what appeared to be one of Maggie's mortal lovers and then leaving his body in the closet? Perhaps Simone felt forced into such actions in order to permanently sever the connection.

Eleisha had viewed only the one scene, the one night from Maggie's memory, and she was not about to judge Simone yet. They had all done terrible things.

But after the initial shock of meeting others like herself, she hoped Simone would be glad to learn that she possessed telepathy, that she could feed without killing, that she could live in an equal community with her own kind and not have to hide who she was among her companions.

Eleisha couldn't help Maggie anymore. Maggie was gone. But she could help Simone, and perhaps salve some of her own remorse.

First, though, she had to find a way to make Simone listen for a few moments . . . to understand they were not a threat.

Reluctantly, she walked to the window and joined Philip, not wanting to upset him further but feeling she had no choice.

"Would Maggie . . . ," she began, faltering once, "would she have told Simone about any of us, about you?"

She expected him to flinch and pull away, but he didn't.

"I don't know," he said softly, his French accent so thick, she almost couldn't understand him. "But she never told me about Simone."

"Did you speak to Maggie very often?"

"Sometimes, but not much after she left for America. Julian said we should exist alone, and I . . . all I cared for after that was hunting. After a while, I stopped thinking about Maggie."

She watched his profile glowing in the low light, and her sympathy—or perhaps empathy—for him grew deeper.

"Everything's different now," she whispered. "You're different."

He looked down at her. His voice turned hard, almost angry. "I am different. I forced myself to be different."

What did that mean?

He turned away. "We cannot try to make contact with Simone at her house," he said abruptly, changing the subject. "She would feel invaded, and if she flees at the sight of us again, and we do not catch her, I think then she would run to a different state or country."

He was changing subjects erratically. Now he wanted to talk about the best way to make contact with Simone?

The air shimmered, and Seamus suddenly appeared near the television.

He looked so tired. His transparent colors were faded.

"You need to get back to Rose," Eleisha said immediately.

"Look at that," he answered, pointing toward an end table near the door.

"At what?" She walked over.

"The small newspaper," he said. "That one. I saw that lying open at her house just a few moments ago."

Someone from the hotel staff must have arranged the neat stack of brochures and local papers on the table. Eleisha picked up the thin newspaper Seamus referred to and opened it.

Philip was watching them. "What is it?"

At first, Eleisha had no idea what Seamus wanted her to see, and then her eyes hit a list of local entertainment.

"Simone is singing tomorrow night at someplace called the Mercury Cafe."

Even while reading the entry aloud, Eleisha felt stunned. Simone was singing? In front of a crowd? Drawing all that attention to herself? It was unthinkable.

Philip walked over in five rapid strides. He took the paper from her hand and scanned it. "Good. We'll try again there. Make contact with her among the crowd so she'll feel safer."

Eleisha still couldn't believe a member of their kind would do anything so public, but this was a good lead, a good opportunity. They needed her to listen for just a few moments.

"Did you see anything else we might be able to use?" Eleisha asked Seamus.

"No, but I only looked around the downstairs. Then her taxi pulled up outside, so I came here."

His words brought some relief. It wasn't that she doubted Philip, but she was glad to know that Simone had indeed simply left the Samba Room and gone home. Tomorrow, Simone had a singing engagement—hopefully she'd keep it.

"Well done," Eleisha told Seamus. "You should go home now, stay with Rose. Tell Wade what's happened, but I think we can take it from here."

As if too tired to speak further, Seamus vanished, leaving her alone with Philip again. They had a few hours until dawn.

"That's all we can do for tonight," she said. "I'll make us some tea. What do you want to do now? Would you rather play cards or watch a movie?"

As soon as those words left her mouth, his eyes flew to her face. Without warning, he dropped the newspaper and grasped the sides of her face with both hands. His grip was so solid, she couldn't move, but she wasn't afraid of him. She trusted Philip. His hands were shaking.

"Before you," he whispered, "I never played cards. I never watched movies. I never drank tea."

Poor Philip, she thought again. This entire journey, this task, must be so hard on him.

"Do you like watching movies and drinking tea?" she asked, not even trying to break away from his grip.

He was quiet for almost a full minute and then said, "Yes."

He took his hands away, but she grabbed the right one, pulling him toward the couch. "Come on."

Using the remote, she was surprised to find that Turner Classic Movies was playing Bela Lugosi's 1931 *Dracula*. Philip didn't usually like black-and-white films, but he soon became caught up in this one, behaving more like himself. He even laughed when Lugosi walked straight through the enormous spiderweb.

Eleisha began feeling a little better. They would try again with Simone tomorrow night, and hopefully win her trust. Soon, they could all go back to the underground together. It would be good for Eleisha and Rose to have another woman in the household.

Maybe they couldn't have Maggie with them, but Simone was the next best thing.

chapter 6

The following night, Rose woke up and dressed quickly, taking less time than usual to brush out her hair. The unwanted psychometric flashes were getting worse when she touched random objects, and so she put on a pair of black gloves.

Tonight, she and Wade would need to begin addressing this new manifestation, and she was determined to learn to control it.

As she was heading for the door, a blur of blue and yellow caught her eye, and the barest transparent outline of Seamus appeared.

"Seamus!" she said in alarm. "I can hardly see you."

Even his voice sounded faint. "I'm going to wish myself to nothingness for a while, stay near you, and rest . . . here, but I won't materialize."

"Yes, go! Hurry."

At her urging, he vanished, and she stood there watching the empty spot. Would he be all right? She'd never seen him so weak before. She was going to speak to Wade about this. Seamus played an important role, but he could not be pushed this far ever again.

With two things on her mind—the psychometry issue and Seamus' well-being—she headed downstairs to find Wade, but she heard him before even entering the apartment. He was clanking around loudly in the apartment's small kitchen.

"Wade?" she said, moving through the living room.

All the kitchen cupboards were open. He'd pulled out their few plates and mugs, along with several boxes of cereal and crackers. The refrigerator door was open, but it contained only a half-full jar of mayonnaise and a bottle of Aunt Jemima syrup.

As he half turned and she saw the tense, almost angry expression on his face, all other thoughts left her mind. Something was wrong here. She hadn't known him long, but Wade wasn't the type of man to exist in a state of anger, and he'd been quietly angry since the night Philip and Eleisha left. In Rose's experience, this brand of anger was usually born from fear. What was he afraid of?

Wade needed to have a purpose. Did he fear that Eleisha and Philip did not find him adequate? That his purpose and usefulness here were slipping away?

"What?" he asked, somewhat shortly, and then took a long breath. "I'm sorry, Rose. What did you need?"

"I don't need anything. What on earth are you doing?"

His hair was a mess, and he was wearing the same clothes he'd had on the previous night.

"I'm looking for something to eat."

"Are we out of groceries?" She stepped in to pick up a nearly empty box of cereal. "Philip asked if you had food."

That was the wrong thing to say, and Wade turned his back to her, looking into the barren fridge. "Yes, but he didn't give me time to shop, did he?"

No, he hadn't. He and Eleisha had packed quickly and taken a taxi to the airport, leaving Rose and Wade behind with barely a good-bye.

Rose stepped up behind Wade. "They need you very much. You must be aware of that." When he didn't answer, she tried a different tack. "Think how it is for me. At least you *can* go with them."

With his back to her, he shook his head. "It's not the same, Rose. . . . I'm sorry to say that, but it isn't. Eleisha and I planned all this. We planned to help vampires like you. Philip was just along for the ride, and now . . ." He trailed off and half turned again so she could see his profile. "I know how I sound," he said, "but this situation is all wrong. I should be in Denver. I should be analyzing Simone. I never should have let them leave without me."

Perhaps he was right. Eleisha, Philip, and Wade functioned as an almost perfect triad, with Eleisha as the heart, Philip as the strength, and Wade as the mind. But if Wade understood this, why was he working so hard on building his body? Even with all his professional training and intellect, did he fear being viewed as less valuable than Philip?

She couldn't bring herself to ask him. It was too personal. But she did want to help, so she turned to the task at hand. Stepping around him, she peered into the open refrigerator. "Well, you can't live on mayonnaise and maple syrup. Why didn't you go today when the sun was up?"

"I didn't want to leave you here alone."

That was noble of him but foolish. "Can't you just call and order something for delivery?"

He leaned against the counter and closed his eyes.

For some reason, she couldn't seem to stop making what she considered sensible suggestions—which clearly were not helping.

"I don't want to order delivery and stick money out the door when it arrives," he said quietly. "I don't want to be trapped inside this church. Why are we working so hard to bring lost vampires out of hiding when we're afraid to step outside ourselves?"

And then she understood another piece of his frustration.

Upon returning from San Francisco, they had reasoned that it would take at least two of them to fight Julian should he attack. His gift of fear was overwhelming, so one of them would need to stun him, via a mental attack or multiple gunshots, so that Philip could take his head. Unfortunately, none of them knew how to use a sword except Philip, and taking off Julian's head wouldn't be a matter of just a blind swing. Too many things could go wrong.

This created a problem for Rose and Wade in their current circumstances. Philip had mentioned teaching Wade to use a sword, but nothing had come of this discussion yet.

"As soon as he gets back, we're going to start training," Wade said, as if aware she followed his train of thought.

But there it was again . . . a need to be more like Philip.

In this instance, she couldn't disagree, but his determination didn't help him right now, and if there was one thing Rose understood, it was the despair of hiding away for worry of going outside into the darkness. She'd existed like that for decades. What *was* the use of all their grand plans if Wade couldn't even go out to buy groceries? Besides, they'd been back for months without the hint of a threat.

"You get your gun, and I'll get my bag," she said.

He took his hands off the counter. "What?"

"We'll take the public streetcar to Whole Foods and get you stocked up."

He didn't answer for a few minutes and then asked, "You sure?"

"Of course." She straightened, knowing he'd never leave her here alone. "You'll need me to carry a few bags."

The lines of his face softened, and he glanced down at himself.

"Okay, let me change clothes, and I'll meet you up in the sanctuary."

Rose turned to go get her bag. She kept the gloves on, deciding that work on her psychometry could wait.

Wade needed to get out of the house. He needed to feel in control again.

In spite of her anxiety over finding a way to make Simone trust her, Eleisha couldn't help feeling the sensation of pleasure upon walking into the Mercury Cafe. It was somewhat dim inside and jam-packed with small polished wooden tables and chairs. Antique chandeliers hung from the ceiling, along with string after string of tiny blue and white lights, which gave the entire place the illusion of being covered by a night sky.

Short dividing walls and slender poles helped break a large main room into more individual spaces. The place served dinner and drinks, but even at eleven o'clock, most of the patrons she could see were drinking coffee and eating desserts, like blackberry cobbler with ice cream.

She liked this place much better than the Samba Room.

They'd timed their arrival to coincide with the last part of Simone's performance.

"I don't hear any singing," Philip said. He'd taken even more time than usual with his hair tonight, and the layered ends had an almost pointy look.

Eleisha glanced around. "I think the stage is over there."

They walked through a maze of tables, and as they approached the stage, she realized that this wasn't exactly a professional venue. She'd noticed that the ad in the local paper also mentioned poetry readings, and the situation began to make more sense.

The stage itself was low, only a single step above the floor, with tables nearly pushed up against it. A purple curtain served as a backdrop, with a few plunging drapes of forest green to create a little more drama.

A piano stood off to one side, and the man sitting at it was dressed like the other bartenders. A slender, black-haired woman was speaking to him while handing him a sheet of music.

When she turned, Eleisha could see her delicate profile.

Simone.

She must be in between songs.

Eleisha looked around at the tables and did not see the man Simone had been with the night before. Good. The last thing she and Philip needed was to have some mortal lover getting in the middle of this.

She motioned Philip to a table on the far left side of the stage, and they both sat down to listen.

Simone didn't see them. She moved gracefully back to the microphone. Her silky hair swung gently every time she moved her head. Tonight she wore a low-waisted red dress with a string of black beads tied in a loose knot, still reminding Eleisha of a lovely, almost boyish, flapper from the twenties.

Simone smiled at the audience, coy and warm at the same time.

"Last number," she said gently.

The piano player started, and a few beats later, Simone began to sway ever so slightly, singing "A Good Man Is Hard to Find."

Each word of the 1920s blues lyrics described a forlorn woman with a sad heart, whose man is "treating her mean."

Sitting there, listening, Eleisha went rigid. She'd heard several recordings—on vinyl—of Bessie Smith performing this number. Bessie always chose a throaty, gravelly way of delivering the song, almost as if teasing the audience about how they should interpret the meaning of the lyrics.

But the quality of Simone's rendition was entirely different . . . haunting and filled with need. Why would Simone choose such a self-pitying song? Even with the little Eleisha had seen of her, it hardly seemed her style.

But then Simone put both pale hands on the microphone, and she began singing into it as if it was her priest, her confessor. Rather than throaty, her voice was clear and soft. She was somehow using the lyrics to make the audience feel for her, feel with her.

Although Eleisha was still having trouble believing one of her own kind would get up on a stage, exposing herself to a crowd, she was not prepared for what happened next.

As Simone started the next stanza, she began to exude the power of her gift.

The audience was enraptured. The mood in the room changed, and Eleisha could feel the envy washing through her. She forgot all about the sorrowful words drifting from the speakers and gave herself over to a longing to be just like Simone.

Philip was staring at the stage, his eyes glassy.

Simone sang on, and the lyrics altered—reminding women to treat a man kindly if they found a good one.

When she finished, her last note lingered long in the air. The audience didn't even clap for thirty seconds and then burst into applause. Simone smiled coyly again, stepping off the stage. Several people surged forward, trying to engage her, to touch her.

Eleisha just sat there, reeling. Simone had used her gift when she wasn't even hunting! Perhaps she was hunting and was simply trying to lure someone away. Eleisha had known a few vampires who'd sometimes done this.

She shook her head to clear it, knowing this was their chance to make contact in a public forum where Simone would not feel so threatened. They wouldn't be able to speak too openly, but they didn't need to yet.

Eleisha could see Simone coming toward them, still smiling and chatting with some of the audience members who tried to follow her. Then Simone saw Eleisha, and she stopped cold.

Her expression shifted, and Eleisha feared she would bolt. On instinct, Eleisha flashed out telepathically.

Wait. Please.

Then she glanced down at Philip's chair. It was empty. She moved her eyes back to Simone and saw that he was already at Simone's side. How had he gotten there so quickly? He didn't touch her, but he said something in her ear.

Watching Simone's face, Eleisha felt hope begin to grow. Simone didn't look so frightened anymore, merely wary and uncertain.

And then, Philip was leading her to their table.

He'd done it.

Everything would be okay.

As Simone let the tall man lead her to the table, she began to realize that something enormous was happening . . . she simply didn't know what yet.

She had heard something, words, inside her head just before he'd asked her to come and sit.

But at close range, she finally realized what was different about him—and what was different about the girl at the table. They gave off no heat, no scent of blood.

She reached the table.

"Sit down," the man said. His French accent was thick. He wore the same black Armani coat buttoned at his waist.

She decided to keep on standing for now. "Who are you? Why are you following me?"

"I'm Eleisha," the girl answered, "and this is Philip."

The girl still reminded Simone of some otherworldly stalk of wheat: pretty, but the type who would blend into the wall at a party.

"That doesn't answer my question."

Eleisha studied her briefly and then said, "We knew Maggie long ago. Philip knew her when she was just a girl."

Simone almost gripped the table from shock. Maggie! She looked from Eleisha to Philip, cursing herself for the loss of composure, but she'd been taken too off guard. She almost couldn't process the words.

We knew Maggie long ago.

Vampires.

Maggie had told her there were a few others but to stay away from them. The only one she'd ever mentioned by name was Julian.

"Sit down," Philip repeated.

She slid into a chair, looking at him.

Up close, he was even more perfect than from a distance. He sat down as well and then leaned back.

"I'm sorry we startled you last night," Eleisha said, and to Simone's further surprise, she really did sound sorry. Vampires with pity?

No, not both of them, just Eleisha. Philip looked as pitiless as a leopard. Simone kept her expression still as she fought wildly to get a grip on the situation. Neither one of them seemed to want to hurt her. But they had gone to great effort to seek her out.

"We didn't know any other way," Eleisha went on.

Eleisha's expression seemed almost . . . warm.

Simone had no idea how to respond. But she glanced at Philip. He was still watching her.

"What do you want?" she asked finally, and she allowed a small bit of her gift to flow out.

Eleisha glanced around. "We shouldn't speak too much here," she said quietly. "We just came to let you know that there are others like you, that we've purchased a large home, and that some of us are choosing to live together . . . that you don't have to be alone."

She might have been speaking a foreign language for all the sense she made. Vampires? Living together in a group? Hardly. What was their game?

But as Eleisha spoke that last phrase, Philip shifted his eyes toward her, and Simone felt the world turn under her chair.

The expression in his amber eyes changed as soon as they focused on Eleisha, to something Simone almost couldn't identify. She'd never seen anything quite like it before: a mix of possession, gratitude . . . and need.

Not the kind of need a mortal would express, but something else entirely, something savage and eternal.

Simone forgot all about Alex and Hailey.

They were nothing, shadows next to this.

Then Simone realized Philip was watching her again.

"Turn off your gift," he said.

She jumped slightly, cursing herself again. Of course he would know! Maggie always had. Then again, Maggie had always succumbed. She was weak.

This thought brought up another suspicion. Opening her small bag, she pulled out a cigarette case and lit one, taking pleasure at Eleisha's shock. Good. It was time to get control of this and stop looking the fool.

"Did Maggie send you?" she asked.

Philip flinched.

"No," Eleisha answered quickly. "She's . . . this isn't the best place to talk."

Simone smiled at her. It certainly wasn't. She could feel the excitement building inside her. She should take them home, let them see how she lived.

Eleisha smiled back.

This was going to be so sweet. The best game Simone had ever played, even better than Maggie and Cecil. She put her cigarette out before one of the waitstaff could come over. Smoking wasn't allowed indoors anywhere in Denver now.

"We could talk at my house," she suggested casually. "I have a few good bottles of merlot I've been saving."

"No," Philip said.

Eleisha blinked at him. "But don't you think—"

"No," he repeated more firmly. "We've talked enough tonight. Maybe too much. She should have time to think before we talk more."

Simone wanted to glare at him but fought to keep her face serene. So now he was talking about her like she wasn't there? She'd make him suffer for that later.

"Oh," Eleisha said, like a child. "Yes, of course."

Then she seemed at a loss about something—Simone had no idea what. Suddenly, Eleisha looked directly into Philip's eyes, and her own squinted ever so slightly, like she was concentrating.

Neither one of them spoke, but he nodded. Then Eleisha grabbed a napkin, took a pen from her canvas bag, and wrote something down. "Here's my cell phone number. Once you've had time to process some of this, call us. We'll meet again."

Philip stood up.

Eleisha leaned toward Simone, her small face earnest. "I know this must be a shock. But please believe us. We would never hurt you."

Simone smiled again. "I believe you."

"Oh, and don't forget a carton of eggs."

Rose walked up Twenty-third Street beside Wade, chatting about the groceries he should buy, allowing herself to enjoy the oversized trees and streetlamps glowing in the darkness. She'd told him about Seamus' weakened condition, and he'd agreed that something would have to change.

It made her feel more at ease just being able to express her concerns and have him listen. She'd existed for so long with no one but Seamus.

"You've taken to wearing gloves?" Wade asked, pointing at her left hand.

"Yes, it's best. Perhaps later tonight we can work together? You can help teach me to control it?"

"Of course. I've already gathered up a few items for you to test out—don't worry, nothing of Philip's."

So he'd already been planning to help her? This put her further at ease, making her grateful for his company. Since leaving the church, he'd seemed much like his normal self again.

He'd changed into a loose button-down shirt and a light canvas jacket. She suddenly wondered why he'd never married. Perhaps he could not find a woman who wanted a telepath for a husband.

"Here we are," Wade said, moving toward the shelter where they could wait for the streetcar. A redbrick hospital stood just across the street, casting shadows, but Wade peered at a small digital reader board just inside the shelter.

"We've got ten minutes until the next arrival," he said, sitting down on the bench. No one else was waiting.

Rose remained standing with her bag over her shoulder. Wade had mentioned the possibility of them buying their own car several times, but the public transportation system in Portland was so extensive that so far, no one had felt the need to act on his suggestion.

A long row of shops stretched down the street behind the shelter, and she noticed a display of imported furniture in a front window. One of the low tables would be perfect for an empty spot in the sanctuary, and she walked a few steps to the corner to get a closer look—maybe see the price.

Leaning down, she spotted a white tag that read, "$1,200." Ouch. That was probably more than they should spend on a table.

"Don't say anything, and gimme your bag," a harsh voice said from beside her.

She straightened in alarm and found herself looking into a tragic, wretched face. He was in his early twenties and had black circles under his eyes. Sweating with a wet sheen, he held a knife toward her throat, and his body blocked hers in front of the shop. She wasn't afraid. A mortal with a knife was no real threat, and she could sway him with her gift if need be.

"Give it to me!" he ordered.

His knife hand was shaking, and although she didn't know much about addiction—at least mortal addictions—she could see he was suffering some form of withdrawal.

"Don't move," Wade said, and his voice was so cold, she almost didn't recognize it.

He was standing a few feet away with his Beretta pointed straight. He'd been sitting in the shelter, and the drug addict must not have seen him, thinking that Rose was a woman alone.

The would-be thief's head swiveled toward Wade, and he sucked in a loud breath.

"I mean it," Wade said. "You twitch and you're gone. Rose, step away from that window."

The man with the knife was desperate, beyond desperate, but it was Wade's calm face that frightened Rose. Her friend had no expression at all. He didn't look angry. He didn't look alarmed. He just held the gun in his right hand, pointed straight at the drug addict, with his finger on the trigger, and she had no doubt whatsoever that he would shoot at the slightest provocation.

His eyes were hard glass she could not penetrate—a stranger she did not know. He must be aware that she was in no real danger. He almost acted as if he had something to prove.

"Run," she whispered to the drug addict.

The man blinked his glazed eyes once as Rose rapidly moved in between him and Wade. Then he bolted around the building. Within seconds, it was if he'd never been there.

Wade was at her side instantly. "Jesus, Rose, are you all right? We have to stay close together. What were you doing back here?"

Looking at him, she couldn't answer. He seemed like Wade again. But she'd seen him clearly when he'd pointed that gun. Something about him had changed.

Philip walked into their hotel suite at the Oxford, fighting his own rising panic.

He kept his face calm, so Eleisha would not know.

Simone was a predator. Like he was.

For all his promises to help Eleisha find these "lost" ones hiding from Julian, it never occurred to him that they'd find anyone besides an elder like Robert (who functioned purely on outdated moral reason) or a damaged, stunted creature like Rose.

He'd been shortsighted.

Simone liked to inflict pain.

He could sense it in her every word and gesture. He did not blame her for this. In his darker moments, he liked pain, too. She was . . . a hunter. Just sitting there with her, sensing the flickers of her emotions, had filled him with a longing to hunt.

But he couldn't let Eleisha anywhere near Simone. Not yet anyway.

So he'd pulled her away from the cafe, and now he struggled with what he had to do next.

"What's wrong?" Eleisha asked him, dropping her bag onto a chair. "It went well, Philip, and you were right about giving her some time to think. I always want to rush things. But I know she'll call us. She was smiling."

He watched as she headed for the electric teakettle in their half kitchen. She wore a new pair of jeans and a little red tank top. She'd even tried doing something with her mass of hair tonight and had woven the long side strands into a thin braid over the top of the rest.

She could never even begin to understand Simone. She still viewed Maggie as some kind of savior—but Philip knew Maggie better.

He did not believe that Maggie would have joined Eleisha's little community. He didn't believe that she would have been satisfied with altering the memories of her victims and leaving them alive or with following some dried-up old laws that their predecessors had worshipped. Not for love. Not for anything.

He didn't know whether Simone would find such an existence attractive in the end, but if she was to be presented with the possibility, he'd have to do it alone, see how she reacted, and then . . . he'd have to make some hard choices.

Eleisha could not be involved.

"I want to go to her house and talk to her by myself," he said abruptly.

She stopped walking and turned to face him. "What?"

"Tonight," he added.

Upon seeing her hurt confusion, he wished he was better at speaking. He could not ever remember being skilled, or even competent, at expressing himself with words.

He knew that Eleisha had killed to survive for many years, but not like Maggie.

His mind slipped back to a night in 1836, when Maggie still lived in France, to one of the rare occasions that he, she, and Julian had joined up and gone hunting as a pack. They'd murdered an entire family in Wales and then burned the house down. Maggie had latched onto a young teenage boy and drained him while he wept and begged. Afterward, she'd laughed.

Without warning, he flashed that memory into Eleisha's thoughts, shocking her so quickly, she wouldn't have the presence of mind to shut him out. He did not stop, even when she gagged and fell to her knees.

"Philip!"

In two strides, he was kneeling at her side. He pulled out of her mind and let her hang on to him.

"That is the Maggie I remember," he whispered, "and she trained Simone to hunt. You cannot believe Simone's smiles. Maggie could smile, too." He waited until she stopped shaking. She wouldn't look at him, but he didn't care. Better that he hurt her a little himself than allow her near Simone. "Let me tell her about the underground, about how we feed there, about why . . . about the laws. It has to be me."

She let go of his coat, still kneeling and looking at the floor. He didn't mention the memory he had just forced upon her, and neither did she. They just sat there until she began to recover.

"What about Julian?" she whispered. "We're supposed to stay together. We all agreed it would take two of us to fight him."

"We've seen no signs that he's here. But I'll keep sharp, and you'll be safe in this room. He'd never risk a frontal attack after you invaded his mind in Seattle."

She crawled away from him, leaning against a couch.

"So that's why you took me out of the cafe?" she asked. "To tell me you wanted to go by yourself? You don't think I'm strong enough?"

"No!" This had nothing to do with strength. "She is *like* me. She won't understand anything you say to her. But she might listen to me."

Eleisha didn't answer or look at him.

How could he explain himself? After searching for the right words, he gave up.

"Do you trust me?" he whispered.

She nodded, still looking at the floor.

"Then let me do this alone."

Simone was upstairs in her bedroom at home when she heard the front door open, and she frowned, thinking it must be Alex coming for a late rendezvous.

She'd nearly forgotten him. He was nothing now, not after she'd seen the way Philip looked at Eleisha.

Maybe she should just feed on Alex and be done with it. Hailey didn't know about the two of them yet, and neither did anyone else, so nothing would connect his disappearance to Simone. She loved feeding on victims who had been obsessed with her in one way or another. All their recent memories focused on images of her. This was the sweetest way to feed.

Yes, she might as well enjoy herself tonight.

Walking from her bedroom, she noted the new shade of light beige she'd had the hallway painted, thinking how well it worked with the dark trim around the doors. She was endlessly particular about this Tudor-style house, as it was one of the few things she truly cared about.

She'd bought it in 1972, having fallen in love with it at first sight while visiting the botanical gardens with her current target for the game. The man's name was Henry Folger, and he'd already given her a small fortune.

The house was two stories and looked rather like an enormous cottage, with V-shaped points across the top stretching toward the sky. She loved the mix of red brick and timbers on the exterior. The yard was landscaped liked an English garden, with a wide variety of flowers growing in the front and back.

Despite her penchant for decorating her own body in a theme from the past, she always decorated her living spaces by the fashion of the era, and so the interior in the seventies had been somewhat garish, but she now had the entire place done in soft neutral tones, with simple but upscale furnishings, leather couches, granite countertops, and art by locally celebrated painters and sculptors.

Alex had wanted to photograph the inside and publish the pictures, but she wouldn't let him.

This place had had been her home and refuge ever since the night she found it, and no matter where she traveled, she always came back here. In recent years, she'd gone farther and farther away, staying in lavish suites for months at a time in order to pick the right couple and then play the game, lest someone in Denver connect the disappearances to her. This game with Alex and Hailey had been the first one she'd played near home in about five years, and she'd made certain none of their acquaintances had ever seen her.

The thought of Alex brought her back to envisioning the pleasure of feeding on him, and she walked down the hallway. But as she neared the staircase, she sensed no life force in the house. She could smell no hint of blood pumping just beneath the surface of his skin.

"Simone?" a masculine voice with a French accent called out.

She stopped.

Philip was here, and he hadn't bothered knocking. She liked the way he said her name, and how he stretched out the long "o" sound.

Excitement built in her stomach. He and Eleisha must have changed their minds.

She moved down the stairs, still wearing her red dress from the cafe.

"Here," she called back casually.

He was standing in the foyer, and to her disappointment, he was alone. She'd wanted Eleisha to see the house. She'd wanted to keep this a series of friendly meetings a little longer, while she slowly worked on Philip.

But if he was here by himself, he was after something, and it certainly wasn't her. Not yet.

How to proceed?

She considered herself a good judge of character, and he wasn't the type to be impressed by places. But still, she let a bit of her gift seep out as she drifted toward him. He was watching her, unblinking, and she could see something in his eyes akin to hunger. She wasn't vain or stupid enough to believe he'd already forgotten Eleisha and fallen madly in love with her, so what was he hungry for?

She had no experience with male vampires.

This was new.

It was exciting.

"Turn it off," he said.

She nearly quivered. How long since she'd played with someone who was consciously aware of her gift? She loved this.

"Don't you like it?" she asked, tilting her head.

He took off his coat and dropped it on the floor, exposing some kind of sheathed blade hooked to his belt, but the sight didn't frighten her. If he was going to kill her, he would have done it by now. He unhooked the short sword and dropped it. Through his T-shirt, she could see that his body was lean and long and hard muscled.

"Turn it off," he said, "or I'll turn mine on."

Oh . . . he had a gift, too. Of course he did. What was it?

"Go ahead," she teased him, still not afraid. Maggie's gift had been strong, and it had never overcome Simone.

"You won't like it," he said.

"Why not?"

"Because it will make you act like a simpering girl."

His arrogance astonished her. He still seemed to think he had the upper hand here.

She smiled. "I showed you mine. You show me yours."

His face didn't even flicker. For a few seconds, nothing happened.

Then an uncomfortable feeling began growing inside her—one she didn't recognize. He was different from other men and not just because he was undead. She took a step toward him, suddenly realizing that his face was beyond handsome.

She wanted to touch him, to run her hands down his chest, put her face into his hair. The drive was overwhelming.

"Philip," she rasped, moving toward him with her hand out.

Just as she reached him, just as she was about to touch him, he stepped away, and the mad desire vanished.

He'd turned his gift off.

She stumbled forward, almost falling, realizing in the same moment how awkward and ungraceful she looked. Rage replaced desire. Her hand formed into a claw, and she half turned to slash her nails across his face.

Moving faster than she could see, he caught her wrist.

"I told you," he whispered.

On instinct, she tried to jerk away and realized she couldn't break his grip. She couldn't even make his arm move. For the first time since he'd entered the house, discomfort began creeping up the back of her neck . . . uncertainty.

"What do you want?" she asked raggedly, still shaken by the foreign desire she'd just experienced. A part of her wanted to kill him, and another part still wanted to touch his chest.

"To know you," he answered. "I want to see what Maggie was to you, what you were to her, how you hunted, how you were together."

Simone was rarely surprised, but this answer was so confusing and unexpected, she didn't know what to say. What did he mean by "see"?

"Eleisha does not understand her own kind," he went on. "She knows things . . . many things that can't be taught, but not how to read one of us. She wants you to come home with us, but I need to *see* you first."

When he mentioned Eleisha's name, his voice softened, and Simone's mind finally cleared. She had to stay focused on the game. The stakes were growing higher by the moment.

"I don't know what you mean," she answered softly, trying to figure out whatever it was he wanted, so she could give it to him. "You can see me right now."

"No."

He shook his head and led her toward the living room.

Sinking down upon her Asian area rug, he gently pulled her after him. She settled down upon her knees, all the rage and embarrassment fading while the excitement began building again. The entire past three decades seemed dull. It had been so long since she'd experienced anything new—truly new.

"What are you doing?" she asked.

"Our kind has more tools than just our gifts. If you think back, think back to Maggie, I can see your memories."

Disappointment replaced excitement.

Was he delusional? If so, the game lost some of its shine.

But he was studying her face, and without warning she began to feel his gift again; the desire to touch him nearly overwhelmed her, and he leaned forward, moving his fingers lightly down her wrist until he grasped her hand.

"Close your eyes and think back," he murmured in her ear. "All the way back."

She closed her eyes.

chapter 7

Simone

Simone Stratford was born in Boston in 1913, but she retained few memories of this city. Her father was a doctor, and he moved his family to Denver, Colorado, when Simone was only seven years old—an act for which his wife never forgave him.

He said that Boston was already chock-full of doctors, and he wanted to set up practice someplace new, someplace with less competition.

It wasn't that he didn't enjoy competition. He simply didn't like being the one involved. But he loved to instigate it in the people around him. This was how he married Simone's mother, the lovely debutante Victoria Grayson, who then became the lovely Victoria Stratford.

Most people wondered how he'd managed to win her consent—as he came from decent money but no bloodlines to speak of. However, if there was one thing he knew, it was how to pit women against one another. He'd simply manipulated her into competing for his attention, and before she realized it, she was married to him.

Afterward, she wondered why.

Their union produced three daughters: Miranda, Kristina, and

Simone. After Simone's birth, Victoria announced that she wasn't going through the indignity of childbirth again and moved herself to another bedroom.

Her husband did not object.

Three daughters were enough. He didn't particularly want sons, and he didn't wish to ruin Victoria's figure.

Then in 1920, he decided to move his medical practice to Colorado.

Victoria did object, but to no avail.

Simone did not learn of these familial dynamics until much later. At the age of seven, all she remembered was her mother quietly weeping on a seemingly endless train ride, and after days of travel, she remembered looking out a window at the flattest, driest, loneliest land she'd ever seen racing past her.

"What is that, Daddy?" she asked.

He liked them all to call him Daddy.

"Wyoming," he answered.

She had no idea what this meant.

Two days later, when she finally stepped down onto the platform at Union Station in Denver, she felt a little better. People bustled around her, men wearing crisp white shirts and ladies in stylish felt hats. Perhaps Mother was wrong, and they would not be living among savages. These numerous people all looked quite similar to the ones in Boston.

But that day was also the first time Simone noticed what would later become a pattern. Miranda was twelve by this point, with black shining hair and milk white skin, like both her sisters.

But Miranda looked older than twelve, with the curves of her hips and breasts visible beneath her muslin travel gown. As she stepped from the train onto the platform, men from all around turned their heads to look at her.

Then Simone's mother stepped down, and the men turned their silent attention to her.

Simone looked up at Daddy, wondering whether he would be offended. He was not. His eyes glinted with pleasure, and his mouth formed the barest hint of a smile. He was more than pleased.

Kristina was only ten, but she was watching Daddy's face as well.

He bought them a house in the Capitol Hill district of Denver, where the best people lived. Their home was not as large as the great mansions, such as the Byers-Evans House, with its three wings, but it was large enough to satisfy Simone's mother.

They did not employ an army of servants, but they had two maids and a cook. Simone's mother considered the "society" here beneath her. So, with little else to do, she kept careful watch over the household menus and management. She paid little attention to her daughters other than maintaining firm control over their wardrobes, hair, and social graces.

This pleased Daddy, who liked to have his new colleagues to dinner, and he expected all four of his women to look perfect at the table . . . to look perfect walking in and out of the room.

Later, at his request, Victoria began having some of the more socially prominent ladies over for afternoon tea on Thursdays.

But as the years passed, Simone became more and more aware of how the entire house revolved around pleasing her father.

When she was eleven, she overheard him instructing Mother to wear her red velvet gown for a dinner party. Victoria came downstairs in her soft yellow silk. She'd always preferred that gown. Simone didn't think anything of it.

Three weeks later, she walked into her mother's room on an errand from the cook.

"Mother, Cook wants to know . . ." She stopped.

Her mother's face was drawn and defeated, and she was attempting to sew up a hole in a pair of stockings.

"Yes?" she asked tiredly.

Simone wavered. She'd never seen a hole in Mother's stockings. "Cook wants to know whether the fish will keep until tomorrow. She thinks she ought to dress the turkey today."

"Tell her that will be fine."

Simone walked down the hall to find her oldest sister coming up the stairs. At sixteen, Miranda had grown into a great beauty, with generous curves and a mane of shining black hair.

"What's wrong with Mother?" Simone asked.

"Daddy's cut off her allowance. She can't go out for tea. She can't buy herself new handkerchiefs or stockings or lipstick. She can't buy anything."

Simone didn't quite understand. "Mother has money. She orders our clothes and our curtains and tells Cook what to get from the butcher."

Miranda looked her up and down as if she was a simpleton. "Daddy gets the bills for all that, and he pays them. Mother has to go to him if she wants a dime."

Simone was upset at the thought of her mother darning stockings. "Well . . . couldn't you give her a pair of your stockings?"

"Me?" Miranda asked in surprise. "If I help her, he'll cut off *my* allowance."

But Mother was especially attentive and sweet to Daddy for the next week, and soon she was back in new stockings.

By the time Simone was fifteen, the ritual of dinner had become grueling. When the family dined alone, Daddy would study all four of them carefully. The one who most pleased him gained not only his verbal approval and open pleasure, but also little rewards such as a night at the theater or the largest allowance or choice of the next night's dinner. The one who least pleased him won his derision and open scorn, and he expected the others at the table to follow his lead. To Simone, it was a painful game.

But even Mother played—every night.

The problem was that by the age of twenty, Miranda still lived at home and showed no interest in marrying one of her many suitors. She knew exactly how to dress and wear her hair for Daddy. She knew how to lean forward with graceful but intense interest when he spoke.

Kristina had recently turned eighteen, and she had grown into a different type of beauty, with smaller curves and curly black hair she wore pulled up in a bow. She also knew how to flatter Daddy and how to tease him in all the right ways. She most often won his pleasure.

But even in her middle age, Victoria could still stop a man at twenty paces.

Simone, on the other hand, couldn't get a man to look up from a plate of roast beef. At fifteen, she was long legged, but as slender as a railroad tie, with little sign of developing breasts or hips. Her dresses tended to look bunchy and bulky on her slight frame, and her black hair wasn't thick like Miranda's or wavy like Kristina's. Although she could sometimes think of ways to flatter her father, she could never outdo Kristina, and then always ended up looking young and foolish when she tried, thus winning his frown.

She began to hate family dinners, and she ate less and less, making herself even thinner. The situation might have been bearable if her mother or sisters had ever defended her—even once—or offered a word of comfort afterward in privacy. They didn't.

They didn't stand up for her, and they didn't stand up for one another. They just went on and on trying to please Daddy, trying to win his game.

Then one day, when the new school year began, Simone met Pug Vanguard, and life became a little easier. Pug's real name was Georgiana, but her slightly upturned nose had resulted in a nickname. She was stocky, with unruly hair and thick glasses and rumpled clothes. She loved music and motion pictures and playing board games, and her smile reached all the way to her eyes.

"I'm Pug," she said the moment she sat down beside Simone. "God, I'd give both my thumbs for your hair."

And a friendship was born.

Pug's family lived in a small, cluttered house just off Broadway. They did not have servants.

Mrs. Vanguard was short and chubby and sometimes wore mismatched shoes. She spent her spare time doing volunteer work for the poor. She was a terrible cook and a worse housekeeper, but she always seemed to produce gallons of hot chocolate from their disorganized kitchen.

Mr. Vanguard adored his wife.

He adored Pug.

Simone had never seen anything like them, and she spent as much time in their home as possible.

Often, seven o'clock would roll around, and Pug's mother would realize she hadn't given a single thought to dinner.

"Oh," she would say as if this development surprised her. "Let me see what I can find."

Then she would serve up something bizarre like baked beans on toast with a side dish of sliced apples. The family would eat and chat about their day, and no one cared how anyone else was dressed, and no one seemed to find the food lacking, certainly not Simone. She even began putting on a little weight.

But finally, Daddy grew tired of her absences from the dinner table two or three times a week. Later, she suspected her mother and sisters were the ones who insisted upon her more frequent appearance, as she nearly always drew the short straw with Daddy.

Then, to Simone's horror, Pug was officially invited to the Stratford house for dinner.

The evening followed a nightmare sequence Simone fully expected.

Daddy stared at Pug's face and unruly hair and faded wool sweater as if Simone had made some kind of mistake and accidentally brought home the wrong person.

Pug looked around at the house with her mouth half open and almost balked when she saw the long dining room table, set with three forks to a plate and two candelabra centerpieces.

Miranda and Kristina both smiled over the soup course and asked Pug politely pointed questions about her house or which afternoon her mother preferred to serve tea. They flicked their eyes repeatedly at Simone in glee as if to say, "Oh, you are going to pay for this."

By the time the cherry-glazed game hens came in, Simone could barely eat.

Mother said about three words through the entire meal, but she didn't seem displeased. She already had three daughters for competition, and Pug was certainly no threat to Daddy's finite approval.

At the appointed hour, Pug's father stopped by to pick her up in his motorcar, and Simone walked her toward the front door when he knocked.

"Jesus!" Pug whispered. "Why didn't you tell me?"

"I've tried," Simone answered miserably. "A couple of times. I just didn't . . . I didn't know what to say. I'm sorry."

"You're sorry? I'm the one who's sorry." Pug grabbed her hand. "See you at school tomorrow."

"Okay."

Pug's father did not come inside the house.

Slowly, Simone walked back into the dining room. Daddy was still there, standing beside the table. She steeled herself for whatever was to come.

But he only shook his head. "I would have thought even *you* could do better than that."

He walked away.

Hating herself for it, Simone realized she was embarrassed by Pug. If she had only brought home some lovely girl who lived in a manor house on Bannock Street, Daddy would be showering Simone with love by now or offering to take her to the theater—while aiming his disapproval at one of her sisters or Mother.

But the next day, she tried to forget her embarrassment. After all, Pug was her best friend.

Three years slipped by, and life only grew worse. Simone tried and tried to please her father. The thing was . . . in addition to wishing for an end to the suffering of his cutting words, she longed more and more to be the "winner" at their evening meals.

She liked having money for herself. She liked taking Pug to the movies or out for ice cream. Money meant freedom, but the only path to gaining money was by winning Daddy's love, and she lived with three other women who were far better at the game.

Then in 1931, a miracle happened, and Miranda finally announced her engagement to a bank manager named Walter Smudge.

What a ridiculous name.

His institution had survived the onset of the Depression, and it even appeared to be doing well. He was the oldest son of a wealthy Denver family, and Daddy approved the match. Walter was balding at the age of twenty-nine. He had a bland face and a thickening waistline.

But Simone didn't care who he was. Had decorum allowed, she would have kissed him. Daddy, Mother, Miranda, and Kristina all became obsessed with the impending wedding: cakes, dresses, flowers, guests, invitations, and so forth. The list went on. They nearly forgot about Simone.

She was in heaven.

She and Pug had just graduated from high school, and it seemed they had an entire summer to themselves.

Now that they were both eighteen, several new doors were open to them, and one night in July, they went to a musical performance at the Bluebird Theater on Colfax Avenue. Simone knew this establishment would not have gone over well with her parents, as the Bluebird was hardly a place Daddy would consider "the theater."

But she loved anything new.

Torch songs and blues music weren't exactly new to America, but Simone had never heard such sounds before. Settled at a table, she let herself get lost in the gravelly voices and sorrow of the singers.

"This is wonderful," she whispered to Pug.

The sultry woman on the stage finished her song and sauntered off to a table. Then the music grew raucous as five young women burst from the sides of the stage, kicking their feet backward and moving their arms in harmony.

"Oh, flappers," Pug said, smiling. "This kind of dance was all the rage in New York a few years back. Mama showed me some photos."

Simone stared at the women, wordless.

Their dance did not seem physically difficult. It just involved rapid, fluid movement, and yet they commanded every eye in the room. They were all slender, with boyish figures like Simone's.

They wore sleeveless, straight-cut dresses with low waists, and long knotted beads around their necks.

Their hair caught Simone's attention the most. Whether blond or brunette, their hair was cut into razor-straight bobs at chin length, and it swung with life as the girls danced and moved. Their lips were red, and a few strokes of black accented the outer corners of their eyes.

Simone breathed in sharply. "Do you think Daddy would like me if I looked like them?"

Pug glanced over in surprise. "What? Why do you care?" She paused. "Simone, you do realize your father's kind of perverse, don't you? I'd worry less about him liking you and more about how to get out of that house as soon as possible."

But Simone couldn't stop watching the girls onstage, studying everything about them. When their number was over, and they walked to join members of the audience, they moved with an entirely different kind of grace than what Mother had always taught. Rather than moving like graceful ladies, they moved more like graceful cats, sure and fluid.

Simone watched them, forgetting everyone else who took the stage that night.

The next day, she took a cab to the shops on Sixteenth Street, and she pawned a small emerald left to her by her grandmother. She bought three dresses cut just like the ones worn by the flappers, knowing her mother would probably faint at the sight of them. She bought long strings of dark beads. She bought little flat shoes. She bought lipstick and eyeliner. Then she gathered her courage and went into a barber's shop and started explaining what she wanted, but he interrupted.

"I know what you want, honey. Don't worry. I've done lots of these."

Her hair reached all the way to her bottom.

"You sure?" he asked, picking up the scissors.

"I'm sure."

When he was done, she hurried back home and slipped up to her bedroom before anyone saw her. She put on one of the dresses—a rich shade of blue—and the shoes and a single string of knotted beads. She put on just a bit of the lipstick and the black liner at the outer corners of her eyes. Her head felt so light now.

She swung her head, feeling her new bob move back and forth . . . and then she looked into the full-length mirror.

A completely different girl stood staring back at her.

She was beautiful.

The dress showed off her small figure and exposed her pale arms. The haircut completely altered the shape of her face, making her features softer and more delicate. The lipstick gave her a bit of mystery.

The dinner bell rang.

She walked down the stairs and into the dining room on her long legs, the light dress making her feel free and confident.

Mother, Miranda, and Kristina all gasped at the same time.

Fortunately, Miranda's fiancé, Walter Smudge, was dining with them that evening, and his mouth fell open.

Daddy noted the state of Walter's mouth.

Then he looked back at Simone.

"Simone?" he asked, as if in doubt.

"Yes, Daddy?"

For once, he was momentarily speechless. Then he said, "You bought a new dress."

Obviously.

"Yes, I thought I'd try something different." She tilted her head. "Do you like it?"

He didn't need to answer.

Mother, Miranda, and Kristina didn't even look angry, as she expected. They looked . . . frightened. Mother didn't say a word about Simone's sleeveless dress or her clear lack of adequate undergarments.

Simone sat on Daddy's left that night, listening and nodding and smiling.

The next day, he tripled her allowance.

She had power in the house now, and she wasn't going to lose it.

But to her surprise, her mother and sisters weren't the ones who didn't care for her transformation.

Pug didn't like it all.

"What are you doing?" Pug asked one night in August. "I've never seen you spend so much time in front of the mirror."

But Simone couldn't stop looking in the mirror. She liked what she saw there far too much. She liked the way Daddy looked at her. She liked the fear and worry on Kristina's once-smug face.

In early September, Pug left Denver to attend a small women's college on the East Coast. She'd badly wanted to go west to Seattle, to the point of showing Simone numerous photos of that city. But choices were limited for women, and her parents didn't have a great deal of money, so she'd settled on a private college in Pennsylvania, to which she'd received a scholarship. Even amidst a tearful good-bye with promises to write every day, Simone couldn't help feeling they were both a little relieved at the parting. In just two months, she and Pug had grown apart.

Miranda got married as quickly as possible and went to Italy with Walter for their honeymoon.

Simone learned how to move, how to walk in her light dresses in a way that could make Daddy's colleagues drop their coffee cups.

Soon Mother was drawing the short straw every night—or sometimes Kristina.

As a reward, Daddy let Simone go out to local nightclubs or theater clubs almost every Saturday night, as long as she was home by a respectable hour (eleven at the latest), and she always remained in a group. She had a new set of girlfriends from her own neighborhood that he'd approved. They weren't like Pug. No one could ever be like Pug. But they were fun, and they liked to dance.

Simone made sure they were never loud or drunk or silly, though. Drinking was illegal, and silliness was a sin in her father's eyes, and she wanted no damaging reports getting back to him. She liked being allowed out in the nightclubs too much.

She was admired and adored there.

Two years slipped by. She turned twenty in June of 1933. The night after her birthday, she first saw Pierce McCarthy, and everything changed again.

Simone and two of her girlfriends were walking toward a cab on Colfax when she passed the mouth of an alley and saw a tall young man dumping garbage from the back of a restaurant into a row of trash cans.

He looked up and saw her.

She froze at the sight of him.

He wore a white T-shirt and an apron, like some kind of cook or dishwasher, but he was tan, with chiseled features, and his hair was cut in a stylish fashion: short in the back with a thick shock of bangs hanging forward over one eye.

They just stared at each other a long moment, and then Simone forced herself to toss her head and walk away. Daddy would kill her if he heard she'd been talking to a dishwasher. But that night in bed, she kept thinking about the young man's face.

The following Saturday night, she was in the Bluebird Theater again, when three men came through the door, laughing and joking with one another. They all wore tailored suits and polished shoes.

Simone's heart nearly stopped.

The one in the lead was the dishwasher from the alley. He stopped at the sight of her and flashed a smile.

He walked over.

Her mind raced for something witty to say, anything, but the sight of him towering over the table left her speechless.

"You recognize me," he said, putting a cigarette in his mouth and offering one to her.

She shrugged. "You look different."

"I'll say." He sat down, so sure of himself. "Pierce McCarthy," he said as if his name should mean something. "You're Simone. Dr. Stratford's daughter."

He knew who she was?

"What were you doing in that alley?" she asked abruptly.

"Working," he answered. "I'm in my final year of law school at Harvard, but I come home in the summers, and my father thinks I should learn the value of honest labor. So I always get a job somewhere on Colfax or Broadway."

Simone put her hand under her chin and leaned forward. This was getting more interesting by the second.

"Oh," she said. "Where do you want to practice when you graduate?"

"New York."

She tried to keep her expression still.

He was going to be a lawyer. He was going to New York.

Simone spent the next few weeks hanging on his every word and studying him the way she'd studied Daddy, taking careful notes of what he liked best and doing everything she could to make him fall in love with her.

It wasn't hard.

Daddy quietly checked out Pierce's family and must have been pleased by what he found.

"Invite him over for dinner," he told Simone.

That dinner was one of the best nights of her life. To make the deal even sweeter, Miranda and Walter were visiting that evening. Walter was bald and bland and thickening rapidly.

Miranda stared at Pierce with open envy. Even Mother looked slightly green. But after the initial shock of Simone bringing home a good-looking Harvard lawyer, Kristina kept her eyes downcast on her plate, demure and shy.

Simone was slightly disappointed. She'd most wanted to rattle Kristina.

The next two months were a whirlwind of new experiences. Pierce said that he adored everything about her, and because of this, she fell deeply in love with him. She loved the feel of his hands on her back, and the minty, smoky sensation of his mouth pressing down on hers. He talked about New York a great deal, and she knew he would marry her and take her away from Denver.

Daddy seemed almost . . . fond of Pierce and invited him to dinner several times a week. Kristina began changing her style of fashion, opting for white or cream dresses, and she always wore a white bow in her hair. Silly cow. At the age of twenty-three, Kristina was in danger of becoming an old maid, and dressing like a pristine schoolgirl wasn't going to help.

Pierce liked Simone's bob and her sleeveless, low-waisted dresses and her black eyeliner. Kristina should take a hint.

Then in late August, Pierce began to claim he was busy on many evenings. This hurt Simone a little. She knew he was preparing for his final year, and so she tried not to complain. But when she did see him, he seemed different somehow, more distant, and sometimes, when he looked at her . . . even disapproving.

She told herself she was imagining things. Pierce loved her.

One Saturday night when he was busy, she decided to go out with her girlfriends, but the nightclub held no amusement or glitter for her, so she went home early. Walking into the house, she heard soft voices in the sitting room, and she walked to the archway.

Her legs began to tremble.

Pierce was standing near the fireplace, holding Kristina tightly while she cried on his shoulder.

"It's all right," he was saying, over and over. "I'll tell her tomorrow. It's nobody's fault."

Then he looked over and saw Simone standing in the archway, and his face went white.

"Simone . . . ," he stammered.

Kristina turned quickly, not wiping away her tears. "Oh, Simone," she said. "I'm so sorry. Please forgive me . . . it just . . . happened."

Simone was numb, but she could see the glint of wild triumph in Kristina's eye. A part of her wanted to scratch Kristina's face, and another part wanted to vomit on the carpet. Pierce took a step toward her but stopped when he saw her expression.

"I'm so sorry," he said.

She couldn't even scream.

She turned and walked away, going upstairs to her bedroom and sinking down onto the bed.

Not long afterward, she heard footsteps in the hall. She went over and opened the door. Kristina was passing by.

"How did you do it?" Simone asked.

Kristina watched her warily for few seconds and then said, "Acting concerned for his future, convincing him you were the wrong sort to be the mother of his children. We met for tea, at the library, that sort of thing."

Reality hit Simone in the face.

Kristina's new *look* had been carefully calculated down to the color of her hair ribbon . . . along with the shy stares at her dinner plate.

"I love him," Simone whispered, knowing it was a stupid thing to say and that it would only make Kristina's victory sweeter.

"He's asked me to marry him," Kristina answered coldly. "I'm going to be living in a town house in New York next year. I'll have a better husband than Miranda does, and you get to stay here and try to please Daddy."

She swept down the hall, into her own room.

Simone walked slowly to her dressing table, sinking down. Kristina had taken Pierce away. Kristina was going to New York. Simone sat for hours staring at herself in the mirror, and then she looked down at a few photos Pug had given her of Seattle. Poor Pug had truly wanted to see Seattle.

Simone looked up at herself again, visualizing the exhausting stretch of dinners with Mother and Daddy. Worse, she pictured next Christmas when Pierce would be home for the holidays and Kristina would be busy planning their wedding. She'd probably ask Simone to be a bridesmaid. Wouldn't that be lovely?

Almost without thinking, Simone got up and took her suitcase from the closet. She packed everything she could possibly fit inside. She took all the money from her dresser drawer and every piece of jewelry she owned.

Dawn was breaking outside.

She wasn't staying in this house.

Pug had been right.

Pug was almost always right.

She walked downstairs, phoned a cab, and went outside to wait.

When she got to Union Station, she simply stood in line for a ticket.

"Where to?" the ticket agent asked when she reached the window.

She blinked. Where was she going? Not New York. Not anywhere near New York.

"Seattle," she said. "One way."

SEATTLE, *1935*

Simone kicked her feet and waved her arms in time with the other girls. She liked dancing onstage at the China Doll Club on First Avenue, even though the place was a dive, but she liked singing better.

Before arriving in Seattle, she hadn't given much thought to anything so mundane as "a job," and she didn't know anything about managing money, so the first few months had been rough. She'd cut all ties with her family—and they had no clue regarding her whereabouts—but she'd finally written to Pug, who wrote back immediately, and to Simone's simultaneous embarrassment and gratitude, Pug sent ten dollars in cash.

But even in her darkest moments, Simone never considered going home.

Now Simone had a job at a club, mainly working in the acts between performances by the real talent. She shared a shabby apartment with three other girls, and she was learning to take care of herself. All the girls here were self-centered and competitive—they had to be. But this was nothing new to Simone. These girls could take lessons from her sisters.

Besides, she was no different.

But she had to be careful and watch her own back. Most of the girls hated her because not only was she prettier than they were, but she also possessed certain qualities they lacked. Most of them had grown up in some kind of shack eating salt pork for dinner.

Simone knew how to move, how to smile, and how to speak in ways they couldn't copy. Both her verbal and her body language were deeply ingrained.

She paid a few pennies each month for a little post office box. She wrote to Pug every week, and Pug always wrote back.

Tonight, she smiled, waving her hands in front of her chest and kicking her feet back by bending her knees, dancing gleefully as if it was the most fun in the world.

The audience loved it, and she could feel numerous eyes upon her.

When the dance ended, the crowd applauded from their tables, and Simone knew the drill. She walked off the stage on her long legs, heading out to mingle with the patrons. Prohibition had ended, and she didn't mind letting a man or two buy her a drink. She could take care of herself.

But as she headed through the dim, smoke-filled room, she saw a woman staring at her.

Not just any woman, but someone . . . exotic. Her age could have been anywhere from twenty to thirty. Her skin was pale, and it glowed softly against dark brown hair that hung in waves down her back. Her eyes were dark and large and slightly slanted.

She wore a black dress and held a glass of red wine.

"You want a drink?" she asked with a French accent.

Simone didn't trust other women. She didn't trust men either, but she knew how to play them.

Then she got a better look into the woman's eyes. They were

lonely. Simone could see the scars of loneliness behind the woman's beautiful face, and the strangest feeling washed over her, a kind of attraction, not the kind she'd felt for Pierce, but to her shock she found herself drawn to this woman.

Cautiously, she sat down.

"You looking for work?" Simone asked. "I probably can't help, but I can show you the stage manager."

The woman smiled. "No, I am here to see the show." Her accent sounded like music, and her smile seemed genuine. Simone began to relax a little.

"I am Maggie," the woman said, motioning to the waiter. "What will you drink?"

"Champagne. My name's Simone."

She still wasn't sure what was happening. Women didn't normally ask her to sit down for a drink.

"I've only recently moved here," Maggie said, "so I have few friends, and tonight I found myself missing my family. I have not seen them in a long time. I came to watch you girls dance."

"Your family?"

"My sisters. We used to laugh and dance together."

"You miss your sisters?" Simone asked, incredulous. "I'd gladly drop both mine off a cliff and then wave when they hit the bottom."

She almost put her hand to her mouth. Had she just said that out loud? Of course she thought such things all the time, but she never *said* them, not even to Pug.

Maggie laughed. Then she leaned forward, and her dark eyes grew intense. "You are different. You are different from anyone I've met here. You've known pain, haven't you? Not hunger or cold or poverty, but the pain of killing yourself every day to please someone else."

Simone sat stone still. A part of her wanted to cling to this total stranger and pour out the torture she'd endured at home. But she wouldn't. She couldn't trust another woman.

"Forgive me," Maggie said.

Simone glanced away. The waiter set down her glass of champagne, and she sipped it.

"Have you been in Seattle long?" Maggie asked, changing the subject.

"Almost two years."

"And you've found a home?"

"In a way. I share a small apartment down the street with three girls." Simone paused and then said, "It's awful."

What was wrong with her? Why did she keep speaking her thoughts?

"I have an extra room in my house," Maggie said, "and I'm looking for someone to rent it. The house is large, and I sleep much of the day. If you are interested, I can show you."

The very idea of going home with a foreign woman she had just met would have been unthinkable five minutes before. But for some reason, the thought of sharing an entire house with just Maggie—with no one else hogging the bathroom or stealing her food—seemed so attractive, she almost stood up.

"How much?" she asked, trying to hold on to her good sense.

"Just see the room, and then we can talk."

Knowing her actions were bordering on madness, Simone nodded. "Wait here, and I'll get my coat."

The house far exceeded Simone's expectations, in a decent neighborhood on Queen Anne Hill.

She couldn't help feeling delight as they moved from room to room—and she was presented with the prospect of living almost as she had back in Denver.

Maggie did not appear to employ live-in servants, but she said, "I have a maid who comes in twice a week to clean."

Oh, Simone thought in bliss. *A maid.*

No more stinky nylon stockings in the rusty kitchen sink.

Maggie must be some kind of heiress or perhaps a divorcée. Simone didn't think she could ask such questions yet. The thought of living there was so enticing, she didn't want to hurt her chances.

But suddenly, Maggie said, "You grew up someplace like this, no?"

How could she possibly know that?

"Yes," Simone found herself answering. "Very much like this."

Maggie walked down the upstairs hall and opened the door to a bedroom. The curtains were lace, and a thick Indian carpet of cerulean blue covered the floor. There was a large closet, a dresser, and a four-poster bed.

"You like?" Maggie asked.

Simone more than liked the room, but the location of the house presented one problem. "I can't afford to take a cab to the club every night, and it's too far to walk."

Maggie waved her pale hand. "Forget the China Doll. I'll get you an audition at the Triple Door tomorrow. Then you can afford all the cabs you want."

"The Triple Door?"

Maggie smiled again.

A week later, Simone was beginning to think her luck had finally turned.

She was in the chorus at the Triple Door theater. It was the hottest place in Seattle. Maggie would take no credit for the stage manager hiring Simone on the spot.

"No, no," Maggie said. "He only had to see you. That was enough."

Her first night onstage was glorious, with Maggie in the audience, cheering her on, and afterward, they drank French champagne.

Simone wrote to Pug and told her everything.

The housing situation turned out even better than expected. Maggie wouldn't take any rent money yet, promising that Simone could catch it up later when she was more established. So Simone used her salary to buy a few new dresses, stockings, and eyeliner.

She and Maggie were normally up all night, so they slept all day.

Some evenings, Maggie didn't come to watch the show, but Simone didn't mind. Although she was grateful for Maggie's kindness, she preferred to trust only in herself, and she was working hard to become a standout member of the Triple Door chorus. The other girls watched her carefully.

One night, after the show had ended, she decided to go backstage to freshen her lipstick before mingling, when she heard the sound of someone weeping.

She looked around and saw Mabel, one of the other chorus girls, leaving through a back door, sobbing quietly. Another girl, Riana, was also watching Mabel slip away.

"What happened?" Simone asked.

Riana hadn't heard Simone come in and glanced at her warily. "She got cut from the chorus. She turned twenty-six last month, and the manager says she's too old."

"Too old?"

Riana turned away. "She's lucky. Most get cut when they turn twenty-five. Managers like 'em young. Brings in the men."

An uncomfortable feeling began growing in Simone's stomach. "How old are you?"

Riana's expression flattened. "None of your business! But I ain't waitin' around to get thrown out." She took a step closer. "You know Tim Hale, the carpenter who builds the sets?"

Simone had barely noticed him, but she nodded.

"He's not married," Riana said harshly, "and he's got a little place near the waterfront. So I got my eye on him. You keep your hooks to yourself, understand?"

She stalked off.

Simone just stood there. So Mabel was thrown out, just for turning twenty-six, and Riana's only plan to save herself from the same fate was to marry a stage carpenter?

Suddenly, Simone didn't feel like mingling or drinking champagne.

She got a cab and went home.

The house was empty, and she walked up to her bedroom, lighting one small oil lamp and looking in the mirror, wondering whether tiny lines might be forming near her eyes. Was that possible? She was only twenty-two.

She wanted to weep but couldn't.

Simone never cried.

The sound of the front door opening reached her ears, and then she heard Maggie's high heels against the floor.

The footsteps stopped, and Maggie called, "Simone? You are home?"

How could Maggie know that?

"Here," she called.

A moment later, Maggie slipped inside the dim room, illuminated only by the small, glowing oil lamp. She looked a little different tonight. Her dress was common, and her makeup was slightly overdone.

"Are you all right?" she asked.

"A girl got fired. She's a good a dancer and she's still pretty, but she turned twenty-six."

Maggie came up behind her. "Oh, my sweet . . . ," she began. "That is the way of things."

"What am I going to do in a few years?" Simone turned in her chair. "The other girls can only think to get married. I don't want to end up washing some man's coveralls and raising his kids just so I can eat and have a roof over my head."

A flicker of something like pain crossed Maggie's features. "Of course you don't. You're nothing like them, Simone. You are different."

Maggie always said things like that, but different or not, Simone was going to turn twenty-three . . . and then twenty-four . . . and then twenty-five.

"Come with me," Maggie said, reaching out and grasping her hand, pulling her toward the door. They went down the hallway to Maggie's room; only the glow of a streetlamp streaming through the window offered any light.

When Maggie drew her over to the dressing table, her ivory face was glowing with intensity, and she kept on gripping Simone's hand. Simone looked down and saw Maggie's antique set of silver brushes and the hand mirror.

"This . . . this is sooner than I planned," Maggie said, "but you don't have to age another day."

Simone tensed, thinking perhaps she had jumped into this friendship and home too quickly and Maggie might be slightly mad.

"No, no," Maggie said quickly, reaching past the brushes to unlock a small box. "Look at this."

She held up a miniature portrait of herself, wearing a red gown. The streetlamp illuminated the date at the bottom: 1874.

Simone wanted to back up. Of course it was a fake. Anyone could do that.

"And this."

Maggie held up a daguerreotype with a clear date stamp of 1901. Her face looked exactly the same as it did now.

Was this real?

Simone looked up in surprise.

Maggie nodded. "It's true." She paused, and then she began to whisper. "Our meeting at the club that night was no accident. I saw you weeks before, coming out the back, and I could not forget. You look just like my sister, Amélie, and I am so tired of being alone."

Simone tensed. Maggie had seen her weeks before their first meeting? Followed her? Watched her?

She knew she should be afraid, but she reached out for the daguerreotype.

"How is this possible?"

"Magic," Maggie whispered.

"And I could go on looking twenty-two for years and years?"

"Forever."

Maggie slowly took the photo from her hand and put it back down. Then she led Simone over to the bed, sinking down onto the edge and pulling Simone to sit beside her.

"You can do that?" Simone asked in a hushed voice.

"Only if you make me a promise."

Ah, there it was. Maggie wanted something from her. There was always a deal. Always a game.

"What promise?"

"That you will stay with me. Men come and go. I had a great love once, that crossed wealth and poverty and death and time, but it ended. Men will always come and go, but women can hold to each other. I want my sister back."

Simone did not believe in the love of sisters, but she would have promised Maggie anything. What had Maggie said . . . magic?

She didn't care. She only wanted to look twenty-two forever.

"I swear," she said.

Maggie's closed her eyes in relief. "Do you trust me?"

Simone didn't trust anyone, but she wasn't backing down.

"Yes."

Maggie was silent for a few moments, and once again, Simone experienced that sensation of attraction, of finding Maggie beautiful and comfortable to be with, of being attracted to everything about her.

The sensation increased until she became lost in a fog.

It did not even seem strange when Maggie leaned over and gently pushed her back on the bed. Then Maggie leaned down and embraced Simone.

"I've never done this," Maggie whispered, "but I had it done, and I promise it will be different for you than it was for me."

Simone could barely hear her on the edge of consciousness. She felt Maggie's face close to hers, whispering in her ear, then Maggie's mouth on her throat, and she tensed.

What was happening?

Before she could protest or pull away, a sharp, blinding pain struck her throat, and she felt Maggie holding her down. She bucked once, and then the fog filled her head, easing the pain, making her wonder whether she was lost in a dream.

She could feel her heart slow and slow and nearly stop.

Then she heard a soft tearing sound, and suddenly, Maggie's wrist was in her mouth.

"Drink," Maggie whispered. "Take it all back, and this will be over. You'll forget the pain and be forever young."

Without letting herself think, Simone put her lips over Maggie's bloody wrist. She began to swallow.

Forever young.

Simone didn't remember blacking out, but when she woke up, she had blood on her dress and she could hear insects moving outside.

She wasn't cold. She wasn't warm. She couldn't feel anything.

"Simone . . ." Maggie was suddenly at her side, helping her to sit up.

Memories and the reality of what had just happened came crashing down, and Simone knew she should be horrified.

But she wasn't.

"Is it done?" she whispered.

"Yes, my sweet, all done." Maggie stroked her forehead. There was a time when Simone would have given anything for her own mother to have stroked her forehead like that. But that time was long past.

"Come and we'll change your dress, and I'll tell you everything," Maggie was saying. "You have so much to learn."

"To learn?"

"How to hunt, how to feed, how to keep safe."

Again, such words should have shocked Simone to her core. But they didn't. She got up and followed Maggie like a child.

*   *   *

A few nights later, Maggie took her down to the waterfront, near Elliott Avenue. Large numbers of the homeless—people out of work—tended to gather down here, standing around burning barrels for warmth.

Simone had not gone back to the Triple Door, but Maggie assured her everything had been smoothed over with the stage manager; Maggie had told him that Simone was simply indisposed for a few nights.

Simone had been going through "the change," her body dying and adjusting to its new existence. She could barely contain her joy.

Her pale skin glowed as never before. Her hair hung straight and shining. Her lips were red.

"You've never been so beautiful," Maggie said, and she was right.

But tonight, Simone had awoken with her body feeling uncomfortable, hollow.

Maggie began explaining some facts about the hard truth of this new life, and Simone listened without blinking. Of course there was a price. She'd expected that. She didn't care.

Whatever it was, she would pay it.

Now they were near the waterfront, dressed in long coats with hoods, standing alone in a side alley, but not too far from the homeless and the hopeless and destitute.

"The easiest way to hide a body is to not *have* to hide it," Maggie said quietly, her voice different tonight, harder and almost like that of a schoolteacher. "The police don't bother with some nameless, shabby body. They just turn it over for burial."

Simone heard truth in this. In large cities, in 1935, the homeless and the hungry died for all sorts of reasons. The scant police force could not possibly keep up, and most of them were beyond caring.

However, that didn't mean she liked being down here. This place was far beneath her. Maggie didn't seem to notice. "All you have to do is lure a man off into an alley by himself. It's not difficult. But don't let anyone else see you. Use your gift to seduce him, and then feed. Cut his throat so it looks like he bled to death, and take his money if he has any."

"His money?"

"So it looks like a robbery."

"Oh, of course."

Maggie was sounding more and more like a schoolteacher. "Just stay here and watch me this time. I'll bring someone soon."

She walked away and stood outside the end of the alley, dropping her hood back. Again, Simone experienced the attraction that Maggie emanated when she chose to. Would Simone's gift be the same? She couldn't wait to find out. Maggie had said it would take only a day or two to manifest, and Simone was eager to feel it . . . to use it.

She heard voices and looked up. Maggie was backing down the alley with a heavyset man following her.

"Just down here," Maggie said in a husky tone. "No one will see us."

"Who's that?" the man grunted.

"My sister. Don't worry, you'll like her."

Was she drawing him away with the promise of sex?

Then Simone got a good look at him. He was revolting. Filthy, unshaven, and reeking of gin.

Didn't he find this situation unbelievable? But he followed Maggie eagerly, glancing at Simone with a glint in his eye.

Disgusting.

To Simone's further shock, Maggie seductively leaned back against the alley wall, and the man grabbed her with his dirty hands and began kissing her.

The aura of Maggie's attraction filled the alley.

Then, almost faster than Simone could see, Maggie whipped the man around until he was the one pressed against the wall. She bit down on his throat, tearing and drinking blood in fast gulps, savage and violent. An expression of joy crossed her twisted features.

Simone's revulsion faded as the hollow feeling in her stomach grew.

Maggie stopped suddenly, lifting her head. "Now you."

In spite of his stink and his soiled clothing, Simone rushed over and took Maggie's place, holding the man's full weight as he sagged in her hands. She bit down, drinking in mouthfuls of warm, sweet fluid. In her mind, she saw images of him working on the docks, calling to a lost dog, drinking gin . . . and drinking more gin.

She shoved against him harder, draining him wildly.

His heart stopped, and Maggie pulled her away. Simone winced in sorrow that it was over. She felt different, stronger, and she had wanted it to go on.

Maggie produced a thick butcher knife and jaggedly cut the man's throat. Then she searched his body.

"Can we find another alley and do it again?" Simone asked.

"You want more?"

Simone wasn't sure. But she wanted something. She could feel something building inside her. Without knowing why, she focused on Maggie. Even with all Maggie's beauty, did she ever want to be more like Simone, dancing on the stage with long legs and shining, swinging hair?

Maggie's eyes widened.

"Oh, my sweet," she said. "It's envy. Your gift is envy."

As those words sank in, Simone's joy at her new existence began to swell again.

*   *   *

The next ten years passed quickly.

Simone decided not to stay in the chorus at the Triple Door. She still loved to perform sometimes, but by using her gift, it was easy enough for her to land short engagements at any club or theater in the city. She soon stopped dancing and began to sing exclusively—it suited her new existence better.

Maggie's mortal social circle was small, but the people she chose tended to be interesting, artists and actors and even a few members of Seattle's financial elite. Simone was content to go to parties and nightclubs with these friends. They all liked her and often told her how lovely she was.

"You can't feed on anyone with whom we have a social connection—ever," Maggie warned. "If someone in our circle went missing, the police would investigate."

Maggie also occasionally took a mortal lover, but she was careful to never let him meet any of their other friends. As time slipped by, Simone understood that this was often where most of Maggie's real money came from. She would seduce a wealthy man, and when he wanted to show his appreciation, she would express a preference for gifts like diamonds or sapphires.

Sometimes the men just vanished, and sometimes, Maggie simply broke it off with a tearful good-bye. Then she'd take the jewels, leave town for a few nights, and come back with a large amount of cash.

She shared everything with Simone. There was no jealousy between them and no competition. Maggie made her feel loved.

Of course, men were always vying for Simone's attention, and she did try to play Maggie's game a few times—letting a man romance her for a while—but it never felt right and certainly offered her no satisfaction. She'd never been able to heal the wound left by Pierce McCarthy, and the thought of merely dating or taking a lover didn't interest her. However, she smiled and laughed and said clever things to inspire admiration.

Adoration fed her more life force than blood.

Several times a month, she and Maggie would go off alone to some shabby, bleak place where the homeless had migrated, and they would feed together. Their routine was nearly always the same.

After the first year with Maggie, Simone stopped writing to Pug, as that too felt wrong. After several further attempts at contact, Pug stopped writing, too.

Simone tried to forget Pug and everything about her previous life.

This routine was only briefly shattered in 1944 when a letter arrived one early evening with Pug's familiar handwriting. The return address was different from the one Pug had used before. This one was from Greensburg, Pennsylvania.

Simone took the letter home from the post office without opening it. She considered throwing it on the fire. But she opened it, finding a folded sheet of stationery, with the words *Read this first* written in large letters on the outside and a folded newspaper clipping tucked behind it.

She opened the letter.

Simone,

> *I hope this reaches you. I know you wanted to cut the ties between us a long time ago, but I was worried you might see this on your own or hear it from someone else. I just learned about it myself, and my mother sent me the enclosed clipping.*

About a week ago, your mother shot your father in his sleep and then shot herself. They are both dead.

Your sisters moved away some time ago, and your parents have been living alone in the house. God knows what's been going on there.

I don't know how this news will make you feel. If you are in mourning, I understand. They were your parents. If you need me, I am always here for you. I've received a teaching post at a small women's college. Please reach out to me at any time, and I promise I will reach back.

If you are not in mourning . . . I understand. I have some idea how you suffered for years. If my father had ever treated me the way your father treated you, my mother would have gone after him with a baseball bat.

No one should tell you how to feel about this outcome.

I've enclosed the clipping with more details. I just thought you should know. I am here for you.

> *Love,*
> *Pug*

Simone opened the clipping and glanced at the headline: PROMINENT DOCTOR'S WIFE SHOOTS HIM IN BED, TURNS GUN ON HERSELF.

She scanned the news story, pausing over only one sentence: *The couple is survived by two daughters, Mrs. Miranda Smudge of Philadelphia and Mrs. Kristina McCarthy of New York.*

Kristina had married Pierce and gone to New York.

Simone had never wanted to know.

She closed her eyes for a moment.

The clipping didn't even mention her, as if she didn't exist. She couldn't bring herself to feel pity for Mother, but she could imagine what life must have been like once Mother was the only target for Daddy.

Well . . . her parents were dead, and her sisters had moved away.

Simone had no family left in Denver—not even Pug.

Maggie came through the front door and saw her there.

"Are you all right?"

Simone dropped the letter and the clipping onto the fire.

"I'm fine."

Over the ten following years, Simone began to lose her feelings of contentment. A certain "sameness" about the nights began to wear upon her, and she found herself becoming bored.

Being eternally young had more than one price, and she had not seen this one coming.

She occasionally broke the boredom by attempting something new—such as learning how to drive a motorcar—but in the end, all the clubs, the people, the hunting . . . everything all began to feel exactly the same.

She suggested they move to a new city.

But Maggie refused. Seattle was her home.

They traveled occasionally, but only in America. Every time Simone brought up the idea of going to Europe, Maggie nearly panicked and gave her the same lecture on how they needed to avoid a violent vampire named Julian—who could not know of Simone's existence. Simone found this cowardly. Europe was an enormous place, and wasn't a visit to Paris worth a bit of risk?

They never went.

To make matters worse, Maggie started insisting that no matter whom they fed on—even the shabbiest of hobos—they needed to start hiding bodies by dumping them into a lake or the bay . . . or down a sewer grate. Maggie said that the practices of the police were changing, and that she and Simone needed to be much more cautious.

Then, after a while, it began to bother Maggie that Simone refused to update her look as time passed and the current fashions changed. Sure, she ordered new dresses and new flat shoes, and she never looked out of place per se. But she would not change the cut of her dresses or the long knotted beads or the razor-straight bob.

This *look* had saved her from Daddy long ago. It had beaten her mother and sisters. It was her trademark. It was her identity.

But besides feeling restless, something else was wrong. At first, she'd found Maggie's complete lack of competition with her to be a lifeline. She'd found peace in Maggie's unconditional love. Lately, Simone had felt that something was lacking in her own existence. Something she couldn't name.

That December, she discovered the missing element when Maggie took her to a new club on Madison Avenue.

They were barely inside the door when a familiar voice called out, "Maggie, come and meet my nephew, Ethan."

Jessica Arkon, a new friend of Maggie's, was standing by a table just ahead. Jessica was about thirty-five but looked younger, with naturally red hair. She owned a posh town house over near Union Bay, and she'd thrown some elegant parties.

A jazz band was playing on the stage, filling the room with raucous sounds.

Simone followed Maggie to the table without much thought, but when she looked down at the couple sitting there, she froze.

"This is Ethan," Jessica said over the squeal of a trumpet, "and his wife, Alice. They're visiting from my brother's home in Dallas."

Ethan was tan and muscular, with chiseled features and a shock of bangs hanging over one eye. He lit a cigarette.

Alice was petite, with light blue eyes. Her blond hair was pulled up into a high ponytail. She wore a short-sleeved white sweater and a pearl choker, looking like a pretty girl who'd stepped straight out of church.

When Ethan looked at his wife, his expression softened, as if she was the finest thing in the world.

Alice smiled up at Simone. "This place is so exciting. Come sit with us."

Simone sank down into a chair.

Ethan looked at her with the same startled expression most men did the first time they saw her, but tonight, she took more pleasure in his expression—a great deal more. She ignored him and turned to Alice.

"So, you're from Texas?" Simone asked. "I've never been. What's it like?"

"Oh, gosh, too big to describe."

"How long are you staying with Ethan's aunt?"

"Only about a month."

Simone made a point of lavishing all her attention on Alice that night, but she slowly . . . ever so slowly allowed the aura of her gift to increase, focusing upon Alice and Ethan, watching small changes in both their expressions as Alice began to envy Simone and Ethan began to envy anyone sitting near her.

Maggie glanced over in alarm a few times, as they never used their gifts on their friends, but she didn't say anything.

Two nights later, Simone made arrangements for them all to meet at a little club called the Snow Spruce, and about an hour after they were settled with drinks, the club's host went out onto the stage and announced a special treat.

"Tonight, Miss Simone has agreed to sing for us."

She didn't sing often anymore, so the people here had probably never heard of her. But they still applauded when she smiled and stood up.

Maggie looked startled.

Tonight, Simone had taken special care with her emerald green dress and black eyeliner. She moved up onto the stage like a cat, stood near the microphone, and nodded to the pianist.

The slow notes began.

Simone had come to learn that society did not become more progressive in a straight chronological time line. In her view, the 1930s had been much freer than the 1950s. The music of the thirties was far richer and more passionate than the light sounds of the fifties.

She began to sing a sultry piece from the thirties called "Body and Soul." It was one of her favorites, and she knew exactly how to pitch her voice.

The lyrics told of someone sad and lonely, pining for a lost lover.

For two verses, Simone sang with a sweet but sorrow-filled tone, as if her heart was breaking. Then she gripped the microphone and leaned into it, exuding the power of her gift, moving her body slowly to the music while lowering her voice to a softer pitch, filled with longing.

She sang of how her life was a wreck, and how she would surrender herself to her lover, body and soul.

The last note rang through the room a long time, and then the mesmerized audience burst into applause. She smiled again, as if her ability to hold the crowd spellbound was nothing, and she walked off the stage. The look on Ethan's face filled her with more pleasure than she'd felt in the last twenty years. His eyes were glassy and hungry. He seemed to have to forgotten Alice sitting beside him.

Simone needed more.

"What are you doing?" Maggie asked as soon as they got home that night.

Simone shrugged. "Nothing. I just wanted to sing."

Maggie didn't press the point.

Seattle nights were long and dark in the winter. Simone's next move was to send a private message to Ethan, inviting him to join her for tea at five o'clock. This was the test, to see whether he'd meet her alone.

If he didn't, the game was over.

But she believed he would.

He showed up right on time, a mix of hunger and guilt washing over his face the instant he saw her. She just pretended they were two friends, meeting for tea. Afterward, they both went home to get dressed for the evening, and nobody knew they'd even met. But after that, the game got easier.

Ethan and his father owned a company that engaged in something called "property development." Simone let him talk about this at first. She tended to steer him away from talking about Alice, trying to create the illusion that he was a single man courting an exciting girl.

They continued to meet just for tea at first, and then later, they both started canceling plans with Jessica and Maggie—making a variety of excuses—and Ethan would send Alice off with his aunt for whatever entertainment had been planned.

After this, they met in little dark restaurants. Simone thought carefully about how Kristina had handled Pierce, how she'd managed to win the game, and Simone came at Ethan from the opposite direction.

She subtly expressed pity and concern over how someone like him could have ended up married to anyone so simple, so unsophisticated as Alice. How would Alice ever be able to entertain the kind of businessmen that Ethan would be dealing with as his company grew? As she did this, she exuded the power of her gift, making him envy her, making him envy her life.

One night, he pinned her to a wall and kissed her so hard, he cut her lip. She didn't care. He tasted of smoke and mints, and his hand felt good against her back. She stopped him from going further than the kiss, but finally, after all these years, she was swept away by a romance that made her feel something.

This was what had been missing.

He promised he'd leave Alice and marry Simone.

Then Maggie planned a night at the symphony, and Simone knew this was an opportunity for the final win.

She made excuses that she had another engagement and told Ethan that if he'd meet her at the Ashbury motel, room five, she'd give herself to him freely.

He agreed immediately.

Simone sent a note to Alice, asking her to come to the motel, room five, at eight o'clock.

> *Please, my dear, come alone, and don't tell anyone. I have something important to tell you.*

Regardless of her simple demeanor, Alice was not stupid. She must know something was wrong with her husband, and she considered Simone her best friend here in Seattle.

Ethan arrived shortly before eight o'clock. He always came in his own motorcar. Simone had given the motel manager a fake name and paid him in cash.

"Let me make sure the door is locked," she said.

Instead of locking it, she left it cracked.

But when she turned, his eyes were on her, and he was kissing her wildly before she reached the bed. She kissed him back, feeling the excitement build. He wanted her more than any other woman in the world.

A gasping sound broke their kiss, and Ethan jerked his head toward the door.

Alice was standing there, staring at them in disbelief.

The look on her face brought Simone the sweetest sensation she'd ever experienced, far sweeter than Ethan's kiss.

"Oh, Alice," she said, "I'm so sorry. It's nobody's fault. It just happened."

Ethan's breathing was ragged, but he didn't take his hands off Simone. "I was going to tell you, Alice. I was going to tell you tonight."

Even with his wife standing there in horror, he made it clear that he'd chosen Simone. She wanted to laugh and sing.

She'd won.

She would never lose again.

Alice turned and ran.

Ethan took a step after her, but Simone held him.

"Give her some time," she whispered. "She'll just go back to your aunt's. Stay with me."

When he looked back down, hunger filled his eyes. He kissed her again, and she drew him to the bed. She let him run his hands all over her body, and she reveled in this closeness to someone who was clean and handsome, who smelled of smoke and mints and cologne—not some filthy bum from the waterfront.

She pushed him back and nuzzled her nose into his neck, hearing his sharp intake of breath.

Then she drove her teeth into his neck and felt him buck beneath her. She held him down, gulping in mouthfuls of his blood until he weakened. She saw images of horses and his father, a few fleeting scenes of Alice, and then she saw what she wanted—memory after memory of the past month, and all of Simone: Simone singing, Simone smiling, Simone's slender backside as she walked away, Simone sipping wine and tilting her head. All of his most important memories were of her.

And she was beautiful.

His heart stopped beating.

She looked down at him, sorry it was over. But she was more filled with life than she'd felt in her entire undead existence. What a glorious way to feed.

But this night wasn't finished.

There was a price for everything, and now she had work to do.

Ethan always drove his own car, and he always kept a full can of gas in the trunk.

Simone peeked outside and saw no one. She wrapped one of Ethan's arms around her neck and half dragged, half carried him to the car as if he was drunk. Once she had him inside the car, she drove to Jessica's town house, where she knew Alice would be weeping alone.

Maggie and Jessica were both at the symphony. They wouldn't be back for hours, but Alice could not be allowed to speak to either of them.

She couldn't be allowed to speak to anyone.

Simone used Ethan's keys to let herself in, but once the door was closed behind her, she pulled the string of beads from around her neck and called out, "Alice?"

A sniffling sound reached her, and Alice came from the kitchen, her face red from crying, her eyes shocked at the sight of Simone.

"What are you doing here?" she spat.

At least she had enough spirit to be angry.

Simone never answered. She walked straight across the room and whipped the beads over Alice's head and around her neck, jerking them back tightly and twisting. Alice fought and gagged, but only for a second. Simone was filled with life force and strength. Using both hands, she twisted with enough force to break Alice's windpipe, listening to the last choking sound.

Only one task left now.

She dragged Alice's dead body to the car and slid it into the backseat.

Simone drove toward the waterfront and turned down a dark, deserted street—she wasn't sure which one. When she saw an aging brick building ahead, she hit the accelerator and slammed the car straight into the wall. The impact jarred her, and she hit her head on the steering wheel, but she was pleased with the result of her actions. The entire front of the car was smashed.

After sliding out the driver's-side window, she went to the trunk and found the gas can. She doused the front of the car with gasoline, lit a match, and set it on fire.

It exploded into flames.

She watched it burn for a while. Then she slipped away and disappeared.

But before falling asleep that morning, she went over and over the sweet events leading up to Ethan's final kiss, to the smell of his clean neck, to taking her time to drain him, and to his many memories of her face.

She had won.

She couldn't wait to play again.

chapter 8

"No!"

Simone heard a masculine voice shouting on the edge of her awareness.

She tried to open her eyes.

Where am I?

She had just been falling asleep, still glowing with the warmth of Ethan's blood and the lingering taste of his sweet memories, and now she was facedown on a rug.

Somebody nearby made choking sounds.

Philip.

The previous events of the night came rushing back, causing her to panic. Had he seen all of that in her mind? If so, he knew almost everything about her.

"What did you do?" she cried, sounding shrill and not remotely sultry, but she didn't care.

He turned his head toward her, and she saw the hunger in his eyes again, wild and brutal. When he opened his mouth slightly, she could see his eyeteeth.

He pushed himself up to all fours, and she was afraid of him. It was an odd feeling. Quite foreign.

"No more," he whispered.

He had seen it. He'd seen it all.

But then he said something that surprised her even more than the events of the past few hours.

"I'm sorry."

Her fear faded, and a kind of anger replaced it. He had somehow reached into her mind and forced her to relive much of her life while he watched. She was more distraught that he'd seen her years with Mother and Daddy than anything that came later.

"How did you do that?" she asked, slowly sitting up.

He didn't answer, and then she wondered what made him pull away from her memories. He could have kept on through the following decades.

"Why'd you stop?" she asked.

He just looked at her, his eyes still filled with hunger, his red-brown hair hanging forward over his cheekbones. "I couldn't keep on . . . the way you hunt." He choked again. "The way you hunt."

Then suddenly, she understood him. He didn't care about anything she'd done in her past. He didn't care about her family's humiliations or her own shabby treatment of Maggie. He cared about only one thing.

She *knew* what he wanted.

"You like how I hunt?" She crawled over to him.

The sky outside was growing lighter.

She let her gift seep out, engulfing him, making him envy her, and he didn't tell her to stop.

His eyes glinted, and she wanted to rejoice. She took in every line of his face, the solid shape of his collarbone, the sinews in his hands.

She had him.

For some reason, he'd not been hunting in the way he needed . . . the way he wanted.

"Stay with me today," she said softly in his ear. "Sleep here today, and we'll go hunting tonight. You can show me how you hunt. I'll go anywhere. We can feed on anyone you want."

His body was tight and poised, like he wanted to lunge at her. But he didn't.

He just nodded.

Mary hovered in the dim shadows beneath the staircase, watching Philip with Simone.

She didn't like this house. She didn't like even being in here. The place reminded her too much of her Aunt Lorraine's: cold and sterile. The couches were leather—stretched over chrome frames—and the coffee tables were glass. Not a spec of dust would dare exist here. Not a centerpiece was out of place. Every painting and sculpture looked as if it had been chosen to impress guests, rather than because it was interesting or even pretty. The rooms were artificial and staged.

Mary hated places such as this, but she held fast and stayed.

She watched the events play out from the moment Philip entered the house.

Why had he come here alone? Why wasn't Eleisha with him?

Mary saw the whole episode of Philip turning on his gift, making Simone try to crawl all over him. But she kind of understood that . . . as he seemed to be proving his own power.

Then she just hovered in the shadows for several hours while they sat on the floor, locked together. She knew they were probably in some kind of mental contact, but this left Mary completely out of the loop, and she was getting worried that Philip still hadn't asked Simone many verbal questions. Mary would need to make a full report, and not much of what was going on between them would be of any use to Julian.

At one point, a ringing sound came from Philip's coat—where he'd dropped it near the door—and it took Mary a few seconds to realize he must have a cell phone in the pocket. It rang six times. Neither Philip nor Simone even reacted to the sound. They seemed lost inside each other.

But then . . . when they broke apart and starting choking, Mary forgot all about the phone, and she focused entirely on Simone's face.

Philip wasn't using his gift anymore, and Simone still wanted him. No, she more than wanted him.

She was crawling toward him like a cat.

"Stay with me today," she said, her voice like honey. "Sleep here today, and we'll go hunting tonight. You can show me how you hunt. I'll go anywhere. We can feed on anyone you want."

When Philip nodded, Mary wished she could chew on her own lip just to think more clearly. Something was very wrong here. Still floating near the stairs, Mary began to realize that Simone would do anything to get what she wanted. And for someone like Simone, the possibilities were endless.

Mary had nothing concrete. She had no facts. She had no specific events or useful conversations to tell Julian. Then it hit her that he'd already gone dormant for the day—as northern Wales was seven hours ahead of Denver.

She'd have to wait for him to wake up.

But he needed to get here as soon as possible.

Mary blinked out.

As dawn grew closer, Eleisha sat on the floor of their hotel suite.

Where was Philip?

Although she'd been stunned by his decision to go alone, she did understand his reasoning . . . and she even knew he might be right.

Philip had once been a lot like Simone. Eleisha had not.

Granted, communication wasn't exactly Philip's strongest suit, but he might be able to handle this situation better—simply by virtue of knowing the right things to say. But still, Eleisha hated sitting here, waiting, doing nothing, and he was really pushing his window of time before the sun rose.

She'd tried to pass the night as quickly as possible: reading, watching television.

Then she'd given up all attempts to distract herself and moved to the floor, keeping her eyes on the door, listening for the sound of him coming down the hall.

Finally, in desperation, she dug into her bag and took out her new cell phone. It felt unfamiliar in her hands, and so small. Opening it, she pushed a button that displayed a short list of names. Then she pressed PHILIP and put the phone to her ear. In all the time she'd known him, she'd never called him on a phone. She'd never had to.

Upon hearing the first ring, she tensed, hoping he would answer and scoff at her, telling her not to worry so much, that he was in the lobby on his way up.

The line rang six times and then went to voice mail. The voice wasn't even Philip's, just some cold digital words telling her to leave a message. She hung up, dropping the phone back into her bag. Then she returned to staring at the door again.

The minutes clicked past.

The sky outside was drifting toward dark gray.

Suddenly, her cell phone rang—well, it didn't actually ring, but rather it burst into Beethoven's fifth symphony. Was that what Wade had programmed?

She jumped a little, startled by the unexpected sound. Then she grabbed the phone from her bag, opening it quickly, and put it to her ear again.

"Hello."

"It's me," Philip said.

For a few seconds, Eleisha couldn't speak. She was too confused. The sky was growing lighter.

"Where are you?" she asked.

"I need more time. This is taking longer than I expected. I'll call you tonight."

He sounded strange. Cold.

"What do you . . . ?" she asked. "You're sleeping there today?"

"I'll call you tonight."

He hung up.

Eleisha just sat there on the floor, staring at the silent phone.

Julian's eyes clicked open just past dusk. Cliffbracken Manor was dark and quiet.

He hoped Mary would come to him tonight with a report.

He'd slept in his pants, so he pulled a sweater over his head and then walked downstairs to his study.

Even with the windows completely covered, he could feel the darkness outside deepening. He lit some candles and began paging through a book lying open on the table, *The Makers and Their Children*, looking for any possible reference he might have missed to a vampire named Simone or some variation of the name.

The three fat candles burned brightly, and he turned another page, well aware he was wasting his time, as he knew the book by heart, but he needed to do *something*.

He suspected this vampire would turn out to be a worthless

pursuit, some murdering member of the new breed who knew nothing of the history of her kind. If so, she was no threat to him, and he needed to get Eleisha back to hunting someone who mattered.

He stood up, walking out into the hall of the main floor, looking left toward the vast dining hall. The furniture was dusty, and cobwebs hung in the corners of the ceiling. He would need to hire some help soon. Perhaps tonight he'd contact a service in Cardiff and have someone sent out.

The air beside the table shimmered, and Mary appeared.

"Oh, God," she said with what sounded like relief. "You're finally awake."

For once, her voice didn't grate on him. He turned toward her, taking in the tense expression on her transparent face.

"What's wrong?" he asked.

"You've got to get to Denver, tonight."

She sounded so serious, he moved closer.

"Mary," he nearly snapped. "What's happened?"

"Nothing . . . nothing yet, but if you want to keep Eleisha safe enough to do your hunting, you'd better head for the airport."

She wasn't making any sense, and he did not enjoy feeling either anxious or confused.

"What are you talking about?" he demanded.

Finally, she attempted to calm herself, and she started again. "Philip's gone to Simone's house alone. He left Eleisha at the hotel, and Simone is . . . doing stuff to him. I don't exactly know what, but she likes to play games with people, and I think she wants Philip."

Julian shook his head in disgust. "You came all the way back to tell me that?"

"Listen to me! I've got the feeling Simone doesn't like to lose, and I can't tell how this is going to play out. Philip doesn't ever sleep away from Eleisha anymore, and he stayed at Simone's today. What happens if Simone starts to see Eleisha as a threat?"

"Doesn't sleep away?" Julian frowned. "You make them sound like mortal lovers."

"Well . . . he sleeps in Eleisha's bed every day."

Julian froze. "What?"

Mary tilted her head. "Yeah, he's been doing that since San Francisco."

"And you didn't tell me?"

"It didn't seem important. I didn't think you'd care where Philip slept." She floated a few inches off the ground. "But it's important now! You should see the way Simone looks at him. You really need to get to Denver."

He turned away, pacing, trying to absorb what Mary was telling him. This was a worst-case scenario. It was sounding more and more as if not only was Simone of no interest to his own purpose, but she now might pose a danger to Eleisha.

"You're certain Simone's not telepathic?" he asked.

"No, she didn't even seem to believe Philip when he talked about it, but I think he was trying to read her mind anyway."

"All right," he said, coming to a decision. "Jasper's only a few hours from Denver. Send him to the airport the moment he wakes up tonight. Tell him to take her head as soon as possible, but he cannot be seen by Philip or Eleisha."

"Jasper?" she gasped—which sounded harsh coming from a ghost. "No way!"

Mary had never truly surprised Julian until that moment.

His mouth fell half open at her refusal.

"He can't handle Simone," Mary rushed on. "She's got a face like a black-haired angel, and her gift is envy. You think he can stand up to that?"

"Envy?" Caught off guard by the fact that she was arguing, he answered, "I can't be seen anywhere near this. Spooking Eleisha could keep her from searching, and I need to save my involvement for when she finds an elder."

Then he stopped, shocked that he was openly explaining himself to Mary. She was his servant.

"Well, Jasper can't do this alone," she said, crossing her arms. "You should at least go there and meet him at a hotel, so you can help him from the background and stay close if he needs you. Will you at least do that?"

The conversation was rapidly growing out of hand. She'd never spoken to him like this.

"You'll understand when you see her," Mary said. "Please, Julian."

And now she was *asking* him . . . as if seeking a favor?

He let his gift seep out until her face flickered with a hint of fear. "You don't ask me for anything," he stated. "You do as I order, or I'll send you back where you came from."

To his further disbelief, she looked him in the eyes. "Fine. Go ahead." Then she glanced away, and her transparent features shifted to frustration. "I'm not trying to make you mad. But you need to come with us. I swear to God you'll understand when you see her . . . when you hear her."

He glanced over at the clock on the mantel. If he left now and arranged the correct flight, he could follow the sun backward, take off in the dark, and land in the dark.

"Have Jasper on a flight as soon as dusk sets in San Francisco," Julian said coldly. "I'll book a suite at the Brown Palace in Denver. We'll meet there."

Her booted feet touched the ground.

"Okay," she said in relief. "Thanks."

He didn't want her thanks, but she blinked out before he could speak again.

Alone now, he went over everything she'd said. As grating as she could be at times, Mary was not given to exaggeration. Perhaps it was best that he follow her instincts in this. But such a long trip was unexpected. He'd made no arrangements for his horse, and he had no time to hire a groom. Frowning, he decided he could let the creature out in the north pasture; it would be all right for a few days. The grass was thick and the stream was high.

But he should book his flight first.

Moving quickly, he headed upstairs to pack a few things and box up his sword properly for the airline.

Just before dusk in San Francisco, Mary was inside Jasper's room, watching him sleep.

She found it telling that Julian always slept on his back, stretched out like a corpse, but he sometimes wore expensive pajamas. Philip never liked sleeping in any kind of a shirt, as if he found it too con- stricting, but he did like Eleisha's head on his chest.

Jasper slept on his stomach with his face half in the pillow, like a mortal, and he tended to fall dormant while still fully dressed in whatever he'd been wearing all night—occasionally with his boots on.

She floated closer, looking down at his short dark hair.

For some reason, she couldn't stop thinking of Rose and Seamus. Ghosts who were tied to a person here on the living plane could stay here only as long as the other was still alive. But when their anchor died, both ghosts would travel instantly to the in-between plane . . . and then most commonly on to the Afterlife plane.

Seamus was still here after nearly two hundred years. He was tied to a vampire. At first, Mary had triumphed over his condition, as it had seemed so limiting. She was free, tied to no one. But now she wondered whether he had it so bad. Maybe it would be okay to be tied to someone.

When Julian first called her from the other side, all she'd wanted to do was punish her parents. They'd left her home alone, like always, the night she died. They'd gone to an art opening. She'd attempted suicide with some of her mom's pills, knowing both her parents would run home when she called them for help. But her Dad had turned his cell phone off, and by the time she'd wised up and called an ambulance, it was too late.

Julian promised that if she served him for a period of time, he'd release her on the living plane and let her go wherever she wanted. He also threatened to send her back if she didn't obey him. In the first few days, all she'd wanted was to make her parents pay for ignoring her.

By now, she was well aware that his aforementioned "period of time" was indefinite. She understood his goals, and they could prove to be very long-term.

But that didn't matter.

Once she started working with Julian—and then Jasper—she started to see things a bit differently. When she looked back on how she'd treated her parents, an unfamiliar emotion washed over her: shame. She'd ruined so many nights for them with her expanding bids for their attention.

How could she not have seen that at the time?

No, she had no wish to hurt them anymore. They were probably better off without her, and she was in a different existence now. The problem was that without a body, without the rage of parental blame, without an actual life to live, she wasn't sure what she wanted.

She didn't want to go back to the gray plane. She didn't want to go to the Afterlife.

That left her here with Julian and Jasper.

Julian could barely stand the sight of her, but he needed her, and they were both well aware of it.

Jasper was different. He was always glad to see her, even hoping for more time with her. In addition, he was undead, so he'd never get old or die.

Maybe someday . . . maybe when Julian's work for them was over, they could form a link like Seamus and Rose, only theirs would be by choice.

Maybe.

The sun set, and Jasper's eyes clicked open. He sat up instantly in the bed.

"Mary?"

She knew he didn't care that she was in his room. He never minded if she watched him sleep, but she could see anticipation growing on his face. He *wanted* to serve Julian, like it was some kind of high-paying job.

She floated closer, noting his rumpled T-shirt. "Yeah, you need to get your sword and go to the airport right now. He wants you heading for Denver on the earliest flight possible. He's already on his way."

Jasper nearly flew out of the bed, running for his phone, pulling a credit card from his wallet. Having unlimited funds also allowed for freedom in booking last-minute plane tickets. He booked a flight and nodded at her.

"Done. Tell him I'll be there before midnight. Where are we meeting?"

"The Brown Palace Hotel on Fifteenth Street." Her voice wavered slightly. She didn't like this.

He pulled off his shirt and moved to the closet. "What's wrong?"

That was something else about him; he listened to what she said, and he cared when something bothered her.

"Stop for a sec," she said.

He looked back at her, his hand halfway to a clean shirt.

"I wish you didn't have to do this," she told him, not exactly certain what to say. "Simone's not like any vampire I've spied on before. She needs to be the center of attention and . . . I don't know. I think she has issues."

"Is that all?" He grabbed the shirt. "Mary, don't worry. I can take her head."

"Her gift is envy. She makes everyone want what she has, what she is."

Jasper smiled, walked to the bedroom door, and opened it, pointing out at the living room. "How could I want more than this?" Coming back toward her, he grew serious. "I have to do this, Mary. I like who I am now, and he pays the bills."

It was easy for him to say all this. He hadn't seen Simone yet. Neither had Julian. They'd both understand soon.

"Just be careful," she said.

"Sure, and I'll have you at my back, right?"

She nodded. "Always."

But she couldn't help wishing that Eleisha had never found Simone and never gone to Denver.

chapter 9

Philip woke up on the floor in one of Simone's guest rooms that night.

For some reason, he didn't want to sleep in the bed, not even in a guest room.

But he'd fallen into dormancy with images of her hunting and feeding playing over and over in his mind. . . . Nothing he'd seen in either Rose's or Eleisha's memories had ever affected him like this. He had *felt* what Simone had felt, and he was starving for the release of warm blood in his mouth and for the feeling of fear and death washing through him.

Once awake, he just lay there staring into the darkness.

Without Simone's gift dulling his mind, his head was clear, and he didn't like it. He didn't want to think.

He hadn't lied to Eleisha—or at least he hadn't meant to. He *had* come here to tell Simone about the underground . . . to see whether it was even possible for her to exist there.

But everything was different now.

All the hunger and the need boiling just beneath his skin had burst inside him, and he'd stopped fighting himself.

He was going to hunt.

The overhead light clicked on, and Simone stood in the doorway. She looked down at him, and when she moved, her black hair swung back and forth. She was already dressed, sporting fresh black eyeliner.

She let her gift wash over him, and he absorbed it in a rush, welcoming the feeling of wanting to be like her . . . wanting to hunt like her. It lulled his mind into a fog and kept him from thinking about anything else.

"You ready?" she asked. "Come on, and I'll show you something."

He got up and followed, leaving his coat and his machete behind in the living room. Both items made him feel bound and restricted. Tonight he wasn't protecting anyone.

Simone walked out a back door and into a garage.

She turned on the light, illuminating a black 1972 Thunderbird.

"You like?" she asked.

Walking to the car, he reached out to touch the driver's-side door.

"I don't drive it much," she said. "Normally I just take a cab."

He didn't want to make small talk. "Where are we going?"

"Boulder. You want to drive?"

He held his hand out for the keys. She raised one eyebrow and passed them over.

Twenty minutes later, they'd made their way out of Denver, and Philip was racing down I-25, whipping around other cars with practiced ease. Simone laughed. She didn't put on her seat belt, and she didn't tell him to slow down.

He could feel excitement building inside his chest.

"Keep your gift on," he said.

This felt like the old days.

No rules. No regrets.

"Exit here," she told him, pointing down 36 West.

They kept driving.

Then, even through the darkness, he could see the Rocky Mountains looming over Boulder. The town itself did not impress him as they entered.

"Don't worry, it's perfect," she said. "A university town, full of the richest and the poorest. Those are always best." She watched the streets pass by out the window. "You feel like college girls or homeless winos?"

He didn't even need to think. "Winos."

"Good. Turn up there and park behind that Liquor Mart."

He whipped the car into the lot so fast, she had to grab the dashboard.

Simone had never felt anything like this. She'd hunted with Maggie for years and years, always being cautious, being careful.

Philip was wild and reckless and unpredictable. He didn't slow down for anything. He was like a bomb waiting to explode.

She tried to appear nonchalant, unflappable, but just the sight of him getting out of the car and slamming the door filled her with anticipation. Still, she didn't hurry, and he stopped to wait for her.

"Where?" he asked.

"Over here," she said, moving forward, "along the creek."

Her legs were long, but he towered over her, staying close beside her, and for the first time since Pug had moved away, Simone didn't feel alone. She suddenly knew why the game was losing its shine these past years, why it had grown so stale.

It wasn't real.

This was real.

He was real.

With an unexpected stab of guilt, she finally understood what Maggie wanted: a companion. But Simone had been a poor choice for a vampire who wanted a sister.

She heard voices through the trees, and Philip turned his head.

"There," he said.

"No, that sounds like a group," she said, pulling back.

"I know. Keep your gift on."

He walked toward the voices, and after a moment, she followed. She could barely wait to see what he was going to do.

Philip liked feeling so hazy. It let him get lost in the need for release.

Up ahead, he saw four people among the trees near the creek, three men and a woman. They were standing beneath a large Douglas fir. He could smell cheap vodka from a distance, and he started to let his own gift flow, knowing full well that Simone would be just as affected as his prey.

When he drew closer, he could see that they were just as shabby as he'd expected, with yellow teeth and red noses. But not a single one looked to be more than thirty-five. The woman's hair was long and unwashed. She was holding a thin bottle.

Feeling him approach, feeling his gift, she turned to look at him.

In times past, when he'd hunted on his own, he often spent a good part of the night with his victims before feeding on them or even just killing them. He realized now that must have been due to boredom and loneliness, but he wasn't bored or lonely now.

He couldn't hold himself back. He couldn't wait.

It had been too long.

He simply relied on his gift and on the power of Simone's as she came behind him. All four of the people were caught by the spell, and Philip walked right up to the closest man, grabbed him by the shoulder with one hand and snapped his neck with the other, letting the body fall while the others watched.

Simone gasped.

Then he turned off his gift.

The woman and the youngest man backed against the tree in shock. The third one turned to run, but Philip lashed out telepathically.

Stop!

The man froze, his eyes wide.

"Don't move," Philip said aloud to the other two. He could feel their fear soaking into him.

He walked up to the frozen man and jerked him closer while turning around so the others could see. Without even pausing, Philip used his teeth to rip the man's throat out. He didn't even feed.

He just dropped the body.

Simone was watching with fascination.

But he wanted more fear. He could feel months and months of pent-up hunger, and now that he'd started, he had no intention of stopping.

He turned his gift on again and moved closer to the woman.

As he approached, the young man next to her bolted, but Simone flew into action, catching him easily. Philip ignored them both, and he walked up to the trembling woman, increasing the power of his gift. Still shaking, she reached up to touch his face.

He lunged.

★　　★　　★

Simone had never fed like this.

Her body was stronger and faster than she'd ever realized, and she bit savagely into the man's throat, draining him in hungry gulps, not even paying attention to the images of his life passing through her. She just ripped his throat deeper, letting him bleed, and she drank until his heart stopped beating. She'd never felt so satisfied after a kill.

She dropped him and watched Philip.

He was glorious.

She could almost feel him feeding on the fear as much as the life force. He shook the woman's body by the back of her neck as he fed. His face and shirt were soaked with blood. Simone suddenly felt a stab of sorrow that she was just finding him now. Why hadn't she found him years ago?

When he finished, he dropped to his knees, his eyes glazed over like he was drunk.

Maybe he was.

She walked over and fell to her knees beside him. Without warning, she grabbed the back of his head and kissed him fiercely, letting her gift flow. He kissed her back so hard that the blood on his face smeared up her cheek.

Then he pulled away, and his eyes cleared slightly. He seemed calmer, looking around at the bodies.

"That was good," he whispered.

"Yes."

After a while, he stood up.

"Come," he said, walking farther along the creek.

She faltered. "Wait. Shouldn't we take their IDs, cut their throats, anything?"

He glanced back. "Leave them. They have nothing to do with us, and no one will care."

"Where are you going?"

"I'm not done yet."

For so long, Simone had liked to be the one in control, in charge. This felt new. She followed him with her eyes on his back. She'd finally found someone she needed, after all this time.

Julian paced the floor of a suite at the Brown Palace in Denver.

Jasper had just arrived. He was sitting quietly in a chair, and they were both waiting for a report from Mary regarding Simone's location. But while waiting . . . they had little to say to each other.

Jasper's appearance had certainly improved, and he was holding his sword across his knees.

"Have you been practicing with that?" Julian asked.

"Yeah. I even hired a guy at a Shaolin school to give me lessons. He's pretty good."

Julian stopped pacing. "When?"

"Couple of months ago. I like this arrangement. I want to be able to do whatever you need."

This news both pleased and disturbed Julian. Of course he wanted his servants skilled and useful, but at the same time he wanted Jasper to continue functioning on a combination of fear and greed. He wanted someone easy to control.

The young vampire sitting across from him looked almost . . . composed, nothing like the damaged creature Mary had found wasting away in that rat-hole apartment.

Julian wasn't sure how to feel about Jasper's transformation.

The air shimmered, and Mary materialized, looking chagrined.

"I'm really sorry," she said immediately. "Eleisha's still at the hotel, but I can't find Simone or Philip anywhere. I'll keep looking, but right now, I can't even sense them."

Jasper stood up, holding his blade by the hilt.

"Don't worry, Mary," he said. "If Eleisha's at the hotel, then she's safe for now." He glanced at Julian. "That's what you want, right? You want me to take out Simone before she gets near Eleisha?"

Julian shifted his weight from one foot to the other, growing more uncertain about both his servants.

But in essence, Jasper was right.

"Find Simone," Julian ordered Mary. "Don't come back until you do."

She looked quickly at Jasper. "Be back."

Then she blinked out.

Julian walked off toward his bedroom. He did not relish the thought of just standing around here the rest of the night with Jasper.

He wanted this over, and he wanted Eleisha safely back in Portland with Wade—so they could continue their search until they found someone who mattered.

At three o'clock in the morning, Eleisha was sitting on the hotel room carpet watching the door with her arms wrapped around her knees.

Philip hadn't called. He wasn't answering his phone.

She had no idea where he was.

She knew only that he'd gone to speak with Simone more than twenty-four hours ago, and he hadn't come back.

Maybe time passes more slowly when a person is alone, but this had been the longest night of her life, just sitting there, watching the door, and going back and forth between ideas of what to do.

Should she call a cab and go to Simone's house?

Philip had told her to stay here . . . but he'd done that last night, when he'd also promised he'd call.

Was he in trouble?

Or was it just taking him longer than he expected to win Simone's trust?

The last thing Eleisha wanted to do was barge in and ruin any kind of success he'd achieved. But . . . it wasn't like him to leave her sitting alone like this.

Something was wrong. She just didn't know what to do.

Finally, she glanced down at her canvas bag on the floor beside her. She didn't want to burden Wade or Rose with all this—especially when they were still in Oregon at her request—but she needed help.

Slowly, she reached over and dug out her phone, opening it and pressing a button to connect with the underground. Wade had told her to call his office first, as he was seldom far away from it, and when he was home, he tended to leave his own cell lying haphazardly about.

The other end started ringing.

Wade sat across from Rose at the kitchen table. She wore a simple cream dress with small silver hoops in her ears.

He'd arranged a string of objects in front of himself.

He was beginning to suspect that Rose's mind-reading abilities were coming along more slowly because her psychometry was so strong. This revelation made him more aware that vampires all developed different strengths and weaknesses.

Eleisha was by far the best able to use her telepathy like a weapon, driving suggestions and visions into someone else's mind—even other vampires if she could hit them before they blocked her—and Julian had no defense against her at all. Wade and Philip could both do this to a point, but not at the level she could.

Philip, however, seemed surprisingly able to control *which* memories he showed to another reader. This was something neither Wade nor Eleisha had been able to master yet. They both tended to be swept away and showed the reader too much.

But Rose's new ability was startling and unique.

"Here," he said holding out an ancient pair of hedge clippers. "Try this one."

Rose had taken her gloves off. She'd been somewhat tense since their short trip to the Whole Foods store. But he made no apologies for his actions. A man had threatened Rose with a knife. If Philip had been the one guarding Rose, he would have killed that drug addict without a second thought. And Eleisha clearly found Philip more useful than Wade.

Wade had some catching up to do.

However, now that he was assisting Rose with her newfound psychometric abilities, she was growing more at ease with him again. She reached out and gripped the clippers with her bare hands.

She smiled, closing her eyes. "Can you see?"

At the invitation, Wade slipped effortlessly into her mind. At first, he saw only Eleisha using the tool on an overgrown rhododendron bush, but then the image grew misty for a few moments, and he saw an old man in coveralls, working quietly in the church garden on a small hedge. The garden looked different, more manicured, and the fence surrounding the church was much more exposed. He could actually see the street and several cars from the early 1950s.

"Oh, Rose," he said.

He could feel that she was in control of this memory—nothing like what had happened with the silver hairbrush. But the images were calm and even somewhat static. He couldn't hear anything, but maybe there was nothing to hear.

Then he saw the clippers in an old-fashioned dry goods store, and the man from the garden was gripping them for the first time. He looked younger, and a golden retriever stood beside him, gazing up curiously. Now Wade could hear the dog whine.

"What do you think, girl?" the man asked her, holding out his chosen tool. "Will these do?" She barked once.

Wade pulled out of Rose's mind.

"It's incredible," he said. "Different from reading a direct memory, more like watching home movies."

She opened her eyes and put the clippers down. "Sometimes, I can feel what the person was feeling at the time, see through their eyes, but not always."

His concern for her comfort and state of mind always took precedence at any of these telepathic training sessions. "Can you block the images if you don't wish to see?"

"Not yet. Do you think you can help? I'd hate to have to wear gloves all the time."

"Try picking up the clippers again," he said. "Only this time, try to force the memories out exactly the same way you'd force me out."

"All right."

She was just reaching for the clippers when the phone rang in Wade's office upstairs.

They both tensed.

"Go," she said.

He walked quickly out the kitchen archway and up the stairs. By the time he reached the office, the phone had rung five times.

"Hello?"

The office was a mess, with maps and pens and notepads all over his desk, half burying the computer keyboard.

"Wade?"

The instant she spoke, his stomach tightened. He knew the various inflections of her voice, and in that one word, she sounded on the edge of desperation.

"What's wrong?"

"I've lost Philip. I don't know what to do."

"Lost?"

"He left here last night after we got back from the cafe. We made a connection with Simone, but he thought he should talk to her by himself . . . that I wouldn't understand her enough to explain things." Her voice broke. "But he hasn't come back."

"What?"

Wade was furious at being twelve hundred miles away.

"Philip told you he wanted to convince her himself, and you believed him?" he nearly shouted.

Eleisha went silent.

Wade closed his eyes, running a hand over his face. Philip had never shown an ounce of interest in pursuing their goal of helping other vampires. He'd made it clear he was involved only because Eleisha and Wade were determined to follow this path.

"I'm sorry," he said. The last thing he wanted to do was make this worse for her. He wanted to help. "Have you tried calling him?"

"He's not answering."

Movement in the doorway caught Wade's attention, and he saw Rose standing there. He reached down and hit the SPEAKER button.

"Do you want me to come?" Wade asked. "I can head for the airport tonight."

"No, don't leave Rose there alone. I don't think any of us should split up further. And even if you were here, you couldn't help me. I just wanted to talk to you."

"Have you heard anything from him at all?" Wade asked.

"He called just before dawn yesterday. I'd have a better idea what to do if I knew where he was. Can you send Seamus?"

"Hang on," he said. "Rose is right here, and I've got you on speaker."

"Oh . . . thank you," Eleisha said softly.

Just talking to them did seem to be calming her a bit. He looked at Rose. "They're separated, and she can't find Philip. Can you call on Seamus?"

"I'll try," Rose answered. "Of course he's nearby, but I don't know if . . ." She trailed off.

Wade understood. Seamus had pushed himself far past his abilities to be away from Rose again so soon. He'd been flitting between London and Denver and Portland too much. Since returning to the church, he seemed to be recovering in a state of invisible limbo, as if even manifesting was too much effort.

"Seamus," Rose called.

Nothing happened.

Wade didn't want to panic Eleisha, but he also didn't want her setting off to search for Philip on her own. For one, none of them knew anything about the level of danger Simone might pose; two, none of them had any idea where Julian might be; and three, Philip could come back at any moment, and her leaving the hotel would simply prolong the separation.

"Just hang on, and we'll send Seamus soon," Wade said.

"Okay." She was quiet for a little while and then said, "Thank you."

She sounded small and sad.

He wanted to get on a plane and go to her.

"Just hang on," he repeated.

She hung up.

When Philip finally climbed back into the Thunderbird, his mind was so thick and foggy, he had no idea how much of the night had passed.

But he was sated.

He couldn't even remember the last time he hadn't felt hunger or need crawling beneath his skin.

Simone had given him this. She'd helped him to shut everything off and do whatever he wanted.

She got in the passenger side, and he raised the keys toward the ignition.

"Wait," she said.

He glanced at her, not wanting to talk. After feeding without restraint, he often had difficulty with speech for a few hours. The words didn't form correctly in his head.

"I wanted to ask you . . ." She trailed off.

She wanted to ask him something?

"Maggie once told me," she went on, sounding desperate now, "that she had a great love that crossed wealth and poverty and death and time. Was that you? Was it you, Philip? I need to know."

The question didn't surprise him. He'd seen her memories and could still hear the sound of Maggie's voice when she'd spoken those words.

He nodded.

"I knew it," Simone said, and her china blue eyes began to glow, as if his affirmation more than pleased her. "I want to see the night she was turned. You made Maggie, and she made me. You and I are connected."

He blinked, just watching her.

She wanted to see and feel him turning Maggie?

"Please," she begged. "She said you were her great love . . . but I think maybe it ended that night, and I need to see."

Had it ended that night?

And why would she want to see it end?

From the moment Rose touched that silver hairbrush, Philip's distant past had been shoved right in his face when all he wanted to do was forget.

Simone increased the flow of her gift, making him envy everything about her, everything about her life. She was free to do whatever she wanted.

Why should he be so uncomfortable with his own past?

"Show me that night," she whispered.

His vision blurred slightly, and the dashboard grew hazy. She wanted this, and he felt that he owed her . . . something.

Simone would not judge him or shrink away from him.

He shot one hand out and grabbed her wrist, sinking his own thoughts into her mind and helping her make a connection.

Then he closed his eyes and let himself go back. . . .

chapter 10

P hilip climbed the trellis up the side of the gray stone house, pulling himself through Maggie's open bedroom window.

He could have used the front door. She'd told him that his money paid the rent on the house and all the furniture belonged to him, but when she spoke of such things, he didn't understand. The only area of the house that seemed familiar was the bedroom, and he always returned there.

He made the short hop to the floor, and he waited.

She wasn't in the house. He could smell her from a hundred yards, so he knew she was nowhere nearby. He crouched next to the bed. His feet were bare, and his long red-brown hair hung in a tangled mess over his shoulders and down his back.

He hadn't come here for a while. He didn't know exactly how long, but he knew a number of nights had passed.

Tonight, he'd woken up longing to see her.

He just crouched on the floor and waited as the hours slipped by. Then, finally, he raised his head, catching a whiff of her perfume.

She was coming.

He heard the front door open and her light footsteps tapping a staccato up the stairs. She came into the bedroom, humming a soft tune under her breath, carrying a candle. She froze at the sight of him.

"Philip."

She almost always wore red gowns. He remembered that much. Tonight was no exception. The color made her pale skin and chocolate brown hair stand out. Her thick hair was piled up on top of her head and held with a set of silver combs. He sniffed the air again, drinking in the scent of her perfume from close range. She put down the candle.

Her eyes were dark and slightly slanted.

When he first began coming here, he did not know why, but he understood that she had meant something to him before. The world seemed clearer to him now, and when she spoke, he was more able to understand and to answer.

"Where were you?" he asked.

Normally, whenever he spoke, she was pleased, and she often told him, "You're getting so much better."

But tonight, she did not seem pleased. She looked at his hair and his bare feet.

"I was out."

"Where?"

She unfastened her cloak, exposing the white skin over her collarbone, and she took a piece of paper from the pocket.

"With friends," she said.

Something was wrong. He could see it in her face. She didn't want to look at him. In some of the first nights he remembered coming here, she had held him and rocked him and wept in the nook of his neck. She'd begged him to come back to her. She had run to him whenever he jumped in through the window, clinging to him, so glad to see him.

She did not run to him anymore. She did not hold him or weep into his neck.

Dropping her cloak on the bed, she showed him the piece of paper.

"Philip . . . ," she began. "If you come tomorrow, I will not be here."

He stiffened.

"This is a letter from my sister Amélie," she went on. "She and Juliette miss me, and I miss them. I'm going home to Nantes for a little while." She held up one hand. "Not long; just a few months."

"No."

He stood up.

He didn't like the quality of her voice, the way she was trying to put him at ease.

She tried to smile. "You remember Amélie, don't you? She adored you. She could not wait to have you for her brother."

That was something else she'd told him, that they had planned to go to a church together and have a ceremony that would bind them. His body remembered certain actions, such as how to ride a horse and use a sword. But he didn't remember events or plans, and he didn't remember Amélie.

"No," he repeated.

He didn't want her in Nantes. He wanted her here.

Her smile vanished, and her dark eyes glinted in the candle-light.

"You never stopped me from visiting my sisters before," she said. "You were always glad for me to see them because it made me happy."

He didn't understand this, and he moved closer.

"Don't!" she snapped. "You're filthy, and you stink."

He flinched, staring at her. She'd never spoken to him like that before. Almost instantly, her expression melted to regret and she came to him.

"Forgive me. I didn't mean that."

But she couldn't take the words back. With a sobbing sound, she turned away and clutched a miniature painting from the top of a chest near the bed, holding it against her stomach. He'd seen it many times. It depicted a handsome man wearing a black overcoat and white cravat. His smooth red-brown hair was pulled back at the nape of his neck.

Touching this painting always made Maggie sad.

She looked up at him and didn't even try to hide her revulsion.

Why was she looking at him like that?

He stepped over to a large mirror atop her dressing table, trying to see himself as she did. His hair was snarled. His soiled shirt was open, and dried red flakes from a kill he'd made last night still clung to his chest. He raised his lips, and his mouth curved into a snarl.

He didn't like what he saw in the mirror, and he didn't like the reflection in Maggie's eyes.

"I'm tired," she said suddenly. "I want to sleep."

He cocked his head in confusion. The bed was only a few feet away. "Then sleep."

"No." Her delicate jaw tightened. "I mean I would like you to go so that I can sleep."

She wanted him to leave? She'd never wanted that before.

"Swear you won't go to Nantes," he said.

She turned on him. "Just leave, Philip! I promise I won't be away for long, but I need to be with my sisters. I need to be away from this house. I need to be away from you!"

At this, he snarled openly, making a sound he'd never aimed

toward Maggie. Why was she doing this? Why wasn't she holding him and begging him to come back to her?

"Go!" she shouted, pointing at the window.

He whirled and jumped up onto the sill, dropping one arm down the trellis and then descending rapidly to the yard below.

Kayli, his bay mare, was tied to a tree, and he strode toward her, grabbing her reins. Then he stopped.

His hand was shaking. Maggie hadn't wanted him in her room. She'd shouted at him. She'd said she would be gone by tomorrow night. Something in her eyes frightened him. She wanted to go away.

In recent weeks, flashes of memories had been returning to him, of his maker, Angelo, holding him down, biting his neck, and then feeding Philip blood from his wrist. These came in bits and pieces at unwanted moments, but Philip was beginning to realize what they meant.

He looked back at Maggie's window.

He couldn't stand the way she'd looked at him tonight, and he couldn't stand the thought of her leaving, even for a few months . . . if it was only a few months. Worse, he'd heard in her voice how much she wanted to be with these sisters, these people who were not him.

She should want to be with him.

The thought made him angry.

He turned and jogged back to the house, grabbing the trellis and swinging himself up. Near the top, he launched himself up onto the windowsill. Maggie was just removing her dress, wearing only the white shift beneath.

When she looked over at him, he saw something new reflect back at him: fear.

Maggie had never been afraid of him.

She dropped her dress and bolted for the bedroom door. He jumped down and caught her before she'd taken three steps, grabbing her arm and jerking her back.

"Philip, don't!" she cried, swinging at him with her fist, hitting him in the face.

He caught her wrist and then used his weight to drop them both to the floor, pinning her with his shoulders. She fought and pushed against him, screaming at him to stop, but he barely heard her.

He existed to hunt and to feed, but never once had even considered feeding on Maggie. She was the only thing that brought him comfort or eased his mind. Now he could see the pulse at the base of her throat, and he bit down into her skin.

He could still smell her perfume.

She sobbed and pushed at him until she grew weak, and his actions turned from memory to pure instinct. He *knew* what to do. Her heart slowed. It almost stopped, and he tore open his own wrist, pressing it into her mouth.

When she latched onto him, draining him back, he was surprised by how much it hurt, but he didn't pull away. He let her drink until he began to feel weakened himself. Her eyelids fluttered, and she fell dormant.

He knew she would.

Disengaging his wrist from her mouth, he picked her up, moving her to the bed. She would sleep for hours. Again, he didn't know how he knew this, only that he was right.

The miniature was on the dressing table now, and he walked over to pick it up, studying the face.

Moving to the wardrobe, he found shirts and boots that seemed familiar. He saw water in a basin. He washed his face and chest and put on a clean shirt. Then he wet his hair down and used Maggie's comb to try to work out some of the tangles.

He would look different when she woke up. From now on, he would try to look like the man in the picture.

An hour before dawn, he closed the shutters tightly and lit another candle.

"What did you do?" Maggie whispered from the bed. "I can't feel my heart."

She was awake, watching him.

He didn't answer. In truth, he did not know what he'd done or why, only that he wanted her to look at him as she had before, with longing.

He remained at Maggie's side for the next few years.

After he turned her, she had mourned for several nights, curled up in a ball, hating the change in herself and blaming him.

Then she began to adjust, becoming a vampire.

A small voice told him that he should stay and teach her what she needed to know. The first few weeks were full of hope and relief. She didn't look at him with revulsion.

But after a while, he began to feel that something else was wrong.

She did not go to Nantes. She never shouted at him or called him "filthy" or told him to leave, but she also didn't touch him or hold him or speak of how they had once loved each other.

He taught her how to hunt and was pleased when he learned that her gift was the same as his own.

Maggie had been alluring before, and she was alluring now. Much more so.

She glittered.

Victims fell into her lap.

He liked hunting with her. But he kept waiting for her to reach out to him, to tell him that she was happy they were the same now, that everything would go back to the way it was when she loved him.

She never did.

Yet, he remained convinced he'd done the correct thing. What else could he have done?

"Tell me again about how I was before," he asked one night, "about how I made my father so angry by promising to go to the church with you."

Not in the mood for an elaborate hunt, they were walking in a small village, looking for possible prey who had stumbled off alone.

To his shock, Maggie shrugged her smooth shoulders.

"I'm sorry, Philip," she said. "I still remember everything from before, but it's like looking at someone else's life."

He stopped walking.

"What do you mean? Tell me how we were before."

She wore most of her hair down loose tonight, with only a few sections pinned up. She was pale and lovely, and her dark eyes seemed hard. She shook her head. "I can't tell you. When I think of you then, I see only some softhearted mortal I'd want to feed on." Moving back beside him, she added, "But I like the way you are now."

His chest felt tight, and he started walking again, not wanting her to see his face. He had not succeeded in building a bridge to close the gap between them.

Instead, he'd broken it.

chapter 11

Simone clawed with her thoughts as Philip jerked away.

"Wait!" she cried.

She wanted to hold on; she wanted to see more.

"That's enough," he rasped, leaning over the steering wheel. "I never should have . . ."

He didn't finish the sentence, and he looked so stricken, she fought to gain control of herself, realizing that while lost in his memories, she'd stopped projecting her gift. She turned it back on, letting it flow into him, clouding his mind and helping him focus on something else.

But on the inside, she was singing. She'd been right.

This was fate.

Philip had turned Maggie, and Maggie had turned Simone, so she shared his blood. Whatever love he and Maggie shared had not crossed the boundaries of death—or undeath. It had been lost the night he turned her.

From that point on, events had been rushing forward to this moment in time.

From him to Simone.

She loved him for exactly who he was and what he was. She had no past comparisons and no illusions.

All the pointless, monotonous nights she'd drifted through in clubs and theaters and lounges only made her value what she saw now.

A line of fate that stretched back almost two hundred years.

It had taken far too long, but it all made sense.

And they were finally together.

As her gift flowed around him, the tight lines of his face eased. After a moment, he reached down and started the car.

She'd never been so happy.

Philip and Simone didn't get back to her house until an hour before dawn.

When they walked in from the garage, he felt numb, like a stranger to himself.

Her lovely face was glowing, her dress was ruined, and she seemed euphoric, nearly dancing ahead of him into the living room.

"There's another bathroom through the kitchen," she said, pointing. "You can use it to clean up." She looked down at herself. "I'm a mess." She smiled. "I'll be myself again soon. We can sleep out the day and go out tonight. We'll go south this time, to Colorado Springs or Castle Rock."

She stepped closer, whispering up to him, "You can show me more. I'll do anything you want." She headed toward the stairs. "Pretend this is your home."

As soon as she was gone, her gift began to fade.

Then it vanished altogether.

He stood looking around the living room. Bits and pieces of the night were coming back to him, along with an unfamiliar feeling in the pit of his stomach.

Had he really shown her the raw emotions of the night he turned Maggie?

He was sated, full of blood and life and the sweet taste of his victims' terror. But without Simone's gift, his head was beginning to clear.

She wanted to go out again tonight?

After living for months with Wade and Eleisha, going hunting only when necessary, the idea of going out again tonight struck him as . . . incorrect. He walked through the cold, sterile furniture of Simone's main room, studying the sculptures and glass tables.

There was no television.

There were no wooden shelves pushed up against the walls.

There were no movies to watch, no cards to play, no books to be read aloud.

What did she do here when she wasn't hunting? He looked down at a tightly stretched leather couch, thinking perhaps no one had ever sat upon it. Upstairs, he heard the shower running.

Simone didn't live in this house. Not really. She went out at night. She went to clubs. She hunted. She played her games with mortal lovers.

His head grew clearer, and the feeling in his stomach turned into a knot.

He'd left Eleisha at a hotel alone all night, and he hadn't even called her. He'd left his phone behind in his coat pocket, lying on the floor. How could he have done that?

But he knew. He'd done it because he'd wanted to, because watching Simone's memories of feeding had driven him to the edge.

Maybe he had even lied to Eleisha about his reasons for coming here.

Maybe he'd lied to himself.

He must have known from the moment Simone sat down at the Mercury Cafe that she'd never be able to exist inside a community at the underground. She was no frightened, lost vampire looking for protection and help and the company of her own kind. She was a killer and a player, and she'd probably laugh out loud at Eleisha's four laws.

He'd wanted to come here alone. He had envied Simone, and he wanted a taste of her existence.

In turn, he'd given her a taste of his—or what it once had been.

But now . . . now the reality of his actions and the possible repercussions were beginning to sink in.

He strode fast through the kitchen into a bathroom and looked in the mirror. His shirt was soaked and crusted with blood. Red, drying flakes covered his face and the right side of his hair.

He stared at himself, and he remembered looking at himself in Maggie's mirror in 1821 like it had been yesterday.

He didn't want to be *this* anymore.

He wanted to go home to the underground.

Looking around in panic, he wasn't sure what to do. He didn't have any other clothes, and he couldn't go back to the hotel like this. And what would he say when he got there?

The water upstairs stopped running.

He looked back into the mirror. He'd left Eleisha alone for two nights.

With a single jerk, he pulled his shirt over his head and turned on the hot water at the sink. Rapidly, he scrubbed his face and hair and chest until he was clean, and then he dried off with a towel. He took the shirt with him when he left the bathroom, thinking he could stuff it into a Dumpster once he got outside.

Out in the living room, he found the sheathed machete where

he'd dropped it the night before. He hooked it to his belt and then pulled on his long coat, buttoning it all the way to his throat.

Simone was coming down the stairs in a satin bathrobe.

"Philip?" she said. "What are you doing?"

She was so lovely dressed in silk, like a porcelain doll.

He took a step back. "I have to go."

"What?" Her eyes grew wide.

She began to let her gift engulf him, but his head was clear now, and he didn't want to feel hazy anymore.

Not noticing the lack of effect, she suddenly nodded. "Oh, you're going to tell her, aren't you? That you're not going back to Portland? I know you want to get it over with, but just wait until tonight. The sun will be up too soon. You can tell her tonight, and then you and I can go hunting."

"No, I'm going home." He took another step back, shaking his head. "Eleisha and I were wrong to come here."

As he moved toward the door, her expression tightened with shock. "Home? You are home."

He kept moving.

"Philip!"

But by the time she called his name, he was outside, running down the street.

Eleisha was sitting on the floor again with her arms around her knees.

Hours had passed. Seamus had not arrived. Dawn was coming.

She shouldn't have waited. She shouldn't have followed Wade's advice. She should have gone out looking for Philip, and now it was too late. She'd have to wait until tonight.

Dim gray from the sky came in through the windows, casting long shadows on the walls, making the furniture appear cold, almost menacing.

She pressed her forehead into her knees. She was alone.

No one knew better than Eleisha that vampires could die—truly die and float away like dust drifting on the air.

Edward . . . William . . . Maggie . . . Robert.

Her chest constricted when she let herself even imagine tomorrow without Philip. The sky seemed even lighter, but she wouldn't go into the bedroom, not without him. Where was he? And what of Simone?

With her eyes closed, Eleisha saw Robert's hawklike face staring back at her. She'd promised him that she'd teach the laws.

She'd *promised*.

And now she was sitting here in the dim light before dawn, helpless, useless, and frozen with fear.

A scraping sound made her look back up.

The hotel room door opened, and Philip nearly stumbled inside. He looked down at her. His hair was wet, but he seemed unhurt.

She jumped to her feet, sick with relief, a hundred questions passing through her mind.

"Philip."

Running to him, she was taken aback when he held his hand up, not letting her touch him.

"Wait," he said sharply. "Wait here a minute."

He brushed past, strode into the bedroom, and closed the door. He was gone less than a minute and then came out with his coat off, wearing a black sweater. He wouldn't look at her.

"Are you all right?" she asked. "Where's Simone?"

His eyes flashed to her face, and her relief began to waver.

"I'm tired," he said, ignoring her questions. "Come and sleep, and we'll go home tonight."

"Home? No, we can't go home."

"Yes!" he shouted. "Tonight!"

He seemed unbalanced, nearly manic, and she knew he must have gone through some kind of ordeal, but she'd been sitting on the carpet in the dark, staring at a door.

"Talk to me! Where's Simone?"

His entire body was shaking.

"In her house," he said more quietly. "She cannot come with us. She belongs here."

Eleisha froze, trying to put the pieces together. Something had happened to convince him that Simone was not capable of joining them in the underground. But where had he been all this time? She wanted to reach into his mind before he could block her, but he'd feel her and blame her afterward.

"What happened?" she whispered.

"Please," he begged, holding out his hand. "Just come to sleep now. I cannot talk."

He'd never done that before. Philip didn't beg for anything.

She felt broken inside that he wouldn't share whatever had upset him so much, had somehow convinced him Simone was a lost cause. But he was so distraught, and the sun was rising. She moved to him and took his hand, leading him into the bedroom. He dropped onto the bed without taking off his sweater.

Then he grasped her and pulled her down hard against his chest. Even through his clothes, she could feel heat coming from his body.

Heat?

"Were you out hunting?" she asked.

Had he tried to show Simone how they hunt already? Had something tragic happened? That would explain his raw emotions.

He tightened his arm. "Close your eyes."

Her eyelids were flickering, and she tried to make herself calm. He was exhausted. Once he woke up tonight, he would feel better, and then he could talk to her.

Letting him go alone last night had been a mistake. Philip was not skilled at explaining either the history of his own kind or the essential nature of the underground or the necessity of the laws. Perhaps now he would realize this as well and not ask to be the envoy again.

He relaxed his arm just enough for her roll slightly inward. She buried her face in his shoulder, still sick with relief that he was back.

But one thing was certain. No matter what he said or did, they were not going back to Portland tonight.

Simone was Maggie's creation, her child, and Eleisha would never just abandon Maggie's child.

Simone went upstairs and sank slowly down onto her bed.

Philip had looked inside of her and seen her life—Daddy and Pug and the early years with Maggie. He'd seen her play the first game with Ethan, and then afterward, he had not turned away. He had reveled in her company and hunted by her side.

He loved her, and he loved her existence.

He wanted to share it all. She knew this as absolutely as she'd known she could make Ethan forget Alice.

Simone didn't lose.

Not anymore.

Philip was not part of the game . . . or maybe he was the ultimate game? Now that she'd found him, she never wanted to play with mortals again. They were shadows next to him. Simone finally understood Maggie.

Simone had found a companion, after all these years.

And then . . . for some reason, he'd run. Something had pulled him back to Eleisha.

But Simone knew what he really wanted.

She lay back on her bed.

No wonder she hadn't been able to interpret the intense expression on Philip's face when he gazed at Eleisha. He wasn't in love with Eleisha—not the way a man loved a woman. He was trapped by some kind of slavish devotion.

Of course he had no desire to go back to a decaying church and live in a tepid "community." That was clear enough from his frenzied, wild feeding.

And after the past two nights, he could not possibly prefer Eleisha's company to Simone's.

No . . . Eleisha had some other kind of hold on him.

Simone didn't know what it was, but she didn't care. The solution was self-evident.

She simply had to remove Eleisha, and then Philip would be free.

Julian's eyelids were growing heavy, and he locked his bedroom door, shutting out the rest of the suite, not bothering to see where Jasper might choose to sleep out the day.

It troubled him that Mary had not even been able to sense Simone and Philip in the city. Anything that kept Eleisha from searching for elders drove him to frustration, and it appeared that she was doing nothing at the moment besides sitting in a hotel room.

He was equally troubled by Mary's omission that Philip had been sleeping in Eleisha's bed for months. What could that mean? From now on, he was going to ask Mary more pointed questions about the details of the household in Portland.

His eyelids fluttered.

He was just lying back onto a pillow when Mary floated right through the wall, startling him. She'd never done that before.

"Good, you're still awake," she said. "Jasper looks totally dead on the couch."

He glared at her, waiting.

"Everything's okay," she said, holding one hand up. "I've got all three of them now. Philip's back with Eleisha at their hotel, and Simone's alone at her house. If you send Jasper as soon as he wakes up tonight, he should be able to take her head."

Mary floated closer, and her expression darkened. "But I'm going with him, and you better warn him to keep sharp and do what he can to block her gift. She's already got Philip half crazy, and Jasper's a kid next to him."

If he could have, Julian would have struck her down to the floor and watched her bleed. But he couldn't.

At least Simone was alone. That was something.

"Be here after dusk," he ordered.

Unable to stay awake a second longer, he closed his eyes.

chapter 12

That night, Eleisha woke up with her cheek pressed into the lines of Philip's sweater. The sensation was unusual, as she'd grown accustomed to the feel of his skin.

She sat up, rubbing her face.

Normally, he woke up a few seconds before she did, but he was still dormant, with his head on the pillow.

Sheer relief at having him safely back, coupled with a day spent sleeping on his shoulder, helped her to begin reasoning the probable pattern of events. Somehow, his attempt to explain their proposal to Simone had gone wrong, and out of pride, he had continued trying until she'd done something to convince him that the attempt to help her was a failure.

Whatever happened must have been ugly . . . if it had sent Philip back shaking and exhausted.

She climbed out of the bed carefully, trying not to disturb him.

Somehow, she was going to have to tell him they weren't going home yet, and after his outburst that morning, she was worried he'd put up a fight. What if she couldn't get him to agree?

She'd never yet faced complete opposition from Philip . . . and wasn't sure she could.

Wandering out into the living room of their suite, she ran a hand through her long hair, glancing around at the unfamiliar décor. She didn't blame him for wanting to go back to the underground, but they weren't finished here yet. They weren't even close.

Suddenly Beethoven's Fifth exploded from her canvas bag.

With a stab of guilt, she realized that in the heat of the predawn events, she hadn't called Wade back before going to bed. She'd left him worrying all day.

She hurried over to get her phone, but the caller ID did not show Wade's name or the underground, and she didn't recognize the number.

"Hello?"

"Don't say my name and don't react," Simone said.

Eleisha was so caught off guard that she just stood there, holding the phone.

"After last night," Simone went on, "I don't think Philip wants me to see you, but you and I need to talk. Can you meet me in an hour at the Starbucks on Larimer?"

"Yes."

"Don't let him know where you're going."

Simone hung up.

Eleisha put the phone down. No matter what her companions thought, she was well aware that Simone was nothing like Rose or Robert, and that she was dealing with a pitiless, self-centered vampire who probably killed without thought or remorse—just like Philip had once been.

She had no illusions in this matter.

But she wasn't just going to give up and leave Simone behind.

Robert's death had placed the burden on Eleisha, and now she was left to teach the four laws.

Walking into the bedroom, she took a hairbrush and a clean

pair of Levi's from her suitcase. Philip was awake, watching her.

"Who was calling you?" he asked.

"Just the hotel, asking if we want Housekeeping to service our suite tonight. I gave them my number when we checked in."

She'd also placed an order not to be disturbed during daylight hours.

"Did you tell them we're checking out?" he asked, sounding so cold, she knew any kind of argument would be a mistake.

"Yes, but I haven't arranged for plane tickets yet."

She studied him as he sat up in the bed, pulling off his rumpled sweater. His pale skin glowed in the darkness. She decided to give him one more chance before embarking upon the plan forming in her mind.

"Philip, what happened last night?"

The hard look in his eyes turned to anger, almost disbelief that she'd asked him again.

"Get dressed and get packed," he ordered. "Then you call for plane tickets, or I will."

This was hopeless. He wasn't going to explain himself—he wasn't even going to try.

In essence, he'd just made the decision for her.

She nodded, stepping closer to the bed. "Your hair's a mess. Why don't you take a shower, and I'll take care of things out here?"

She dressed in the jeans and a light green tank top.

He just watched her, as if suspicious of her for giving in so easily. But then he seemed relieved and climbed off the bed, taking some clothes from his suitcase. "I won't be long."

She knew he did not believe her capable of open deception—not to him.

As soon as the bathroom door closed, she pulled on a pair of sandals. Looking at her cell phone, she briefly considered leaving it behind, but then changed her mind and simply turned it off before dropping it into her bag and slinging the strap over her shoulder.

She wrote a note and left it on the coffee table. Once she'd made sure the note would be the first thing he'd see upon emerging, she slipped out the door.

Philip took longer in the shower than he'd planned, washing his hair twice. He just couldn't seem to feel clean.

Closing his eyes, he let the hot water run over his face, blocking out the sight of the white tiles all around him.

An alien emotion was tickling the back of his brain. He could not name it, but neither could he make it go away. Eleisha had trusted him to sit down with Simone and explain the nature of the underground, the danger from Julian, the four laws, and the benefits of living inside a community. He had convinced Eleisha that his similarities to Simone made him the best choice to present this argument.

But he'd done none of those things.

Instead, he'd read the memories of a lonely, damaged vampire, and when her memories drove him to savage hunger, he'd allowed her to cast a haze over his mind so that he could hunt like the Philip Branté of old once more. He'd used Simone so he could revel in blood and fear.

He didn't recognize the uncomfortable emotion passing through him, but he hated it.

To make matters worse, in his entire existence, he had never once stopped to examine his own actions like this before. Why couldn't he just forget last night and move on?

At least Eleisha wasn't angry that he'd left her alone so long. She was going home with him. In the end, that was all that mattered.

He opened his eyes, still letting the water run over his face, his mind still turning.

Could she really be giving in this easily? He'd expected more of a fight—with him getting mean and having to bully her. He'd carry her to the airport over his shoulder if necessary.

Some of this resolution involved fear for Eleisha, who couldn't be allowed anywhere near a vampire as unbalanced as Simone.

But some of it also involved fear of what might happen if Simone ever told Eleisha about last night. This made him cringe at his own cowardice, but nothing would change his mind.

He was taking Eleisha away from here tonight.

Shutting off the water, he reached for a towel and rubbed his head, knowing that while Eleisha wouldn't lie to his face, she might be trying to lull him into a false sense of security so she could ambush him with another reason to stay here and try a new tactic with Simone.

He was ready for her.

He got dressed and ran some mousse through his hair, starting to feel a little more like himself.

Opening the bathroom door, he called out, "Did you get a flight arranged?"

She didn't answer.

He stepped out into the suite, "Eleisha?"

Using his mind, he flashed out as far as he could reach.

Eleisha?

Running into the bedroom, he swiveled his head left and right. Then he ran back into the living room and saw a note on the coffee table.

Philip,

    I know something terrible must have happened last night, but we can't just give up on Simone. We both owe Maggie more than that, and you know it.
    I've gone to meet Simone by myself. Don't worry. I'm not foolish, and I'll be on guard.
    Please call Wade and let him know you're okay. I called him last night when you didn't come back. I was upset, and I may have worried him.
    Stay in the hotel, and I'll contact you soon. Everything will be all right. I promise.

Eleisha

He dropped the note and ran for the outer hallway, not bothering to put his boots on. The elevator doors were closed, so he took the stairs, jumping down them four at time. When he hit the lobby, people glanced over in alarm, but he didn't stop and ran for the front doors.

Mortal pedestrians walked along the dark streets outside.

Looking both ways wildly, Philip felt his throat begin to constrict.

Eleisha was gone.

Simone was already sitting at a table at Starbucks, pleased that her gamble of calling Eleisha had paid off. But she'd had a strong feeling that Eleisha would play the game, keep a straight face, not tell Philip who called . . . and then agree to this meeting.

Movement at the door caught Simone's attention, and she

looked over, first with hope, and then with a mix of relief and trepidation, as Eleisha walked in.

Now the hard part began.

Simone understood Philip completely—better than he understood himself. She knew what he wanted.

Eleisha was more of a mystery. For one, she had potential, but she tended to wear things like faded jeans and tank tops, with her wispy hair blowing loose, like she hadn't given two seconds' thought to how she looked.

Simone didn't understand her at all, so it would be difficult to figure out what she wanted. Simone had always functioned by finding out what someone else wanted and then providing it—no matter what it was.

This was the only method for winning anyone's trust.

To Simone's further frustration, Eleisha didn't look as welcoming tonight as she had that night in the Mercury Cafe. In fact, she looked . . . cautious.

She came straight to Simone and glanced around, spotting another table in the very back with no one else sitting nearby.

"There," she said, as if only that one word were necessary.

Simone stood up. "Of course."

She headed for the table, leaving Eleisha to follow. She'd almost reached the closest chair when something smashed into her mind like a fist, and she felt a sharp command.

Freeze!

Every muscle in her body clenched, and she could not move. She was helpless for several long seconds. Then her body went fluid again, and she grabbed the back of the chair. Eleisha was right behind her.

"I may not be Philip," Eleisha whispered, "but I'm no sheep. Remember that."

Simone half turned, trepidation turning into worry. Perhaps Philip could read memories, but could Eleisha use her thoughts like a weapon? If so, then winning Eleisha's absolute trust was going to be essential.

But how?

"I wouldn't try to hurt you," Simone said. "I called you so we could talk."

Eleisha nodded and pointed to a chair.

They sat side by side in order to speak more softly. Simone had dressed carefully tonight, in a tan dress with sky blue beads, an ensemble she normally reserved for having evening tea with her current target's wife. She wore her trademark eyeliner, having decided to skip the lipstick.

"How much has Philip told you?" Eleisha asked.

The place was crowded. Over the loud calls of coffee orders and the hiss of the milk steamer, no one could hear them. Still, they kept their voices low.

"About what?" Simone asked in return, not sure where this was going.

Eleisha's forehead wrinkled. "About the underground."

Simone wasn't sure how to answer, so she trod carefully, deciding to drop a few bread crumbs. "Not much. He said he needed to know me, to see my life, so he made me think back."

"He read your memories?" Eleisha's expression altered instantly to concern, even sympathy.

Simone knew she'd hit the right mark. "It was awful. I couldn't stop him, and afterward he said I would never fit into your world."

"Philip said that?"

Eleisha seemed so surprised, Simone wondered whether she had pushed it too far.

But then Eleisha shook her head, and the sympathy in her voice increased. "I'm sorry, Simone. He's just overprotective, and he was trying to make sure you weren't a danger to the rest of us." She leaned forward, her eyes intense. "But his body was so warm when he got back this morning, and he wouldn't tell me what happened last night. . . . I've been wondering if he tried to take you hunting, to show you how to alter a memory."

Simone felt an unwanted flash of rage over how Eleisha would know that Philip's body had been warm that morning, but she kept her face politely distraught, as if she had suffered at his hands, and she mulled over the combination of the words "hunting" and "how to alter a memory."

Afraid of making a mistake, she didn't speak and simply nodded while looking at the tabletop.

"I thought so," Eleisha said, sounding frustrated now. "Something went wrong, didn't it?" She lowered her voice to an almost inaudible level. "He was so rattled this morning. Was anyone killed?"

These words caused only surprise and more confusion. Eleisha genuinely seemed to think that Philip would be upset by the death of a mortal. How was that possible? Eleisha was a vampire.

"I can't talk about it," Simone said. "Don't ask me."

Eleisha shook her head. "At least some of this is making sense now. It's my fault. Philip never should have forced you to show him your memories, and he never should have tried to teach you to alter a memory this soon." She leaned close enough to speak in Simone's ear. "But he thought he was doing the right thing. Please don't think badly of him."

Rage kept on building inside Simone. Eleisha didn't even know Philip. She didn't know the first thing about him, and here she was begging Simone to think well of him? Any other woman would have clawed Eleisha's eyes out by now. But Simone was not any other woman. She preferred to fight with a smile—just like her mother and her sisters.

"You came a long way to find me," Simone said quietly. "Maybe you should tell me why."

This was good. She'd safely established that Philip had told Eleisha nothing of the events that had taken place in Boulder, and Eleisha now believed that Philip had brutalized Simone in his attempt to explain their purpose in Denver.

They were beginning to build a bridge of trust.

Eleisha was quiet for a little while, and then said, "I know you left Maggie, and I think I know why."

In her first unguarded moment since Eleisha walked through the Starbucks door, Simone asked, "Did Maggie send you here?"

"No . . . Maggie's dead. I didn't know how to answer you at the cafe."

"Dead?"

Almost nothing Eleisha said made sense, but the thought of Maggie dead seemed beyond comprehension. Philip had shown her raw memories of Maggie only the night before. How could he not have told her Maggie was dead?

"I can tell you how it happened, but . . ." Eleisha trailed off. "Can we go someplace else? This place is too bright and loud, and I have so much to tell you."

Inwardly, Simone began to feel more confident. She had a plan . . . a good plan, if she could just keep Eleisha with her until morning, if she could just make Eleisha trust her.

So if Eleisha wanted to talk, Simone would certainly let her.

"There's a bookstore down the street called the Tattered Cover. It's huge, with nooks and crannies everywhere. We can find a little corner to ourselves."

Eleisha stood up. "Okay."

She didn't seem quite so cautious anymore.

Mary materialized in the living room of the suite at the Brown Palace, knowing that Julian was going to blow a gasket and that she couldn't even blame him.

"Is Jasper gone yet?" she asked immediately, looking around.

To her relief, Jasper was just pulling his coat on—to hide the sword strapped to his belt.

Julian was dressed in black slacks and a white shirt, but he wasn't wearing shoes. His feet were large and pale. He crossed his arms.

"I was just giving him instructions. What's wrong?"

She steeled herself. "Simone's not at the house anymore. I checked at dusk, and she was there, so I went back to Eleisha's hotel to make sure they weren't on the move yet, and when I checked back, Simone was gone, and now Eleisha's gone. I haven't done a serious search of the city, but I wanted to catch you before Jasper left. Right now, I don't know where they are."

She could see Julian grinding his back teeth, but he didn't explode.

"Find them," he whispered.

Philip threw several twenties at the cab driver and jumped out onto High Street, running up the walkway to Simone's house.

When he found the door locked, he kicked it open.

"Eleisha!"

All he could see was the sterile furniture and art.

"Eleisha!"

He searched every room, even after he realized she wasn't there.

His throat was still constricted, and he couldn't stop thinking of Simone's determination to win the games she played. He'd allowed himself to be sucked right into one of her games. . . . He'd even instigated it.

And now Eleisha was alone with Simone.

In desperation, he pulled the phone from his coat pocket, flipped it open, and hit the button to dial Eleisha's number. He knew she wouldn't answer. He knew she'd probably even turned her phone off. But he had to try.

The line rang six times and connected to voice mail.

He closed his eyes and then closed the phone.

Just as he was slipping it back into his pocket, it began ringing loudly. He almost dropped it as his heart jumped. She was calling him! Relief flooded his mouth as he rushed to answer, and then he stopped at the name on the caller ID display.

UNDERGROUND.

That was Wade's office phone.

Philip stood frozen, letting it ring. He couldn't talk to Wade right now, not after he'd lost Eleisha. He had to find her first.

But he didn't know where to look.

Eleisha found a carpeted spot on the floor between two bookshelves in the art section on the third floor, and she settled down across from Simone. There was nobody else in sight.

This felt so much like being with Maggie.

She had to remind herself that Simone was *not* Maggie and that she needed to focus on her purpose here. There was so much to tell Simone . . . whose impression of the underground must be negatively skewed.

But at least Eleisha was gaining some idea of what Philip had done, first by forcing Simone to expose her memories and then by trying to teach her the first law through a hunting exercise. Why had he been in such a hurry? She could only think he'd done these things out of fear for Wade, that he wanted to make sure Simone was following the first law before bringing her home to the church.

But something must have gone horribly wrong during the hunt, and she wished she knew what had taken place. It would help her proceed here.

Regardless, Philip had inadvertently caused some damage, and she had to find a way to fix it.

Where should she begin?

"Let me tell you how we met Rose," Eleisha said. "She's the one who started all this."

Simone pulled her knees beneath herself and smoothed her dress. Eleisha told her about the letters Rose sent, about buying the church, about going to San Francisco and meeting Rose, and then about being presented with the daunting figure of Robert Brighton, a soldier from the court of Henry VIII.

"He was five hundred years old," Eleisha said with some difficulty. It still hurt to talk about him . . . to think about him.

"Five hundred?"

"Our kind once lived all over the countries of Europe," she pushed on. "They had attachments to one another and existed among humans by always practicing the first law . . . what Philip tried teaching you last night. Vampires are latent telepaths, and they all learned to replace the memories of their victims and feed without killing. Robert taught me the laws, but then . . . Julian caught us before we reached Portland, and he took Robert's head." She paused, closing her eyes for a moment, trying not to see Robert's body lying on the sidewalk. "How much did Maggie tell you about Julian?"

"Just that he was mad, and we could never visit Paris or London because he might find out about me."

This seemed a somewhat shallow response.

"He's not mad in the sense that he has no ability to reason," Eleisha said. "It's just that he's not telepathic, and so he can't follow the first law. He was afraid the others like Robert, the elders, would turn against him. Now, I'm not sure what he wants. But I think he sent some kind of servants after us when we were trying to go home, and then he killed Robert himself."

"Servants?"

"Yes, a slender, dark-haired vampire and a ghost . . . a girl with magenta hair. But don't worry. If you choose to come with us, Philip and I can get you home."

Simone smiled. "I believe you."

Eleisha didn't smile back, but she felt the first real spark of hope.

Sitting on the floor, surrounded by books, Simone absorbed every word Eleisha said, and the way to Eleisha's heart spilled out like a magic elixir.

Simone could hardly believe it.

No wonder Philip fed like a starving man cut loose from his chains.

Eleisha was a zealot. She wanted converts.

She'd become obsessed with some long-dead code created by vampires who'd existed hundreds of years ago. Maybe Julian wasn't so bad. Maybe he'd done them all a favor. From what Simone could follow, Eleisha's goal was to find vampires hiding from Julian, bring them back to Portland, protect them, and then teach them how to feed on mortals without killing anyone.

Astonishing.

Ridiculous.

Unnatural.

But . . . Eleisha had just poured out her dreams and hopes. All Simone had to do now was prove that she was willing to try. This would win Eleisha's trust, and then Simone just needed to keep her away from Philip until morning.

Simone looked down at the carpet. "Before I have to see Philip again," she said, "I want a better idea of what he was trying to teach me last night. He thought I was hopeless . . . and then everything went wrong."

"What happened?" Eleisha asked.

Simone shook her head. "I just want you to show me. I know it will be better if you show me how yourself."

"No, it's too soon. You need a better grasp of your telepathy first, so you can at least observe what I'm doing by slipping inside my head."

A thrill passed through Simone. "Telepathy? You could teach me how you send and read thoughts like you do?"

Eleisha sat back. "Well . . . Didn't Philip explain that before he took you hunting?"

Warning lights went off in Simone's head, and she realized she was giving away too much. "He's not very good at expressing himself."

"Oh, that's true."

"Can you teach me?"

Eleisha looked uncertain, but then she leaned forward again.

"I wanted to give this a few more nights, but maybe he was right to start so soon." She paused. "Just relax and use your thoughts to reach into my mind."

Excitement building, Simone closed her eyes.

Can you hear me?

Eleisha's voice seemed to speak inside her own thoughts. This was unbelievable. A whole new world of power.

Yes, she answered. *I can hear you.*

Let me show you the churchyard.

A picture flashed onto Simone's eyelids of a tall wrought-iron fence, with lilacs and roses blooming all around an aging brick church. She saw a headstone and a young bush of white roses. The headstone read, ROBERT BRIGHTON, PROTECTOR, 1491 TO 2008.

The surreal quality of all this made her dizzy. All this time, she'd had this power inside of her and had never known it.

Eleisha's thoughts lingered on the headstone.

"Okay, now try to push me out," Eleisha said aloud. "Just try to block me. You can't control your power properly until you can block."

Simone began to try.

chapter 13

Shortly after sunset, Wade tried calling Eleisha first, and then Philip. Neither one answered. He sat on his desk, holding the phone tightly.

As yet, Seamus had not materialized, and Rose was pacing in the office.

Wade looked over at her and shook his head.

It wasn't like Eleisha to leave him hanging . . . or maybe it was. In all the time he'd known her, they'd never been separated quite like this.

"We need to do something," Rose said. Her face was tightly drawn. She hadn't bothered getting dressed yet and still wore her silk bathrobe. "You heard her voice. She sounded near the edge of despair. I couldn't stand it."

Wade sighed, all his instincts telling him to get on a plane. But he knew that would be the wrong choice for several reasons.

"The best we can do for now is to stay here and wait for some word and keep trying to reach Seamus."

"That doesn't seem like much," she said softly.

"I know."

She stopped pacing. "Seamus has never vanished like this. He's always been able to materialize even when he was exhausted."

"We pushed him too hard . . . or he pushed himself too hard."

Wade didn't completely understand the metaphysics, but he knew Seamus needed to remain in limbo near Rose and let his spirit recharge from her presence.

Rose looked at the door, and then her eyes seemed to drift. "You stay here, and I'll try downstairs in the kitchen. That's his favorite room."

"I don't think that will make a difference."

"Let me try."

She walked out abruptly, leaving him sitting there on the desk.

Rose slowed when she reached the staircase, waffling back and forth in indecision. She knew Seamus would not answer from the kitchen either, not until he had rested longer. He had gone beyond his limits.

She would not try to call him again just yet.

But she stopped at the bottom of the stairs, turning her head down the hallway toward Eleisha's room.

They knew almost nothing about Simone, and now Philip and Eleisha were separated in a strange city dealing with this child of Maggie's. Upstairs in the office, it occurred to Rose that if she only knew more about Simone—anything more—she might be able to help guide Eleisha from here.

But there was only one place she could think of to learn more . . . the same place she and Eleisha had started.

Still walking slowly, Rose moved down the hall and into Eleisha's bedroom. It was a pleasant room, painted in cream and white, slightly messy, with the lace comforter askew and a few of Philip's shirts thrown over one chair. Several dresser drawers were still open, as if Eleisha had packed in a hurry.

Rose went to the dressing table, looking down at Maggie's set of antique brushes and the silver mirror. Then she looked at the gloves on her hands.

A part of her was afraid to delve into these memories again. She'd felt Maggie's pain so acutely the first time. But she couldn't stop hearing Eleisha's sad, frightened voice over the speakerphone, and Rose hated feeling useless.

Even before she and Eleisha ever met, they'd made great plans together for the underground. Eleisha was so unselfish, so willing to share everything, and a clear path had lain before them. But now this terror of travel kept Rose locked inside the church while Philip . . . *Philip* of all people, had become Eleisha's only source of help.

What a state of events.

Rose peeled off her right glove.

She had to do something.

Upon waking tonight, she'd remembered a detail from the earlier vision.

Inside the memory, although Maggie had been gripping the silver brush, Simone had been holding the hand mirror. Since working with Wade, Rose's psychometric visions were growing clearer, and she was picking up direct memories from people who had touched various objects . . . she was feeling what they had felt. She'd even seen images that occurred "around" an imbued object once the holder set it down.

She gazed down at the hand mirror. A pretty thing, etched with ivy leaves across the back.

Rose didn't want to see any more of Simone.

But she had to.

Sitting on the floor, so she wouldn't fall if the memories struck her too hard, she grasped the handle of the mirror.

Almost instantly, she was pulled back in time, looking out through Simone's eyes.

"Maybe we should head over to the Showbox," Cecil said, his voice tense. "I don't want to just leave Maggie sitting there alone."

Simone couldn't believe what she was hearing.

He was thinking about Maggie?

She turned from the dressing table, still gripping the hand mirror, and tilted her head. "I thought you wanted us to be alone tonight."

He opened his mouth and closed it again, as if he wasn't sure what to say, and her disbelief began to grow. Was she losing him?

Impossible.

He looked nice tonight, freshly shaved, wearing a dark suit. Cecil always looked best in dark colors. Simone had never entertained an ounce of interest in any of Maggie's lovers . . . until him, but only because Maggie had never cared for any of them . . . until him.

Cecil was different.

For one, he was an up-and-coming artist, with paintings on display in two Seattle galleries. Maggie tended to date businessmen who bought her expensive jewelry, but she hadn't connected with Cecil for money.

Most artists treated everyone around them like unwanted baggage. They often locked themselves away and cared for nothing besides themselves and their art.

Cecil wasn't like that. He treated the people in his life as if they were precious to him. He had warm eyes, strong hands, and excellent taste in clothes and wine. He could talk about baseball and French literature with equal ease.

When Maggie looked at him, her face always softened.

The first time Simone saw them together, she knew the game had begun.

She'd come at him first by letting him explain several of his paintings to her—the motivation behind them. Like any artist, he did love to talk about his work, and she played the captivated audience. After that, it had been easy to draw him off alone.

Once she could see his affections switching from Maggie to her, she'd played the reluctant friend, falling madly in love with him yet unable to betray Maggie. Her girlish loyalty drove him wild. Last week, he'd lost control of himself for a moment and kissed her in the hallway of a nightclub.

At that point, she knew the end was getting closer.

He would break it off with Maggie, and Simone would win. In truth, it had all been a tad too easy.

But maybe that was for the best. She was sick of Seattle. She was leaving. First, though . . . first Maggie had to know who had won.

Simone had lost the game only once in her life, and she would never lose it again.

However, after the kiss, Cecil began acting strangely. He seemed far too concerned about Maggie's feelings—even voicing this concern aloud. His behavior stunned Simone. No man had ever done that before.

And now, tonight . . . he was suggesting they leave the house and go meet Maggie at the Showbox?

What was happening?

She turned back to the mirror, examining her reflection. The girl in the mirror was perfect. Tonight, she wore a gauzy purple dress that showed off her slender curves and pale arms. Her china blue eyes were glowing, and her black hair swung when she moved.

Cecil didn't seem to notice.

Maybe she'd been wrong to bring him into Maggie's bedroom. She'd thought seducing him in here would only add to the excitement, but now she second-guessed herself. Maybe she should have drawn him to her own room.

She stood up.

No, she'd rather win in here, surrounded by Maggie's things. Tonight, she'd get him to promise he would leave Maggie—and that he loved only her.

She took a step toward him, tilting her head again. When she got close enough, she reached out and touched the back of his hand with the tips of her fingers. He looked down. His eyes filled with longing . . . and something else. Sorrow? Regret?

"Simone," he whispered sadly, and the word spoke volumes.

She had seen that look on the faces of countless men. She'd seen it on Pierce McCarthy's face when he stood by the fireplace of her parents' house holding Kristina.

She froze.

"We never should have started this," he said softly. "I can't . . . I can't hurt Maggie."

Her entire body felt paralyzed. This couldn't be happening.

Then she found her voice, and she fought down the rising panic. "Isn't it better to hurt her now than to let this go on and on?"

"Maybe it shouldn't go on and on."

Something clicked inside her, like a switch. She had only two options: win him over or remove Maggie.

There was no third option.

Maggie could not be allowed to win.

She moved closer, brushing the front of his suit with her slender body. "You don't mean that," she whispered. "How would you feel next week without me?"

He winced at the image, and the longing on his face increased. He did want her. He loved her. She just had to make him see that he loved her more than he loved Maggie.

Simone turned on her gift.

"You want to be with me," she murmured. "You want to live like me."

Waves of envy passed around him, through him, and his eyes waxed hazy.

"Yes," he mouthed, leaning down.

She had him.

"You'll tell Maggie it's over?"

He wavered for the span of a breath, and then whispered, "Yes."

His hands closed around her arms, and his mouth pressed down over hers. She wanted to sing.

"Here," she said, pulling her mouth away and taking his hand, letting the power of her gift flow outward. "Come in here."

Still holding the mirror, she led him to Maggie's closet and opened the door. He followed her without question. She set the mirror on the floor, then drew him down, kissing him, running her hands under his jacket. Slowly, she pushed him back and moved on top of him, loosening his tie, unbuttoning the top of his shirt.

"You love me?" she asked in his ear.

"Yes."

"Only me?"

"Yes."

Without warning, she sank her teeth into his throat, just below his jawline, ripping and drinking. His body bucked, but she held him down, sucking mouthfuls of his blood as the memories surfaced, passing before her eyes.

She saw an easel and brushes and canvas.

A short professor with glasses and a beard.

She saw a palette smeared with oil paints.

She saw Maggie in a tight black dress.

Finally, she saw herself as he saw her, lovely, young, sweet, full of life. This was what she'd waited for.

Then . . . she saw Maggie again, beautiful, mysterious, exotic, intelligent. . . .

His heart stopped beating, and she stared down into his dead face. Blood still ran freely from his torn throat onto the floor. His last memories had been of Maggie.

Simone jerked away and stood up. Then she calmed. In the end, he had still chosen her. He had still promised to leave Maggie, and he had *chosen* her.

She'd still won.

That was all that mattered.

Leaving him there, she shut the closet door and went back to the dressing table, sitting down and gazing at her own reflection. But she shouldn't sit here too long. She needed to pack.

Maggie would be home soon.

Rose gathered the conscious will to drop the mirror.

She was choking.

Glass shattered around her, but she barely noticed. Struggling to her feet, she stumbled toward the door. By the time she reached it, she was gaining control of her body. Grabbing the knob fiercely, she shoved outward with enough force that it flew from her hand and slammed against the wall.

She started running.

Images of Simone's drives, of Simone's thoughts, crawled in her mind like tiny spiders.

She ran up the stairs, not even caring that her silk bathrobe exposed her legs.

"Wade!"

He wasn't in the office, but then she heard a distant clinking sound downstairs and realized he was using his weights. She didn't bother shouting for him again, but turned in a circle, looking all around at the messy desk and the maps and the atlas.

She put her hand to her mouth, then took it away and looked toward the ceiling.

"Seamus!" she shouted. "Please, Seamus. If you can hear me, let me see you now."

His colorful, transparent form did not appear.

Rose had always considered herself well in tune with her gift—a woman of wisdom. But at that moment, she had no idea what to do.

Leaving the office, she walked out through the sanctuary, past the couches and bookshelves, out the front doors of the church, and before she realized where she was going, she found herself outside in the garden, standing by Robert's grave, looking down at his headstone.

Eleisha talked to Robert all the time.

"Robert," Rose whispered, "what should I do?"

But kneeling down, not caring that she ruined her silk robe, Rose knew that talking to him wouldn't do any good. He was beyond talking back.

chapter 14

Full of self-doubt, Eleisha left the bookstore with Simone, walking all the way to Sixteenth Street. Too many elements about this situation felt wrong.

First of all, back home, she'd sworn to Philip that she wouldn't go hunting without him, and now here she was in a strange city—with another vampire he was supposed to be protecting from Julian—and they were strolling down a busy street. But maybe "busy" was the optimal word. The tall lampposts and all the pedestrians would keep them safe from Julian coming out of the shadows. She ground her back teeth and forced herself to believe that. As long as she saw him coming, she could defend Simone.

But second, she was rushing Simone's entrance into their world, and she knew it. This was too soon to be teaching her how to hunt via telepathy. Simone needed at least a few nights to adjust to all the epiphanies and rapid changes invading her existence. Yet, Philip had already started this chain of events, somehow botched it, and in the back of her mind, Eleisha understood his reasoning.

It was possible that he'd simply wanted to see if Simone was willing to *try* to feed without killing. If she even entertained the idea . . . then there was hope. Philip wouldn't bring her anywhere near Wade unless she'd proven she could be trusted.

No wonder he'd been in such a hurry. Wade would be offended by the extent of their concern. He knew perfectly well what he'd signed on for when he agreed to help.

But while Eleisha tended to side with Philip on this issue, she also couldn't help feeling an almost crushing disappointment that he'd given up so easily. Wade would never have given up. He'd never have abandoned Simone, and he certainly wouldn't have just left her here to continue killing mortals.

Eleisha just wished she knew what had gone wrong last night. But if she even approached the subject, Simone grew agitated.

So she stayed with safer subjects.

"This isn't at all what I expected," Eleisha said, looking at the street around them.

"What did you expect?" Simone asked.

"I don't know. I guess something more rustic."

Simone laughed, and again, Eleisha had to fight down the illusion that she was out with Maggie.

Most of the buildings around them had recently undergone a face-lift. Nearly all large cities sported an uncomfortable mix of the affluent and the poor. Denver was no exception, but the people were more multicultural than she'd expected. She'd envisioned Colorado as a bit more . . . homogenized. The size of the homeless population also surprised her. By the time they'd gone three blocks down Sixteenth Street, she'd been asked for money four times.

"Stop giving them cash," Simone said. "They'll just buy booze."

"They might buy food."

Eleisha expected Simone to frown in disagreement, but Simone's expression remained pleasant. Come to think of it, Eleisha had never seen her frown.

But then, suddenly, Eleisha was faced with the choice of what to do next. A dark parking lot was the best choice for hunting, but she didn't want to take Simone anyplace with blackened shadows—as that's where Julian always hid.

His method of killing other vampires was simple and straightforward. He would keep hidden and wait. Then he would swing from the darkness and slice off their heads before they could attack him telepathically. When vampires died, their psychic energy burst out, momentarily crippling any other telepath around them. As Julian was not telepathic, he was not affected.

Eleisha paused. "Is there a parking lot with decent lighting anywhere around here?"

Simone stopped walking.

"A parking lot?" she repeated.

"Yes, of course. Where did . . . ?"

They always started teaching a new vampire in a parking lot. That's how she taught Philip. What in the world had he tried last night? But as she started the question, Simone seemed to grow anxious again, and Eleisha didn't finish.

"Yes," Simone said, glancing away. "Beneath the indoor mall, over there."

"Okay."

As they continued to walk, Eleisha's spirits rose slightly. This was going much more easily than she'd anticipated. Simone was willing to listen and willing to learn. She was no lost, frightened vampire as Rose had been, so as yet, she was certainly not ready to leave her home and go back to the underground. But she'd listened to Eleisha explain the history of their own kind and the reasoning behind the laws.

And now she was already exploring methods of learning to feed without killing. Wade was much better than Eleisha at teaching someone else how to hone and control telepathy in the early days, but Simone's abilities seemed to be waking quickly.

What more could Eleisha have asked for this soon?

"There's the door," Simone said, pointing toward a stairwell.

In spite of herself, Simone couldn't help her curiosity from rising as she followed Eleisha into a large underground parking lot filled with cars, but nearly empty of people.

Eleisha's long wheat gold hair bounced against her back as she moved quickly down the stairs, and Simone had to admit that, if nothing else, this entire experience was something . . . new.

Is that how Eleisha had managed to trap Philip? With the promise of something new? Simone could at least understand that. Years and years of monotony became a kind of personal hell for someone who never aged. While Eleisha herself was a tedious crusader, Simone was beginning to see how Philip must have become entangled with something, anything, that was different from two hundred years of routine.

But now he had another life waiting, a better life.

Simone had a clear—fairly simple—plan in mind as long she could keep Eleisha with her until dawn. But there were two main obstacles to overcome: (1) For her idea to work, she had to gain Eleisha's complete trust in a matter of hours; and (2) she had to be able to block a telepathic attack.

Eleisha had been more than willing to wake up Simone's psychic abilities, as apparently they were necessary for this method of hunting. But in the few moments of practice at the bookstore, Simone had found "blocking" somewhat difficult.

She needed more practice.

What better way to begin winning Eleisha's trust and gain more experience with telepathy than by seeming eager to learn "the first law"?

"For now, just watch me," Eleisha said, scanning the parking lot. "Get in the car when I do, but if it's a truck, let me get in first."

She continued scanning, and her gaze stopped near a Dumpster. A jagged piece of the hinge was bent outward.

A few moments later, the elevator doors opened, and a young man got off. He was Asian, wearing expensive jeans and a loose white shirt buttoned just below his collarbone. The top of his hair was gelled into small spikes, and Simone could smell CK One cologne all the way from the stairwell.

Eleisha watched him closely as he headed toward the Dumpster and used his keychain button to unlock a black, four-door Mazda.

Again, Simone's interest rose at both the unfamiliar staging and the potential victim. She would not have chosen this man for either the game or any necessary feeding in between conquests.

He wasn't upscale enough for the game, and he was far too upscale to just feed on and dump. If he turned up dead, somebody might investigate with a passion.

But Eleisha moved forward, heading toward the car, and the strangest feeling came over Simone.

As waiflike as Eleisha looked normally, she suddenly appeared even smaller, helpless and lost and pretty. Simone took a step forward to comfort her, to assist her, and then stopped cold.

Eleisha had just turned on her gift.

The strength of it was almost overwhelming, and Simone had to fight to keep her head clear.

"Excuse me," Eleisha said softly, and the young man stopped in his tracks, staring at her.

Simone came up behind, just watching how this would play out.

"Our car won't start," Eleisha went on, her voice hesitant. "Could you help us?"

The need to help her began increasing, and Simone wasn't sure how much longer she could keep herself in check. This gift didn't affect her to the level that Philip's did, but it was much stronger than Maggie's.

The young man took a step toward Eleisha, his face awash with concern. He pulled a cell phone from his pocket. "Do you need me to call a tow truck?" Up close, he was handsome, with artificially whitened teeth.

"No . . ." Eleisha faltered. "I couldn't afford a tow truck. Could you just drive us home? My brother can check the car tomorrow."

This surprised Simone more than anything else Eleisha had done so far. She wanted him to give them a ride somewhere? But then she remembered Eleisha's earlier words: "Let me get in first."

"Yeah, sure. I'll take you," he said, as if her request was commonplace.

Get in the back, Eleisha flashed. *Then read my mind.*

Fascinated, Simone climbed into the backseat of the car.

Eleisha was in the front seat by the time the young man ran around the car, got in, and slammed his door. Her gift was still flowing, and Simone was having trouble concentrating.

"Where do you live?" he asked, still watching Eleisha as if he didn't believe she was real. Even in the moment, Simone could not help feeling a jolt of rage that he hadn't even noticed her. Just as he was moving the keys toward the ignition, Eleisha reached out and touched his hand.

"Wait. You're too tired to drive. You should rest. Sleep. We'll leave soon."

Simone slipped inside her mind, and she could *feel* Eleisha putting him to sleep. His head lolled back against the seat, and his eyes closed. Eleisha scooted closer and lifted his wrist, putting it to her mouth. With what appeared to be great care, she punctured his skin with her teeth and began feeding.

Simone saw a barrage of images of a large family, of dinners with numerous dishes of colorful food, of his father's disappointment that he was not going to study medicine, of a job selling memberships at a local health club, of confusion about the future. . . .

Eleisha stopped feeding. Using one of her eyeteeth, she connected the holes on his wrist. Simone continued to follow along inside her thoughts, and then realized they were both inside the young man's mind. Eleisha took him back to the moment he'd walked out of the elevator. He'd seen no one. While walking to his car, he'd passed the Dumpster. He'd tripped and fallen, cutting his wrist on the jagged, protruding hinge. Without realizing how badly he'd been cut, he'd gotten into his car, still bleeding, and passed out.

Eleisha pulled out of his mind and turned off her gift, looking at Simone.

"Did you see?"

Simone nodded, wordless.

They got out of the car, and Eleisha made sure all the doors were locked—like she was worried about the unconscious man behind the wheel.

Leaving him there, they both headed for the stairwell.

"He'll wake up in a few minutes, and he'll be okay," Eleisha said.

So many things were becoming clear.

This? This was how Eleisha insisted Philip feed himself? This bland, unsatisfying act of luring someone into a car and putting him to sleep? No wonder Philip had been ready to explode. How many times could he do this without going mad?

"All our predecessors fed this way," Eleisha said in the stairwell, moving upward. "They never killed to feed, so they were no drain on the population, and they could exist without fear of discovery. They could exist in harmony with mortals. They could exist without remorse."

Something in that last word had more emphasis, more meaning, than the others. Simone focused sharply, thinking about that word. When they emerged back onto Sixteenth Street, there was no one within earshot, so she reached out for Eleisha's arm.

"Remorse?"

Eleisha looked away, and Simone could feel excitement building inside her chest. She'd hit on something important.

"I didn't know . . . ," Eleisha whispered. "I didn't know any other way to hunt . . . before, and I was turned in the 1830s."

"And you feel regret?"

"We've all done terrible things. We didn't know there was a choice." Eleisha lifted her hazel eyes, and they glowed with a hard intensity. "But we have a choice now."

The last piece of the puzzle fell neatly into place.

Eleisha wallowed in guilt for what she considered to be past sins, and she revered vampires who could experience remorse . . . regret. She would trust a vampire capable of remorse.

Simone had suffered the emotion once.

There was only one way she could prove this to Eleisha, and it was time to put the next part of the plan into motion.

"This was a good beginning," Eleisha said, breaking the moment. "But I've left Philip alone too long. He'll be chewing on the furniture by now."

This casual reference to Philip caused a heated instant of rage and panic.

"Wait," Simone said. "Please stay with me. This has been so . . . different from last night. Please stay. I want to show you something."

The resolute look in Eleisha's eyes faded, replaced by sympathy. Simone still could not believe any undead capable of sympathy. It was repulsive.

"Don't worry, we're not leaving the city," Eleisha said. "I wish you'd tell me what happened last night, but no matter what, I promise we won't leave you. Maybe tomorrow . . . maybe you and Philip can try talking again."

"I'm not ready to see Philip, but I don't want to be alone right now," Simone said. "Would you come with me to a place I always feel safe? I like the Hyatt Regency, and I go there sometimes to book a room up on the thirtieth floor, so high off the ground that it feels like my own small space." She kept her gift off but increased the longing in her voice. "I want to show you a memory, but I want to do it someplace where I know we won't be disturbed."

"A memory?"

"Please."

The sympathy in Eleisha's eyes turned to pity. It was sickening. "All right."

Simone nearly melted in relief. "This way."

Philip slammed open the front doors of the Mercury Cafe, not caring whom he might hit, turning his head as he ran inside.

Several people looked up in alarm, but at the sight of his face, no one said anything.

He'd already been to the Samba Room, and he was going everyplace he could think of to which Simone might have a connection. He felt foolish that he'd not come here first. Eleisha had liked this place. She'd told him so.

Eleisha!

He flashed the thought out as loud as he could, searching the entire room of wooden tables.

No one answered.

He sensed nothing but mortals drinking coffee and eating blackberry cobbler.

He felt sick.

Not only was Eleisha alone somewhere with Simone, but she was in a strange city with an unfamiliar vampire, and the last time that had happened, Julian had come hunting them.

He moved between the tables, still looking around, heading for the stage—just to be sure.

Finally admitting to himself that she wasn't here, he gripped the back of a chair and closed his eyes.

He had nowhere else to go and nowhere left to look.

Mary searched the city, using her senses to try to pinpoint the presence of the undead. The living put off such a strong signal that finding a vampire was simply a matter of locating a hole in the fabric of spiritual energy, or at least that's how Mary viewed her abilities.

She had learned to tell the difference, for the most part, between the signatures of ghosts and those of vampires. A little earlier, she'd located Philip near Simone's house.

He hadn't looked good.

In fact, he'd looked awful.

But she didn't stay to follow him. Her job was to find Simone.

She wished herself into nothingness, and then materialized in an alley off Larimer Square downtown.

Time was passing, and she knew Julian was furious. She didn't blame him. She never should have lost track of Simone.

She kept searching until she felt something—that familiar hole in the night—near Grant Street. She hadn't seen that area yet, so she didn't know where she might materialize safely. But Grant Street wasn't far. She floated upward, over the tops of buildings, blending with the darkness.

Down below, she saw a camera shop closed for the night, and she blinked out, rematerializing just inside the front windows. She reached out with her senses, this time feeling a clear undead presence somewhere close.

Looking across the street, she saw the Hyatt Regency.

People passed by the windows, but she ignored them, just waiting.

Then, finally, she saw Eleisha walking with Simone on the other side of the street. They went into the Hyatt.

This wasn't good. The very thought of Eleisha alone with Simone made her nervous, and how was Jasper supposed to take out Simone without Eleisha seeing him?

First things first.

She had to be able to report their exact location.

She waited about fifteen minutes, and then she began to search for their signatures again. She looked up, near the top of the hotel.

She blinked out, rematerializing thirty-five stories up, realizing she was too high. She floated down five floors and looked inside a window, seeing a man in a suit working at a notebook computer. Then she drifted to the next room and saw a balcony with a sliding glass door. Floating over, she looked inside just as Simone and Eleisha walked into the room from the hallway.

The door opened inward, and Mary clearly saw the numbers: 3012.

Simone's expression was serene and pleasant as they moved farther inside together. Then Eleisha stepped out in front, dropping her bag on the floor.

As Simone glanced at Eleisha's back, her entire face altered for just a second to a visage of hatred so savage that Mary floated sideways on instinct.

Then, as Eleisha turned around, the expression vanished. Simone smiled at her.

Mary wished herself into nothingness, rushing back to Julian.

Julian paced the floor of his suite, beginning to resent the fact that he'd come here at all. Too much pointless time had passed since his arrival, and Mary seemed to be more than slightly off her game.

What if she was wrong about Simone?

What if Eleisha was in no danger?

If he had come all this way for nothing, there would be repercussions.

Jasper sat on the couch, watching an old John Wayne movie. In truth, that at least was a relief, as Julian had nothing more to say to him. He'd given Jasper a fairly lengthy lecture on how to focus his thoughts to avoid being affected by another vampire's gift, but that had been hours ago.

The air shimmered by the couch, and Mary appeared, her magenta hair seeming brighter in the lamplight.

"I've got Simone," she blurted out. "Hyatt Regency, room 3012. But she's with Eleisha. We'll have to split them up somehow."

Jasper stood up, grabbing his long sword and his coat.

"You got any ideas?" he asked before Julian could speak.

She nodded. "Yeah, maybe. I think so. But we need to hurry."

"Okay, meet me there."

Again, this familiar exchange between his servants left Julian unsettled.

"Is Eleisha in trouble?" he asked.

"Oh, yeah," Mary answered. "But I don't think she knows it yet."

Julian watched as Jasper strapped on the sword and buttoned his coat.

"Remember what I told you," he said. "Don't let her gift overwhelm you. Mary told me it's envy, and I've never encountered that before."

"I can handle her gift," Jasper answered, heading for the door. "And I'm getting pretty good with my own."

Jasper's gift was pity. He seduced his victims while they felt sorry for him. Julian would have hated such a gift. He reveled in his gift of fear.

Fear overcame any and all other gifts he'd ever known.

Could pity outweigh envy?

Doubtful.

"Don't worry, I'll take her head," Jasper said, leaving the suite and closing the door behind himself.

Julian wasn't worried about Jasper.

He just wanted Eleisha safely out of Denver—and back hunting for elders again.

chapter 15

Mary remained hidden in an alley on Fifteenth Street, watching Jasper come up the sidewalk on the other side of the street. Their own hotel was only four or five blocks away, so he hadn't bothered with a taxi.

His narrow face was calm as he looked up at the Hyatt. With his black coat buttoned to his chest, he reminded her a little of Philip.

This whole situation pissed her off.

She fully understood that Jasper had been created only to handle Julian's dirty work, but this was different. If Julian wanted Eleisha out of this mess, he should be facing down Simone by himself. Simone might not be as old as these "elders" he was so obsessed with, but she was . . . toxic.

Jasper came across the street.

"Mary?" he called softly.

"In here."

His head turned toward the alley, and he walked in the entrance, spotting her in the shadows.

"I knew you'd beat me here," he said.

"Yeah, but you were pretty quick."

He sometimes liked to fill silences with small talk, but she didn't mind. She liked talking to him.

"So now what?" he asked. "You said you had an idea?"

His black coat swung in a smooth rhythm around his boots when he walked.

She floated a little closer to the mouth of the alley. The doors to the hotel were only a few feet away.

"Go inside the lobby. Find an in-house phone and call room 3012," she said. "We're on Simone's home ground, so I'm pretty sure she'll pick up. When she does, pretend you're staff and tell her there is a Mr. Philip Branté asking to speak with her, but that he wants her to meet him outside the front doors."

Jasper raised an eyebrow and shook his head. "That'll never work. She's never going to come down here and walk outside in the dark to meet Philip."

"Oh, yes, she will. Trust me." Mary paused. "Can you fake a French accent?"

Inside the hotel room, Eleisha looked over at her canvas bag on the floor, debating whether she should call Philip.

By now, he was either in a rage or having a panic attack—or both.

But even if she did call, nothing she could say over the phone would calm him down, and he'd just insist she come back immediately. Within moments, the conversation would turn into a fight.

Simone walked gracefully toward the balcony. Her tan dress clung lightly to her hips, and her eyes seemed far away. She needed Eleisha right now a lot more than Philip did. This was more important. He could wait a little longer.

"Do you like tea?" Eleisha asked, heading toward the coffee-maker. "I could heat up some water."

"That would be nice."

Eleisha reached toward the faucet, and the hotel room's phone rang from the nightstand.

She froze. No one else knew they were here.

Simone glanced at her and then picked up. "Yes."

She just listened for a few moments. Her face didn't flicker. Her expression didn't change.

"Yes, I see," she said. "I'll be right down."

She hung up. "I'm sorry, there's an issue with my credit card. I need to go downstairs for a moment."

"Do you need me to charge the room?"

"No, it's just an error. I'll be right back."

The elevator doors opened on the ground floor, and Simone stepped out into the lobby with a mix of anxiety and hope.

How could Philip possibly have known where to find her?

But since the moment they arrived, Eleisha and Philip had both been exhibiting one telepathic power after another, each more surprising than the last. Perhaps he had some psychic method of tracking her down.

The thought was exciting.

Had he realized the truth? That he belonged with Simone? Had he come to claim her?

If so, the game was over, and Eleisha became irrelevant: just another forgettable woman who'd lost.

Only this time, the game had a different ending, and Simone would leave with Philip, go anywhere he wanted, do anything he wanted. Eleisha could rot in the hotel room until she figured out Philip was gone and Simone wasn't coming back.

The elevator doors closed behind her, and she looked around the lobby, wondering whether he might come inside after all.

He was nowhere in sight.

She moved quickly toward the front doors, suddenly wishing she'd worn a richer color—and some lipstick. She'd dressed for Eleisha tonight, not Philip.

But stepping outside into the warm night air, a moment of fear gripped her when she didn't find him waiting on the sidewalk.

Had he changed his mind again?

"Simone," a low voice called from the alley, drawing the "o" sound out with a French accent.

"Philip," she answered in relief, walking toward his voice.

Jasper stood between two overfull trash cans, the sword in his hand.

But he couldn't help feeling a jolt of shock as the slender woman came striding toward him down the alley. Mary had tried to warn him, but he still wasn't prepared.

He'd grown used to the company of pretty girls in the past few months. His town house, clothes, car, and the money had changed everything.

But in all his life, he'd never seen anything like Simone.

Her skin was pale and perfect, and her hair swung like black silk. She wasn't just pretty . . . she was different. A doll come to life. But she moved like a cat, and her china blue eyes narrowed when she saw him. She looked all around.

"Philip?"

Then she looked back at Jasper, and her gaze dropped to his sword.

He came to his senses and stepped forward, gripping the hilt. He didn't care how pretty she was. He was here on a job.

He let his gift flow outward, surrounding her, engulfing her with the impression that he was pitiful, not a real threat, just some skinny guy trying to act tough. She shouldn't fear him—just feel sorry for him.

He took another step.

In the early days, he'd hated his gift and thought he'd drawn a short straw. But then he'd learned how to use it and decided it wasn't so bad. Drawing his arm back, he increased the aura of his own tragic state, focusing so he could take her head off in one swing. He'd been training hard with the sword and knew exactly how to aim it.

And then something fogged his mind. Almost instantly, he lost his careful focus.

The alley blurred in his vision, making him dizzy. He suddenly realized how much he wanted to be like her. She had it all . . . everything, and he wanted it. He wanted to be with her, to let her show him her perfect world.

Why hadn't he seen this right away?

She was standing right in front him, so perfect. He wanted to touch her, to absorb everything about her.

Growing hazy, he couldn't see the alley anymore, only her.

"Drop the sword," she whispered.

His hand opened. Metal clanked against the pavement.

Upon seeing the dark-haired young man alone in the alley, Simone's first emotion had been crushing, almost crippling disappointment.

Philip hadn't come for her.

But this disappointment was short-lived.

The second she saw his sword, her survival instincts kicked in. In the same instant, she realized he wasn't breathing and had no pulse pounding in his throat.

Vampire.

As with Eleisha, she was stunned by the strength of his gift when he let it loose. The image he created was astonishing, and he seemed to physically change before her eyes—from a threat to a tragedy. She could sense the emotion he was trying to invoke.

But there was one thing he hadn't taken into consideration.

She couldn't feel pity.

It was beyond her.

She turned on her gift and watched his face in satisfaction. He'd raised her hopes. He'd pretended to be Philip, and she would make him suffer.

"Drop the sword," she whispered.

He dropped it.

"Get on your knees," she said softly.

He sank to the pavement.

Mary hid in the shadows at the back of the alley. Her only weapon was the element of surprise, and she couldn't waste it. But as soon as Jasper saw Simone, Mary couldn't stop a creeping feeling that they'd made a horrible mistake in obeying Julian tonight.

They should have told him to get stuffed and then suffered whatever punishment he gave—anything would have been better than this.

The look on Jasper's face made her want to cry. He'd lost before the fight even started. When Simone turned on her gift, Mary felt it, too.

She longed to look like Simone, to be like Simone, to have Jasper stare at her with that same hungry expression.

But then Simone drew closer and whispered something in his ear, and he dropped his sword.

He sank to his knees.

Simone looked down at the sword, and again, Mary caught a flash of vicious hatred flicker across her lovely face.

Simone reached toward the hilt.

Shoving away the thick cloud of envy, Mary blinked out and rematerialized right beside Jasper, screaming so loudly, anyone on the street could have heard.

"Get away from him!"

The scream pierced Simone's ears, and she stumbled backward, nearly falling against the wall.

Twisting back around, she froze at the sight and sounds she saw just a few steps away.

A transparent girl with spiky magenta hair and a nose stud was standing over Jasper. Her translucent face was contorted in rage. She was shaking a fist and screaming loudly enough to bring anyone within a half mile running toward the alley.

"Get away! Get away from him!" she shrieked over and over.

The shock was almost too much, and Simone drew back, not certain what to do. The dark-haired vampire was still on his knees, staring straight ahead, but the girl ghost kept screaming.

People from the street would be coming at any moment.

Simone turned and ran into the hotel lobby as fast as she could.

*　　*　　*

Mary fell silent, tense, waiting to see who else might come . . . police, bystanders, anyone who might have heard her.

But no one came.

Maybe people didn't walk into dark alleys anymore when they heard someone screaming.

Jasper fell forward, catching himself with one hand, gagging as if trying to draw breath he didn't need.

"Jasper!"

She knelt beside him, coming to a decision.

"It's all right," she said. "You're okay."

It took a few moments for his eyes to clear, and then he looked around at the alley, at her, at his sword on the pavement.

"Oh my God," he choked. "Mary, did I . . . ? What did I do?"

The line of his cheekbone twitched as he grabbed for the hilt, trying to gain his feet, but he tripped, falling again.

"Stop it," Mary told him. "It's over. She hit you with her gift, and you couldn't hold it off. That's all."

"Where is she?"

"Gone. I chased her off." She hesitated, hating the idea of lying to him. "Then I left you for a few minutes, and I teleported back to Julian. He says this is too much for you, and he's going to take care of it himself. You're supposed to head for the airport and go back to San Francisco. Right now. If you can't catch a plane that will land in the dark, just get a hotel room and leave first thing tomorrow night."

"What? No! I can do this. I can take her head, Mary."

But she knew what he really feared—being cut loose from Julian for failure.

"He's not even mad at you!" she insisted, trying to sound convincing. "Everything's okay. But those are his orders. Go home. He'll take it from here."

"He doesn't even want to see me?"

"Not tonight. I'm sure he'll have something else for you to do soon, but for now, he wants you out of the way."

He glanced away, hurt and worried at the same time. She felt awful for deceiving him like this, and she knew there'd be hell to pay later. Julian might even banish her back to the gray, in-between plane.

But at least by tomorrow night . . . Jasper would still have his head on his shoulders.

Simone was alone in the elevator, and she pushed the STOP button, leaning against the wall, too shaken to stand on her own.

A number of realizations continued striking her at the same time.

Philip hadn't come for her.

Eleisha hadn't lost the game.

Someone had just tried to kill her in the alley.

She'd been attacked by a slender, dark-haired vampire and a girl with magenta hair. . . . Wasn't that how Eleisha had described Julian's servants?

Julian was real.

She'd never truly believed that before. He'd always been some story Maggie had used to frighten her. But he was real.

Think, think, think.

What to do next?

She straightened and forced her mind to clear. In essence, not much had changed. Philip's apparent "job" on this quest was to protect any vampires Eleisha contacted. This meant he was capable of handling Julian. Since Julian's two servants had gone to extensive lengths to lure her outside, that meant they knew where she was but clearly didn't want any trouble inside the hotel.

All she had to do was keep Eleisha with her until dawn.

Once Eleisha had been removed, she simply needed to contact Philip. Without his chains, he'd be free, he'd be grateful, and he could protect her from Julian. They could leave the city together. Go anywhere.

Yes, in essence, very little had changed.

She started the elevator again, heading up to the thirtieth floor.

Wade made his way up the stairs toward his office.

He was sweating and tired, but working out seemed to make the time go faster while he waited for word—any word.

The phone rang.

Forgetting his sore legs, he bounded upward, three stairs at a time, running for the office. The door was open, and he flew inside, grabbing the phone.

"Eleisha!"

"Wade," Philip said quietly. He sounded broken. "I lost her. I can't find her anywhere."

"What? Where are you?"

"Back in the hotel suite. I didn't know where to else to look, so I came back."

This was almost too much for Wade to take in—or follow. The last time the phone had rung, Eleisha had lost Philip. Now it was the other way around? And Philip sounded desperate, as if calling Wade was a last resort.

"What do you mean, you 'lost' her? When?"

"Just past dusk. I told her we were going home, and she left while I was in the shower." His voice faltered. "She's with Simone, and Simone is damaged . . . a killer, a player. I don't know what to do."

Rather than feeling sorry for Philip, Wade was angry. "Player? What does that mean?"

Philip's communication skills were scanty at best, but now he seemed so scattered that he wasn't making sense.

"Her father was cruel," he nearly whispered, "pitting her and her sisters against each other. It ruined her."

Wade breathed through his mouth in disbelief. "Are you listening to yourself? Eleisha's gone missing, and you're so useless that you're actually standing there telling me about a hundred-year-old vampire with daddy issues?"

He wanted to throw the phone across the room.

The line was silent, and he closed his eyes, cursing himself now. This wasn't helping.

"What do you need?" he asked. "Should I fly out to meet you?"

"I need to find Eleisha."

Anger resurfaced, and he gripped the phone tighter.

Then he heard running footsteps out in the hallway, and Rose rushed in the door, frantic and disheveled—wearing a silk bathrobe, soiled at the knees.

"Is that Eleisha?"

"No, it's Philip."

She ran over, not bothering to try to grab the phone from his hand, hitting the SPEAKER button instead.

"Philip, listen to me," she said, her voice shaking. "You need to gather up Eleisha and come home right now. I don't care how you do it. Force her on a plane if you have to, but get her away from there.

We'll figure out what to do about Simone later, but you must come home. And *this* is important: Whatever you do, don't let Simone see Eleisha as any kind of competition. Do you understand?"

The line was quiet. Was Philip still there?

Rose's eyes flew up to Wade's face.

He shook his head. "They're separated."

"It's my fault," Philip whispered.

At least he was still on the other end.

Rose leaned down closer to the speaker. "You have to find her."

"I've tried. I don't know else where to look. Tell me what to do."

Wade blinked. Philip had never asked Rose for anything. She moved away from the phone, looking all around, her face set in determination.

"Seamus!" she shouted with surprising force.

This time, the air by the desk shimmered, and Seamus' transparent form materialized. He still looked exhausted, the colors of his plaid washed out and faded. But he was visible.

"Go to Denver," Rose told him immediately, "just for a short while. Find Eleisha and tell Philip where she is. That's all you have to do. Then come straight back."

He didn't speak but nodded.

Rose turned back to the phone. "Philip, did you hear? I'm sending Seamus. He'll find her." She stopped and leaned close to the speaker again. "And do not concern yourself with our hopes and plans for the underground . . . not this time. You do whatever you have to."

"I know."

Wade heard a click as Philip hung up, and he took a long breath in confusion.

Both Rose and Philip seemed to know a good deal more than he did.

Slipping back inside the hotel room, Simone knew she had to choose her words carefully. By nature, she was always careful, but tonight was critical.

"Everything all right?" Eleisha asked, turning from the view out the balcony window.

City lights glowed off her light green tank top, and her wispy hair hung forward down her shoulders. Simone had never played anyone quite like Eleisha before, but for once, the "new" experience wasn't completely welcome. She didn't want to make any mistakes.

"Yes, it's fine. I'm sorry it took so long."

Eleisha walked closer. "You said you wanted to show me something?"

Now came the difficult part.

Back outside, in the parking garage, Simone had clearly seen the quickest path to gaining Eleisha's trust: remorse.

Eleisha respected remorse, even revered it. She preferred the company of vampires who deeply regretted having killed to survive. Simone doubted that Philip had ever expressed such a sentiment, but it seemed like he'd been with Eleisha for some time, and she'd come to trust him through other means.

Simone had only a few hours.

The trick was not to let Eleisha see her true motives. She had to come at this from another angle.

"You claim you've done terrible things," Simone said, turning away. "But I don't think you've done the things I have." She paused, looking back, allowing a hint of pain to seep through her voice.

"And I don't want to be hurt when you find out and decide I'm not *fit* for your community."

"No, Simone. I promise that I'll—"

"Just listen!"

Eleisha fell silent, just watching her.

"I want to show you a memory . . . the worst thing I've ever done," Simone said. "If you can watch that and you still want me, I'll go to Portland and see the underground. But I'm not going to uproot myself until I know we're on the same page."

Simone had to fight to keep her expression sad and determined.

"You don't have to show me anything," Eleisha said quietly. "Didn't Philip just put you through this last night?"

"I want to show you. I want to be certain."

Eleisha's mouth tightened, as if in reluctance. Perhaps she didn't like being exposed to ugly memories. But she sank down to the floor and held out her hand.

"Come and sit."

Simone wanted to dance with joy. This memory was the key to Eleisha's trust.

"Just close your eyes and think back," Eleisha said, cross-legged on the floor. "Try and pinpoint the right moment."

Simone closed her eyes.

chapter 16

In the winter of 1982, Simone walked down Broadway in the cold night air, somewhat sorry she had to cover her new dark pink dress with a coat. She'd never been fond of pink, but this particular shade made her eyes shine.

Ah, well.

But Denver winters were frigid. It was snowing lightly, and she would have looked odd indeed walking around without a coat. She also wore a black felt hat to keep her hair dry.

Then she imagined the look on Randal's face when she arrived at the restaurant and took off her coat and hat. She smiled. He'd swoon. Maybe it was better this way after all. This certainly wasn't the most exciting game she'd ever played. Randal sold German sports cars for a living—and he was the type to dye his hair and go to tanning booths. His wife, Ruth, was slightly dumpy, with a hook to her nose, but she was a renowned surgeon at St. Anthony's Hospital, and he showed such deep respect for her, such admiration for her success, that Simone had not been able to resist.

Tonight she was meeting him at a small cafe just off Broadway. The place was far beneath them both, but she wouldn't risk being seen by anyone he knew. Besides, he rather enjoyed the grittier elements of their secret rendezvous.

As she walked past a bookstore, closed for the night, she caught her own reflection in the darkened window, and she stopped, unbuttoning the top of her coat to let some of the color of her dress show. This shade really did complement her skin. She should consider dark pink more often.

"Simone?"

The creaking sound of an incredulous voice caused her to turn rapidly, on guard against . . . what?

An old woman stood just a few feet away. She wore a bulky coat that did little to hide her stout figure. Her white hair was unruly, and a set of thick glasses made her eyes look large.

There was something so familiar about her, something so familiar, Simone forgot all about Randal. The small hairs on her arms began to tingle with warning.

"Simone?" the old woman said again, her voice clearer this time. "It can't be. . . ."

Reality splashed over Simone.

She was looking at Pug.

Even after all these years, in her mind's eye, she always saw Pug at the age of eighteen, quirky, smart, with uneven brown curls. Sweet, funny, caustic Pug.

How old was she? Seventy?

And Simone still looked twenty-two.

Every once in a while since returning to Denver, she'd noticed someone giving her a second glance as if recognizing her, and then shaking his head. She'd never paid much attention. No one had known her well enough to believe his eyes.

Except Pug.

Her mind raced. What could she say?

Suddenly, she smiled and moved closer. "I'm sorry. My name is Victoria, after my grandmother."

"No, no . . . Simone, it's you." Her eyes were milky, and her face was wrinkled, but she still looked like Pug.

"I had an Aunt Simone. But I've never met her."

"An Aunt Simone? Who is your mother?"

"Kristina McCarthy. But we live in New York. I'm just visiting."

The look of near horror washed from Pug's face, and she breathed out through her teeth. "Oh, of course. Kristina's girl? My God, you look just like your aunt. You could be twins." Now she seemed happy, reaching out with one gnarled hand to touch Simone's coat. Simone grasped her fingers.

Pug.

"Did you know my aunt?"

She knew she should make a polite excuse and flee down the street, but for some reason, she couldn't bring herself to leave. Pug was the only person who'd ever truly loved her—well, maybe except for Maggie, but that was different.

"Know her?" Pug answered. "She was my best friend, my dearest friend. I still think of her every day."

Simone almost winced. She hadn't thought of Pug in decades.

"Are you in a hurry?" Pug asked, catching her off guard. "I have a house just over there." She pointed to her parents' old place. "I'm still unpacking. I retired a while back and decided to come home to Denver. But I have a box of photos of your aunt when she was young. Come and I'll show you."

Pug was lonely. Simone could see it in her face. And retired? She'd always liked to be busy, and Denver was so different now. Had she inherited the house? This must be so hard on her, to come back to her parents' old empty home, with everyone she'd ever known gone or dead.

Simone was surprised at herself for reasoning such things.

Again, the instinct to run welled up inside her.

"You won't believe it." Pug said. "You look just like her."

Simone didn't want to leave. She wanted to go with Pug and look at the old photos like some elderly woman dreaming about the past. Without letting herself think, she fell into step, and they made their way down the block.

They climbed the steps to the front porch.

The house looked just the same, maybe a bit shabbier, but Simone could not help remembering the happy years she'd spent here in high school. This place had been her refuge, somewhere safe and comfortable to laugh and eat baked beans on toast.

They went inside, and she looked around, trying not to tremble. Why did this affect her so much? All the memories of those years came crashing back, when she had been valued and accepted by the people who lived here. The shallow, hollow images of the last fifty years echoed inside her mind.

She walked over to the faded couch, upholstered in tacky brown and yellow flowers, chunks of stuffing coming out. It was the same couch she and Pug had once sat and played cards upon.

The entire place was filled with boxes and stacks of books. A half-full cup of cold coffee sat on an aging end table. Simone could almost hear Pug's mother exclaiming that she'd completely forgotten to plan dinner—but promising she'd find something and then inviting Simone to stay.

Simone could feel the relief at not having to go home, not having to face Daddy over the dining room table.

"Are you all right?" Pug asked, clicking on several lights.

Simone turned and saw her clearly. She was so old. Her sweet face so ravaged.

"Yes, I'm fine."

"The box is over here. Make yourself comfortable, and I'll bring it over. Truly, you won't believe the resemblance."

Simone took off her hat and shook her head slightly. Then she unbuttoned her coat and laid it over a chair. Pug lifted the cardboard box and looked up.

She dropped the box.

She gasped.

For a second, Simone didn't understand, and then she caught her own reflection in an antique mirror across the room. Her black hair swung loose in its razor-straight bob. She wore a sleeveless, low-waisted dress with a dark string of knotted beads. She looked like a slightly updated flapper from the 1920s, bright and colorful and fluid . . . just like she always did.

"Simone," said Pug.

The word was not a question.

Pug shuffled forward, squinting through her thick lenses and shaking her head. "How . . . how can you . . . ?"

She stood with her mouth half open, waiting for an answer.

But Simone had none.

And it was no use trying to go on pretending she was Kristina's daughter.

Pug couldn't be allowed to leave this house again. Simone rushed across the room and shoved her back onto the couch, holding her there. Pug gasped again and struggled.

"Simone!"

She didn't want Pug to suffer, and the kindest thing would be to break her neck instantly, but the memories and the ghosts of the house and the distant past called to her. She needed more. Gripping Pug's wrinkled face in her hands, she held it tight.

"You loved me once?" she whispered.

"I love you still," Pug answered, and her eyes were calm. She'd stopped struggling.

Simone drove her teeth into Pug's throat, tearing and drinking. She'd never fed on someone so old. The skin of Pug's neck was loose, and the life force flowing into Simone was weak. But then the memories started, and she forgot everything else.

So many memories.

Memories of her.

She drank more slowly so they would continue. This was better than any man who'd claimed to love her. She saw herself as Pug saw her, back when Daddy called her skinny and awkward, back when her cotton dresses bunched at the sleeves. But Pug saw her as beautiful and unique. Pug loved her as no man ever had.

The memories went on, of Pug as a young woman, teaching and helping students, of walks on a green campus with buildings that resembled churches. And every day, she thought of Simone, always seeing her as a young girl with long hair and cotton gowns.

Pug's heart stopped beating.

Simone pulled back and looked into her friend's dead face.

Something painful began building in her chest.

"No," she said, touching Pug's face.

Waves and waves of pain passed through her. She did not recognize the emotions at first, and then she knew she felt remorse . . . guilt . . . horror and regret at what she'd just done. She'd had no choice, but that didn't matter.

She dropped her head to Pug's chest.

"Pug," she whispered.

The remorse did not fade, nor did the pain. She held Pug's body tighter and stayed there for a long time. She did not know how long.

Finally, she forced herself up. She was a survivor. She had to survive, and Pug could never have been fooled, not for long.

The boxes and books were piled all around the couch. Simone picked up a lighter and started a fire in the middle of the floor.

She slipped out the back door as the blaze began to increase, catching on the curtains. She didn't care if the fire spread to other houses or shops.

She just kept walking.

Pug was gone, and Simone's chest still ached.

chapter 17

"Stop!" Eleisha cried.

She jerked out of Simone's mind and fell sideways onto the floor, catching herself with one hand. She'd read memories before: Wade's, Philip's, Rose's, and Robert's. But she'd never experienced anything quite like this. Lost inside a memory, the reader felt and thought everything as the scene progressed forward.

Philip's emotions were sometimes savage and difficult to share, but Simone's were cold and alien.

Eleisha wanted to wash her face and rinse her mouth out with water.

Then Simone began choking, her face locked in sorrow and pain. Eleisha pushed herself up, trying to clear her head, realizing how hard that memory must have been for Simone to relive. For all her cold exterior, Simone deeply regretted her actions. She was capable of remorse.

Even though Simone could not have intended for Eleisha to come to such a realization, it was more important than anything else that happened tonight.

She crawled over beside Simone.

"Try to come out of it," she said. "You're here in the room with me."

Slowly, Simone stopped trembling. "She was my only friend when I was young and alone . . . and I fed on her."

In truth, this act was the worst thing Eleisha had ever seen from one of her own kind. But she understood why Simone had shown it to her—to expose the darkest moment and see whether they could overcome it.

They could.

Simone had felt remorse.

"You were scared," Eleisha whispered, leaning back against the couch. "She might have exposed you."

"You don't hate me?"

"No."

"Will you stay here for a while?"

"Yes."

Simone's body racked once, and she crawled sideways, putting her head up against Eleisha's stomach. Eleisha reached out like a mortal, like a woman, and pulled her closer, rocking her slowly back and forth.

"It's all right," she said. "Everything's all right."

And it was. She would rescue Maggie's child.

Philip paced the floor of their hotel suite. He couldn't sit down. He couldn't stop moving, but he had to stay in this room. This was the only possible place where Eleisha might return.

Seamus had appeared briefly—several hours ago—and then gone looking for Eleisha. He hadn't come back, and dawn was not far off.

With nothing else to do, Philip had too much time to think.

In spite of this, he still measured the time in seconds.

For some reason, he couldn't stop thinking about Rose. He'd

needed help tonight, and she had helped him. He would not forget that.

Fear made his head pound as he thought about "the laws" Robert had passed down to Eleisha. Robert had been useful in many ways. He could be trusted. So could Eleisha . . . and as much as he didn't want to admit it, so could Rose. They followed the laws. They cared about forming a community.

Simone could not be trusted, and Philip was too aware in this moment that neither could he.

But Rose had helped him.

Maybe Robert had been right all along, and vampires needed to exist with connections to one another, and for that to work, the laws were necessary.

So many years ago, Philip's maker, Angelo, had broken the second law—he'd created three new vampires in the span of a few years. As a result, Julian developed no telepathic abilities, and Philip had come out "wrong," with no memories of his mortal life. This act of Angelo's . . . this transgression had set a chain of events into motion that still haunted the scant few vampires still in existence.

Several things that had never made sense to Philip before were beginning to make sense now. If only he could take Eleisha home to the underground, he would listen to her. He would try harder to understand the ideas she found so important.

He stopped pacing and rubbed his temple.

He knew she was not dead. If Simone had destroyed her, he would have felt the blast of her psychic release.

But he was still measuring time in seconds, waiting uselessly to feel her death.

Simone had no limits.

Once she was locked into a game, she would do anything to win.

Philip wanted to go home to the underground, but Eleisha *was* the underground. It didn't exist unless she was there.

Faint gray streaks began appearing in the sky.

He started pacing again.

Hours had passed, and Julian was becoming concerned. Twice now, he'd almost called Mary back, but he feared pulling her away from Jasper at an inopportune moment.

The faintest hint of gray was beginning to show in the sky.

Where were they? And why hadn't Mary at least reported back?

To his relief, the air by the windows shimmered, and she materialized, looking nervous.

"What's wrong?" he asked.

She didn't answer, but she crossed her arms, not as if being petulant, but more as if she was cold.

"Mary!" he barked. "Is Simone dead?"

"No."

She looked as though she was trying to chew the inside of her lip, and his anger began to rise.

"Where is Jasper?"

"I sent him to the airport. He's going home."

Julian froze. "You what?"

"I told him those were your orders."

"Then get him back."

When she didn't move, he pulled his cell from his pocket and angrily snapped it open.

"It's too late," she said. "Look outside."

Julian took a step, the useless cell still in his hand. "You waited this late on purpose?"

"He can't handle her!" Mary suddenly shouted, uncrossing her transparent arms. "She hit him full force, and he just crumpled to his knees. It's not his fault! Philip couldn't handle her. Nobody can take her out but you!"

He strode across the suite, putting his face close to hers. "And what makes you say that?"

"Because you don't feel anything. She won't affect you."

He stood there, shaking. She was wrong. He could feel rage. He'd banish her for this, send her back where he found her.

"Is Eleisha still with her at the Hyatt?" he asked.

Mary glared at him, as if she thought this change of topic was a trick question.

"Yeah, but you better hurry, and I wouldn't worry about being seen. I'd break the door down if I were you."

While this appeared to be his only option, Julian still feared Eleisha misinterpreting his intentions and invading his mind before he could act. But what choice did he have? If Mary was right about Simone, Eleisha was in danger.

Seething, he grabbed his sword and jogged down the hall. The Hyatt wasn't far.

The sky was growing lighter, and Simone stood inside the balcony window, looking out with her back to Eleisha—pretending she needed to gain control of herself.

"I don't think you'll make it back to your hotel in time," she said. "We should just sleep here today."

Eleisha came up behind her. "I know. But I need to call Philip and let him know."

Simone nodded. "Of course."

If that was the case, she'd have to act quickly.

She reached down to open the sliding glass door. Everything depended on the next few moments.

"I want you to see something first . . . something we don't often get to see." She stepped out on the balcony.

"What are you doing?" Eleisha asked, sounding alarmed.

Did she fear heights or the gray streaks in the sky? Simone moved to the rail. She felt confident, powerful. She had won Eleisha's trust, and she knew it.

"I love to do this," Simone answered. "If you look out just before dawn, you can see the entire city from up here, and you almost feel like a mortal as the sky gets lighter." She half turned. "Come and look with me."

Eleisha wavered. "Be careful. You're facing east."

"We still have time."

Simone knew exactly what would happen. She wasn't even anxious anymore. Eleisha wanted converts. She wanted to please others. She wouldn't refuse.

A few seconds later, Eleisha stepped out cautiously, peering over the edge from just outside the door.

"Over here," Simone said. "It's beautiful from here."

Eleisha joined her at the rail, and indeed the sight before them was a rare experience. The city spread out below them in the predawn shadows. Simone stepped closer to the door, pointing outward.

"Look. It's like we can see forever."

Eleisha's gaze followed where she pointed, off into the distance.

In a flash, Simone dashed inside, slammed the glass door closed, and locked it. Eleisha turned from the rail, not even alarmed yet.

"Simone?"

She stepped back to open the door, finding it locked, and a hint of confusion crossed her features.

Simone waited in quiet joy for her to understand what had just happened.

Simone had just won.

"Open the door," Eleisha said, looking in.

Had Simone panicked and run inside?

But then Simone stepped up close to the glass . . . and she smiled. It was an eerie smile, exposing her white teeth, but the hatred shining out of her eyes was unmistakable.

Eleisha suddenly felt cold.

"Open the door," she ordered, loudly this time.

Simone didn't move. She didn't stop smiling.

Eleisha drew her arm back and slammed her elbow against the glass. It bounced off.

"Double paned," Simone mouthed at her. "Safety glass."

The eastern sky was growing lighter.

Seamus was having trouble sensing anything.

He could feel himself being pulled to the other side.

He'd never pushed himself like this before. Worse, he felt plagued by a hunger—like starvation—to teleport back to Rose.

But he cared about Eleisha, and he would not abandon her . . . even if it meant risking his existence here . . . even if it meant working with Philip.

Hours had passed since his arrival in Denver, and as yet he hadn't been able to pinpoint a single undead signature. Not because they weren't there, but because in his weakened state he needed to be close to even sense one.

So he'd been searching the city block by block, growing more and more concerned that he would fail—while fighting every second to remain in this world.

He'd started out near the botanical gardens, where Simone lived, but now he was moving closer to downtown.

Materializing in an alley on Stout Street, he stopped, feeling something on the edge of his senses. He blinked out and rematerialized in the shadows of a skyscraper on Fifteenth.

He had something: two undead signatures—and they didn't feel like other ghosts.

Throwing caution away, he blinked out and rematerialized as close to the signatures as possible, appearing in a hallway outside a door to room 3012. He wished himself through the door, passing into a hotel room—but he could hear a pounding sound.

Simone had her back to him, facing a sliding glass door. Seamus looked beyond her, and to his horror, Eleisha stood outside on the balcony, slamming her elbow against the glass, as if trying to break it.

She didn't see him.

What was happening?

Then he realized that Simone had locked her outside and Simone was just standing there . . . watching.

He started to rush forward and then stopped. After giving Simone an initial shock, he couldn't do anything. He couldn't take Eleisha off the balcony. He couldn't even open the door. Morning was coming, and he was running out of time.

He blinked out.

Eleisha slammed her elbow against the glass again and again, trying to crack it.

Nothing happened.

She whirled around, looking over the rail, not wanting to let the truth—or any version of the truth—sink in.

Had Simone just lured her out there moments before dawn and locked the door? How could that be? They had spent the entire night together, hunting, sharing memories, talking about the laws and the future.

How was this possible?

She looked back inside. Simone still stood watching her with the same eerie smile.

Let me inside, Eleisha flashed.

No.

Why are you doing this?

To win.

The hatred in Simone's eyes was taking on a kind of madness, and Eleisha felt the first wave of real fear.

She was going to be left out here to burn in the sun.

Summoning all her focus, she drove a command straight into Simone's mind.

Open the door!

Simone's body twitched in shock, and her hand came up. Eleisha kept pushing, repeating the command with force. Simone's hand was moving in harsh jerks toward the lock, and then she stopped. Eleisha felt her creating a block, pushing the command from her mind, forming a barrier.

Simone wasn't smiling anymore.

Philip was still pacing when Seamus materialized across the room.

"You've got to run!" Seamus nearly shouted. His colors were so faint, Philip could barely see him, but his voice echoed off the walls.

Philip tried to let the words register, but Seamus rushed on.

"The Hyatt Regency on Fifteenth! Room 3012. Eleisha's locked outside on a balcony. On the thirtieth floor!"

Philip froze. "What?"

"Run! We're about ten blocks away. But Simone's locked her out, and the sun is going to rise."

Without another word, Philip bolted for the door, stopping only long enough to grab his machete off the couch.

chapter 18

Eleisha didn't know which was worse—the crushing sorrow or the fear.

Simone had never intended to come home to the underground, and she'd been deceiving Eleisha all night. What could possibly warrant this level of veiled hatred?

Simone took a few steps back from the door to avoid the impending sunlight, but she was still watching, as if longing to see Eleisha burn with the arrival of dawn.

Why?

The sun was close to peeking over the horizon.

There had to be some way out of this.

Eleisha had already tried breaking the glass. She'd tried a telepathic attack. Neither one worked. Her phone was still inside her bag—inside the hotel room.

She turned back toward the rail again, moving over to look down. Could she jump? A fall from this height wouldn't kill her, but it would break her body.

Julian had once survived a long fall, but it had been less than half of the one she faced, and his bone structure was much heavier, and he'd taken the fall in the middle of the night.

She gazed down and then up at the horizon. Once she hit the

ground and her bones shattered, she would simply burn there in the sun anyway.

Eleisha turned back to the window, realizing she was about to die.

What would become of Philip?

The exhaustion she always felt this close to sunrise began setting in. She closed her eyes, seeing Philip's pale face. A slight burning sensation tingled down her back.

How much would this hurt? Would it last long?

A loud popping sound echoed out from inside the room. Eleisha opened her eyes and then wondered whether she was hallucinating.

The door between the room and the outer hallway flew open.

Julian walked inside, carrying a sword.

Simone stayed back, away from the window, but still close enough to watch. Her eyelids drooped as dormancy called to her, but she wasn't about to fall asleep.

Not yet.

She would stand here until Eleisha was burned down to nothing. The joy, the triumph of this moment made every other game she'd ever played seem like nothing in comparison.

Tonight, when she woke up, she'd call Philip.

He would run to her, and then her existence would be so different. All the years ahead would make up for the monotonous ones she left behind.

She fought her exhaustion by sheer will.

Only a moment or two now, and Eleisha would ignite.

A popping sounded from the hotel room door, and she whirled toward it.

The door opened, and a large man with dark hair walked in. He wore black slacks and a white button-down shirt. His bone structure was so thick, he appeared almost heavy. No pulse beat at the base of this throat.

He carried a sword in his right hand.

Simone knew who he was without asking. He couldn't be anyone else.

"Julian," she mouthed.

First he glanced over at Eleisha, and then he looked back at her.

She realized she was afraid of him, but vampire or not, killer of his own kind or not, he was still a man.

Summoning all her strength, she straightened and tilted her head, letting her hair swing, and she let her gift begin to flow.

Julian studied Simone for a matter of seconds, and everything Mary had told him began to make sense.

"Julian," Simone mouthed.

His ghost servant had been right.

How could Philip or Jasper overcome this visage in front of him? Her power was too different from theirs. He took in the sight of her lovely face and slender body and china blue eyes, and he absorbed her gift when she let it flow.

It was strong.

He could sense the envy passing through him, how men would envy anyone near her, how women would want to be her. He could sense the intoxication of her power.

But it didn't affect him.

"Maggie told me all about you," she said softly. "I always wanted to see you, to meet you. And now you're here."

Was she really trying this on him?

In answer, he let his own gift flow and watched her coy expression change to open fear. There was no time for satisfaction in the moment.

He took four steps forward, gripped the hilt with both hands, and swung at her neck.

Pressed up against the glass, Eleisha almost screamed at him to stop.

But she didn't.

She could have invaded his mind and stopped him telepathically, but she didn't.

She just watched him draw back his thick arms and swing. The sword sliced through Simone's neck without even slowing, causing black blood to spray from the stump. Simone's head fell to one side, and her body dropped onto the floor with a light thud Eleisha felt through her feet.

She braced herself for the blast, but being prepared never helped.

When vampires died, all the memories of their existence, their victims, their emotions, burst out in a telepathic explosion, hitting other telepaths in close proximity the hardest. But any vampire for miles would feel it.

Except Julian.

Eleisha's legs gave way, and she fell to the balcony floor when the onslaught hit. She writhed and rolled as one memory after another racked her body and mind.

She saw the round, cold face of a father who'd humiliated Simone, of a mother and sisters who'd turned their backs. She saw the face of a girl with unruly hair and thick glasses who gave love and comfort. She saw a string of girls dancing in thin, low-waisted dresses. She saw a young man with chiseled features and a shock of bangs hanging over one eye. He smoked cigarettes. His mouth tasted like smoke and mints.

Then she saw Maggie laughing, sipping wine, brushing Simone's hair, feeding on the homeless and dropping their bodies onto alley floors.

She saw a string of men and women Simone played with like chess pieces.

She saw Philip as Simone saw him, savage and unpredictable and impossible to control. She caught a flash of him with blood smeared all over his mouth, crusting onto his T-shirt.

She saw a misty image of Maggie in a red dress as Philip used his whole body to trap her against the floor.

She saw images of herself as Simone saw her: an obstacle to be removed.

She saw Philip walking away while Simone called his name. . . . Simone's last clear memory was of Philip.

The pain began to fade as she tried to make sense of anything she'd just seen. The burning tingle spread to her shoulder.

A soft click sounded, and the sliding glass door opened. Strong arms lifted her into the air, and then she was inside the hotel room, pressed up against Julian's chest as he carried her across the room. He smelled of sandalwood soap and leather. With a dry sob, she clutched the collar of his shirt with her fingers.

Julian.

He had made her a hundred and seventy years ago by pinning her in his lap, driving his teeth into her throat, and then forcing her to drink from him. He was her maker. He was her enemy. He'd murdered Robert.

She gripped his collar tightly.

"I wanted to help her," she whispered. "I tried to help her."

He carried her into the bathroom and crouched down, laying her on the floor.

Pulling her fingers from his shirt, he said, "Stay there."

She'd almost forgotten the hollow quality of his voice. His footsteps moved away just as dormancy swept her into darkness.

Philip was running down Fifteenth Street when the blast hit him.

He tripped and collapsed, dropping his machete.

His first terror-stricken thought was that Eleisha had been killed and his mind would be invaded by her memories. Then he saw Simone's father.

He saw her entire youth, just as he had before, only much faster and harder, in a matter of moments. His body jerked on the pavement as another memory struck him before the last one fully passed.

He saw himself smeared with blood.

He saw himself turning Maggie.

He saw Eleisha through Simone's eyes and felt a hatred he couldn't comprehend.

He saw Simone calling his name.

When the memories stopped, his left shoulder was tingling with a burning sensation, and he realized the sun was cresting. Was Eleisha still trapped on the balcony? How had Simone died?

Still disoriented, he looked around wildly. The street around him was empty. The tingle on his shoulder grew hot.

In despair, Seamus materialized in the shadows across the street and watched Philip fall, rolling and writhing in some unknown pain. He had decided to follow Philip—to help and guide him if necessary.

But the sun was cresting, and Philip had not reached Eleisha.

Seeking Philip's help in the first place had gone against all Seamus' instincts, but there had been no other choice. And now . . . this failure seemed too much to bear. What would Rose do without Eleisha?

Philip stopped writhing and pushed up to all fours, looking around like a lost child. He did not see Seamus, but he was about to burn in the sun.

Seamus turned halfway, spotting a boarded-up ticket office that seemed long abandoned. It might be a safe place for Philip to take refuge. Seamus began to call out to him . . . and then stopped.

Should he call out?

What if he did nothing? No one would know and no one could blame him if Philip had simply been trapped outside too long. Philip had just failed Eleisha, and he was certainly no friend to Rose. Maybe the world would be a better place without Philip in it.

But then, Seamus remembered the sight of Philip strapping on his machete to protect Rose while she hunted . . . and of Philip sitting on the couch with Wade watching movies with guns and explosions.

If Seamus simply let Philip die today, it would be murder. He would be no better than Philip himself.

With reluctance, still doubting his judgment, Seamus called out, "Here!"

"Here!" a voice called.

Even through exhaustion and the haze of what he'd just been through, Philip recognized the Scottish accent and looked up. Seamus' transparent form floated across the street in front of what looked to be a boarded-up ticket office. Graffiti covered the boards. But Seamus' eyes were stricken and defeated.

They hadn't reached Eleisha before sunrise.

They'd failed.

"Hurry," Seamus said.

Philip crawled to his feet and staggered across the street, breaking off one of the boards and slipping inside right as the sun crested.

Julian left Eleisha lying in the bathroom, and he went to check the door to the hallway. He hadn't kicked it in. Instead, he'd used physical strength to break the lock. The handle was slightly loose to the touch, but the door was intact. Stepping into the hall, he hung the DO NOT DISTURB sign and pulled the door shut.

He couldn't lock it, but he got it to stay closed.

Hopefully, the maids wouldn't touch it—or perhaps Simone had even placed an order for the room not to be serviced during the day.

This was the best he could do for Eleisha, as he could not wake up in the place she did—when she was in full control of herself and her power—and he was about to fall into dormancy himself. But he was trapped inside the hotel, so he hurried to the elevator and went all the way to the basement. When the doors opened, he stumbled out, looking around at small dark offices and janitorial supplies, seeking someplace he could hide and sleep out the day.

chapter 19

Just past dusk, Eleisha woke up on a bathroom floor, uncertain how she got there.

Then everything came rushing back.

Simone was dead.

She pushed herself up and opened the door, looking out into the hotel room. Julian was gone. City lights shone in through the sliding glass door, illuminating the outline of a tan dress and a string of light blue beads on the carpet.

Eleisha walked over and sank down beside the dress. Ashes lay in the pattern of arms and legs beneath the cotton cloth. Eleisha closed her eyes.

"Maggie," she whispered. "I'm sorry."

All the images from Simone's memories were still fresh in her mind, but she couldn't stop thinking of Philip covered in blood and the hazy picture of him holding Maggie against the floor.

Had he shared his memories with Simone? He must have.

Her hand shook as she reached out and touched the ashes. It didn't matter anymore. Simone was gone.

With her eyes still closed, she saw Robert's headless body on the sidewalk as it turned into ash.

Twice now, she'd tried to help one of her own, to bring them to a safe place where they wouldn't have to exist alone anymore.

Twice, she had failed.

Philip woke up with his face pressed against a wooden board. He'd slept facedown? He never did that.

Then he remembered where he was and jumped up.

"Seamus!"

The dark, abandoned ticket office was silent. Seamus had probably not been able to remain. Philip's chest constricted with fear of the unknown—he didn't know what had happened after he'd collapsed. Had Eleisha burned in the sun, and he'd not felt her memories because he'd gone dormant?

He rushed to the boarded-up opening and broke his way out, running down Fifteenth, trying not to let himself think. Reaching the hotel, he bolted through the front and then burst through the doors to the stairwell, knowing he could make it up thirty flights faster than it would take to wait for the elevator.

But when he ran out onto the thirtieth floor, he stopped outside of room 3012 and just stood there for a few seconds.

He was too afraid of what he'd find inside.

Finally, he reached out, wondering whether he'd need to break the door, and turned the handle. It felt loose, and it opened.

He forced himself to look in.

Eleisha knelt there on the carpet beside a tan dress and some small piles of ashes.

She was still here, still with him.

He couldn't even feel relief. He couldn't let himself feel anything.

She didn't look up. He walked in, closed the door, and sank down across from her. Her long hair was a tangled mess, and her cheek was smudged with gray. In spite of fighting to keep control of himself, he noticed the smaller pile of ash a few feet away. Was that Simone's head?

"Eleisha," he said. "Look at me."

Her gaze moved up to his face.

"Did you kill her?" he asked.

She shook her head slowly. "Julian."

"Julian?"

She nodded this time, just as slowly, her eyes drifting away. Her voice was so low, he could barely hear it. "Simone locked me out on the balcony, just before the sun rose. He broke in and cut off her head. Then he carried me inside, put me on the bathroom floor, and he left."

Philip couldn't hold himself at bay anymore, and emotions began to trickle in: sick relief mixed with guilt that he hadn't made it here in time. He wanted to touch her but held himself back.

"Why would he do that?" she whispered.

"I don't know."

A new anxiety began to gnaw at him. When Robert died, he'd seen Eleisha on the edge of a sorrow from which she couldn't rise. He'd managed to pull her out of it, but she looked close to the edge again.

"I don't care why he did it," he said flatly. "He was right."

She looked him in the face, as if suddenly realizing he was there, studying his mouth, his chest.

"Philip," she said, her voice more audible. "What happened that night with Simone? Please tell me."

He locked eyes with her, deciding he wouldn't lie.

"I'll never tell you, and I'll never show you the memories," he said. "But I am beginning to see things as you see them. I am beginning to understand."

Her chin dropped, and she reached out to touch the dress.

"What do we do now?" she whispered.

That was the easiest question she'd ever asked him.

"I want to go home," he said.

chapter 20

Two weeks later, Wade decided to go back to searching news stories on his computer and taking notes as he worked. He hadn't spent much time in the office since Eleisha's return from Denver, but somehow tonight felt . . . correct.

He scanned news reports for a few hours, but he kept glancing over at the file he'd started on the madman from the London alley. He considered calling for Seamus but decided against it. Seamus had looked so much better in the past week, all his bright colors returning when he materialized.

Wade didn't want to send him out just yet.

Finally, he got up to stretch his legs, walking across the hall, through the door behind the altar, and out into the sanctuary.

Rose and Philip were sitting on the floor in front of a couch. They were facing each other with their eyes closed. Neither one of them seemed aware he'd entered the room.

Philip had changed since coming back.

The changes weren't stark, but they were noticeable. While he wasn't exactly kind to Rose, he treated her with respect, and he'd even offered to help her focus her telepathy. Wade hadn't thought this a good idea at first—but he'd been wrong.

"No," Philip insisted, "push harder!"

"I am pushing!"

Rose's face contorted with effort, and Philip nodded.

"Good," he said. "Keep the block up. Keep me out."

Philip was far less patient than Wade and much more aggressive in these training sessions, but for some reason, Rose responded to him better. She fought him. She wasn't afraid to hurt him or push back. The result was astonishing, and she was learning how to block.

Wade had also picked up two wooden practice swords, and Philip was teaching him some of the basics—but even the basics turned out to be more difficult than he'd expected.

The other change in Philip was his attempt to communicate better verbally. The night after returning from Denver, he'd found Wade alone, and he'd actually *tried* to explain what had happened between Simone and Eleisha, at least from his own perspective. He wouldn't let Wade read his mind—which would have been easier—but he'd talked for nearly half an hour.

This was new.

Whatever had happened in Denver, it had altered Philip.

Eleisha, on the other hand, hadn't said a word about the entire journey. And Wade knew better than to press her. After Robert's death, she'd disappeared inside herself for a while, but she'd eventually come out of it.

She just didn't handle failure well, and she always blamed herself.

Tonight, she'd gone into the churchyard to weed the gardens. That was good sign. She always liked working in the garden.

Wandering through the maze of couches and bookshelves in the sanctuary, he walked outside to go find her.

*   *   *

Julian put his horse inside the stall and brought it a bucket of fresh water. Then he put the saddle away and headed back toward the manor.

His mind drifted as he walked, and he was taken unawares by how quickly he reached the mudroom. Stepping inside, he couldn't help remembering a time when this room was filled with barking, wriggling spaniels and men pulling on their coats and loading guns for a shooting party.

In truth, the memory was a welcome distraction. For the past two weeks, he'd been torn over what to do about Mary.

She'd not only disobeyed him in Denver. She had forced him into action.

After encountering Simone, he'd finally understood a few of Mary's desperate speeches. Her instincts had been good, but it would be dangerously wrong to simply let her behavior pass.

Yet what enraged him, what troubled him, was . . . even though he had to punish her, there was nothing he could think to do.

He couldn't strike her. He couldn't lock her up without food.

And he couldn't send her back. That was the crux. Without her, he was blind. He could attempt calling another ghost, but the truth was, she fit his needs perfectly, and he might never find another like her.

He'd never found himself in this position before, and he hated it.

Walking to the study, he pondered this dilemma. Then he opened the study door and started slightly at finding Mary inside, next to the round table. She was waiting here for him?

"Mary," he said before he could stop himself.

She looked at him warily. They hadn't spoken much since that night in Denver. He'd decided not to punish Jasper—who'd believed he was only following orders—and so Jasper was back in San Francisco.

But what should he do about her?

"Yeah, I came to report," she said. "Wade was back at his computer tonight. He took notes and looked at some maps. I think he's getting ready to send Seamus out again. I thought you'd want to know."

"Where to? Are they focusing back on London?"

"I'm not sure yet. He was working alone."

Beneath this tense exchange flowed a volume of words they had not spoken.

"All right," he said. "Just go back and keep a close watch. Let me know as soon as you have a location."

"Okay."

He expected her to vanish. But she didn't. Instead, she floated closer.

"So, we're just going to keep acting like nothing happened?" she asked. Her eyes were challenging, but she wasn't stupid enough to dare him to send her back to the gray plane.

He straightened to full height, looking down his nose. "I have no idea what you mean."

She stared at him and then floated backward as the silent truth became clear. No matter what she did, he wasn't going to send her back.

This changed everything.

"I'll let you know as soon as I learn anything," she said.

She vanished.

Alone in the study, he thought about those last words and her apparent willingness to still assist him. Perhaps nothing had changed after all.

Eleisha sat beside Robert's grave, pretending to pull weeds.

She'd been struggling these past weeks to try to understand everything that had happened in Denver.

She'd failed Maggie.

She'd lost Maggie's child.

But to her shame, she was not in mourning. The emotions passing through her did not feel even close to the pain of Robert's loss.

Worse, the same scene kept replaying in her mind: of Julian taking Simone's head off.

Julian was the enemy. He'd plagued their footsteps and murdered his own kind. She viewed Robert as a paragon on the other end of the spectrum. But what would have happened if Robert had walked into that hotel room and seen Eleisha locked out on the balcony?

He'd have done the exact same thing that Julian did.

In her heart, she knew this.

She had gone to save a lost vampire from loneliness and from Julian. In turn, he'd saved her, and she couldn't even bring herself to blame him for killing Simone. The lines were growing too blurred. Her purpose, which had once been so clear, seemed a dark muddle.

"What do we do now?" she asked Robert.

A twig snapped, and she looked over to see Wade walking toward her though the lilac bushes.

Wearing jeans and a gray T-shirt, he pushed his white-blond hair back with one hand as he walked. There was something different about him, but she couldn't figure out what. Perhaps a confidence or determination she'd never noticed? He'd set up a gym in the congregation's old kitchen, and he'd been spending a good deal of time there. His forearms were beginning to look harder and more defined.

"I thought you were pulling weeds," he said, coming up and kneeling down beside her.

"I am. But I was just thinking."

"Me, too. I think we should send Seamus to London."

She looked away. She wasn't so sure.

"What's wrong?" he asked, and again, his voice sounded . . . different.

She wasn't certain how to explain her doubts. "Julian's tracked us down twice now, murdered a vampire we were trying to bring home, and then left me alone. He carried me in from the balcony and put me inside a bathroom so I'd be safe. Why would he do that? And how does he always know exactly where we are? And if he knows where we are, why hasn't he ever attacked us here at the church?"

Her words were quite a speech for Wade to take in.

"I don't know," he answered, but he didn't sound so sure.

"You think he's using us, don't you?" she asked, nervous that he might agree.

He was quiet for a while.

"The thought has occurred," he finally said. "But we can't just stop looking. There are still vampires like Rose, like Robert, hiding all alone." His jaw twitched. "We do need to change tactics though, work together better, and make sure we get the next one home."

She winced. "You think it's our fault . . . mine and Philip's."

"You shouldn't have split up," he answered coldly. Then his tone softened. "But I don't think anyone could have helped Simone. Not after what Philip told me. And that's another thing. We're going to have to be a lot more careful before we approach the next one. Every situation is going to be different. I don't think I quite realized that before." He paused. "I am sorry that Julian was so close and neither one of you had a chance to kill him."

Her eyes widened. "Kill him?"

He seemed taken aback by her response. "If you had the chance, you'd take him out, wouldn't you?"

She hesitated before answering. "Yes . . . yes, you know I would."

"Good." He nodded. "Because I'd put six bullets in his chest and let Philip take his head in a heartbeat."

She studied his face. He *was* different.

He stood up. "I want to get started again. As soon as possible. Are you on board?"

"Yes."

And she was. As he headed back toward the church, she realized he was right. No matter what, they couldn't stop. Even if Julian was using them like bloodhounds, they couldn't stop. What would Rose's existence be like without the underground? Or Philip's? Or her own?

She'd promised Robert that she would find any others and teach the laws and reinstitute the old ways. Reaching out, she touched his headstone. Then she stood up.

"Wade," she called.

He stopped.

"Wait for me."

Half turning, he watched as she hurried to join him.

Near the end of the wee hours before dawn, Philip stopped by his bedroom and gathered all the pillows off his bed. Since their return from Denver, his clothes had slowly migrated to Eleisha's closet, but he'd decided to move some of his other things to her room.

It made him feel more anchored.

He'd been worried that she'd ask him again what had happened with Simone in Denver, that she wouldn't be able to let it go. Although she was aware that whatever had happened was bad, she had no idea how bad.

But she hadn't asked him.

For some reason, he'd felt an unfamiliar need to make up for his dark secrets by working harder at home, trying to be of more use to Wade . . . even to Rose.

He did not know how the future would play out, if he would be completely able to exist as Robert had, as Eleisha and Rose did now. But he was going to try. He wanted to become the person Eleisha thought he already was.

That was something else he'd learned since returning. He'd always known that Eleisha had a somewhat different view of him than Wade did, but sharing a mental connection with Rose had been even more eye-opening. During their sessions together, she'd tried to hide her opinion of him, but he'd caught several flashes. She viewed him as heartless, self-centered, violent, and childish. Worse, she had no idea what Eleisha saw in him.

This perspective was like a splash of cold water.

Maybe he'd been relying on his gift too long, which made everyone see him as perfect. He had learned a few hard truths from Simone, such as the dangers of believing his own gift.

Walking down the hallway with his armload of pillows, he used one hand to open the door to Eleisha's room.

She was at her dressing table in a white cotton nightgown, using one of Maggie's silver brushes, stroking it through her hair.

Smiling at him in the mirror, she said, "What are those?"

"Pillows."

"I can see that. Don't I have enough in here?"

"No."

He didn't need to use his gift on her. She already saw him as he wanted to be seen. He'd found ways to be more useful to Wade and Rose, but he most wanted to give Eleisha . . . something, and until tonight, he'd had no idea what.

He'd caught a few thoughts in Rose's mind when her block failed briefly.

I wish Philip would let Eleisha talk to him about William, Maggie, and Robert. She can talk to me, but she wants to talk to him. I can feel it. He knew them all.

Philip had no objection to Eleisha speaking of her own past. He just feared it might cross the line into his own—and he didn't want to talk or think about his own past.

He still did not understand Eleisha's need to dwell on things that could not be changed, but he knew that in spite of Simone's mania, of her madness, Eleisha still blamed herself for failing to bring Maggie's child home. She blamed herself for too much.

Walking to the bed, he dropped the pillows.

"You're using Maggie's brushes?" he asked. So far, she'd only laid them out as some kind of shrine.

"Do you think she'd mind?"

"No." He sat on the bed. "You cared for her."

She turned, looking at him almost warily, as if unsure what he meant.

"It's all right if you want to tell me about the time you spent with her," he said. "Or about William. You can even show me memories."

She stood up, walking to him. "You don't mind?"

"No, I don't. . . . I should listen. Just don't ask me anything about myself."

Her lower lip trembled, and he could see she found his offer momentous, which only made him feel more guilty that something so simple affected her this much. He should have offered long ago.

The sky was growing lighter.

"Close the blinds," he said. "We can talk tonight."

While she prepped the room for daylight hours, he stacked all the pillows against the headboard of her bed and then pulled his shirt off. When she came to him, he was half sitting with his back propped up. He'd sometimes slept this way in the past and found it comfortable.

But no matter what position he was in, she always seemed to know what to do. Joining him, she curled up in a ball and laid her head on his stomach with her face looking up toward his.

"Philip?"

"What?"

"Thank you."

He put his hand on the top of her head. "Sleep now."

Just past sunrise that morning, Wade walked through the sanctuary alone. He'd sent Seamus to London a few hours before, and now he was stuck in wait-and-see mode.

He made sure all the doors and windows were locked, and then he decided to go cook breakfast and watch the morning news. But after coming out the bottom of the stairwell, he turned left and went down the hall to Philip's room, cracking the door.

It was empty.

The closet door was open, and half his clothes were gone. So were the pillows from his neatly made bed.

Wade walked farther down the hall and went into Eleisha's room.

Philip's clothes were hanging in her closet. But he'd also piled all his pillows on her bed, and he was sleeping in a half-sitting position. Eleisha was curled into a little ball with her head on his stomach. Wade had never seen them sleep quite like this before.

As he stood over them, he no longer felt like some unbalanced voyeur. He felt more like their watcher, someone to protect them during daylight hours.

Maybe this was just an excuse to himself, but he didn't care.

Stepping closer, he took in the lines of Eleisha's face, of her hair stretched out across Philip's stomach.

Then he left the room.

Hopefully, Seamus would be back before long with some concrete news. Wade wanted to begin a new search as soon as possible.

But one thing was certain.

He was never staying behind again.

Not ever.

Barb Hendee grew up just north of Seattle, Washington. She completed a master's degree in composition theory at the University of Idaho, and then taught college English for ten years in Colorado. She and her husband, J.C., are coauthors of the bestselling Noble Dead Saga. They live in a quirky little town near Portland, Oregon, with two geriatric and quite demanding cats. Visit Barb's Web site at www.barbhendee.com.